PROPHECY OF DUST:
A SUPERNATURAL PSYCHIC THRILLER

WRAITH HUNTER CHRONICLES: BOOK 4

By John R. Monteith

I0640462

CHAPTER 1

Layla writhed on the cross, her skin chafing under coils of nylon. The drug pumping within her veins was yielding to clarity, but it disoriented her, and she fought to remember how a crucifix of four-by-four lumber segments had become her fatal perch.

She forced the memory.

Her young teacher had driven by her on her walk to school. With the rain becoming a downpour, he'd stopped to offer a ride. Since he was her history instructor, she'd accepted to pump him for information on the upcoming exam.

When he'd jammed the hypodermic needle into her thigh, she'd realized his timing had been premeditated, and she was a victim.

Now, in the basement of a suburban house, she faded in and out of awareness. She suspected a date-rape drug, but her clothes were unruffled, and her body felt unviolated.

Her captor hadn't touched her.

Not like her step-father had.

The bastard who claimed guardianship over her had started fondling her as she'd entered puberty, and threats of violence had kept her silent.

With a warranted distrust of men, her heart raced as she heard footsteps descending into the basement.

Handsome in his signature teaching ensemble of beige slacks with a tan sports coat, her teacher smirked as he leered at her. "Ah, I see that you're awake."

She attempted a protest, but a cloth gag held her tongue.

As he crossed the basement, he passed through a circle of candles in the room's center. Resting atop two parallel workbenches that outlined a central aisle along the concrete floor, the flickering flames cast an eerie hue over her captor as he stepped on chalk markings drawn in the form of a pentagram.

Seeing the satanic setup amped Layla's fear, and she launched a muffled scream.

"Resisting won't help. You've been chosen." He moved below her and ogled, but his stare differed from that of high school boys who leered at her chest and buttocks. It was more like that of her mother's fourth husband, the monster who molested her, with its smug pride of conquest. But a peculiarity in his demeanor suggested a lust for something other than her sexuality.

She tried to kick him, but ropes held her ankles. Looking down, she noticed kindling branches and logs stacked below her, and terror coursed through her veins as she feared being burned alive. Unable to cry out her plea, she begged for mercy with her eyes.

But the teacher-turned-beast ignored her and backtracked to the center of the candlelit circle. There, he knelt and produced a bronze-colored dagger. Clutching the knife with both hands, he uttered phrases in a foreign language.

Insane with fear, she writhed and jerked, trying to break any bond she could. A loud crack encouraged her, and she glanced at her limbs in hopes of seeing snapped wood. But she remained bound.

Continuing his chant, the beast looked to the ceiling and then back to his dagger.

As she saw fear in his face, she realized the noise had come from the ground floor. To no avail, she tried screaming again.

The beast finished his incantation. "I told you to stop resisting. Nobody will save you. They know better than to hurry, and I'll be finished with you soon." He rose to his feet.

Her mind raced. Who were 'they', and could they save her?

His knife extended, her captor climbed a wooden stepladder nestled within the kindling wood. When he paralleled her height above the concrete floor, he ran the dagger's tip down her blouse and recited foreign words.

Above the room's far corner, a bomb exploded, and floorboard shards rained in the basement.

The beast half-fell, half-jumped from his ladder, landed on the concrete, and showed her his back. From his pants, he withdrew a pistol, extended it, and aimed it at the stairway. He walked towards the exit, from which flowed new light through an up-stairs door Layla assumed the explosion had broken.

A moment of calmness overcame her in which she sensed her captor's fear and indecision. With clarity, she understood his dilemma. Her would-be rescuers had hurried to save her, and their haste had led them into one of her abductor's grenade traps. The teacher-beast was undecided about verifying their demise. By inspecting them, he'd expose himself to their weapons. By ignoring them, he risked them continuing their assault. She sensed his final decision before he acted on it.

After returning his pistol into the small of his back, he turned, walked to her, and climbed the ladder. Again, he aimed the point at her heart and recited an incantation.

Movement in the stairway caught her attention. In the dim light, a man wearing body armor and carrying a machinegun crept down the steps. His left arm was avulsed below the elbow, and his shoulder was shredded. Missing his left eye, he appeared near death but determined. After staring at the horrific image of hope, she averted her eyes to avoid warning her captor of her rescuer. She watched the knife approach her chest.

Her rescuer sent a deafening burst of gunfire, and the beast fell.

Craving deliverance, Layla watched her abductor squirm on the floor, but the red holes in his upper back appeared outside of his vital organs.

Using his three good limbs, the beast crawled along the con-crete, the nearer workbench hiding him from the rescuer.

Her one-eyed savior reached the bottom of the stairs and walked towards her. Keeping his assault rifle aimed across the room, he scanned for his enemy who remained hidden.

Layla tried to nod towards her captor, but the blunt clue became unactionable as the crawling teacher-beast reached the safety of the room's far corner.

Her rescuer looked up with his single eye, revealing the bat-tered face of an old man. His lips moved, but he could only wheeze. Despite his morbid injury and age, he moved with unbreakable resolve behind her crucifix.

She heard a rope snap. As she looked at her left hand, she saw her savior using his single hand to unravel coils of nylon. When the tightness yielded, she abraded her skin while yanking her arm to her side. Gravity tugged her downward, and she stiffened her leg, stomach, and right chest muscles to prevent herself from flopping forward. Once balanced, she relaxed her jaw muscles and cracked her bottom lip pulling off her gag. She pointed. "He's over there!"

Her rescuer wheezed again.

As her balance waned, she reached for the unraveled rope near her left hand to steady herself. Then she heard nylon snap again by her feet. This time, she waited for her savior to uncoil the strands before struggling to move. She also scanned the room for her captor, but he remained hidden. "I don't see him. I'll keep an eye out for him."

With a steely combat knife, the rescuer tapped the top step of the stepladder, and then he uncoiled more rope.

Layla understood his command. When she could slide her right foot, she drove her weight down into the ladder. While she stabilized herself, she heard her rescuer slice the ropes of her right arm, and within seconds, she was on the tiptoes of her sneakers with her back arched, holding the unraveled lines by her freed hands for balance. As she kicked, lifted, and shimmied her left leg out of the strands, she saw movement. "Over there. By the stairs!"

Her savior limped to position himself between her abductor and her exposed torso, but her elevated perch placed her above her protector. He raised his assault rifle and aimed it at the teacher-beast, but he was late.

The captor fired his pistol into the one-eyed man's chest, knocking him backwards. He banged against Layla's shins, but she'd angled her legs sideways in time to escape harm.

In a huge strain, she grasped her ropes, pushed with her left leg, and lifted her right.

Recovering, her rescuer sent rifle rounds towards her captor, who ducked under a bench before her savior could aim.

She pressed her right leg into the ladder, scraped her left leg free, and then released herself into a freefall. Smacking her knees and palms into the concrete hurt, but escaping the exposed elevation above the pyre was worth the pain.

Her rescuer fell to one knee, and then he collapsed onto the pile of kindling wood. He extended his rifle to Layla.

Clueless about its operations, she took it, glanced at it, and shrugged. "What do I do?"

He flicked his wrist towards their common enemy and then transformed his hand into a mock pistol. Wiggling his thumb, he pantomimed his intent for her to kill the beast.

To test the weapon, she raised it to her shoulder, aimed it at the stairs, and squeezed the trigger. Three rounds burst into the wood, and the recoil surprised her, but she remained standing with renewed courage. "Show yourself. I have a bigger gun!"

No response.

Crouching, she lowered her weapon and examined the view closer to the concrete. At the basement's far end, her captor lay against a wall, motionless. She saw a path between the candles leading to her enemy, and she marched along it, hunched behind her weapon and keeping the beast in her sight. As she stood over him, she saw the slide of his pistol locked back, signaling an empty chamber.

His usable hand pressing a flowing wound at his opposite shoulder, he looked up with defeated eyes. "Go ahead and do it, if you can."

She knew she could. Hate was engrained into her DNA, and she lifted the rifle. But then the glimmer of his dagger distracted her. "Give me that."

He snorted. "You want it. Come and take it."

She pressed the rifle barrel into his foot and squeezed off three rounds.

Blood spurted, and he howled. He grabbed the knife with his bloody hand and hurled it at her chest.

But she was too close for the tip to rotate, and the bloodied handle smacked her rib before falling at her feet. "Asshole. Now toss your gun."

"The hell with you."

Jamming her rifle into his undamaged foot, she glared at him.

"Okay. Okay." He pushed the pistol across the concrete and then covered his shoulder wound again. "What's your next move, sweetheart? You don't look like a killer."

Ignoring his verbal jab, she backed up, stooped, and reached for his dagger.

Before she could touch the bronze handle, time stopped around her, and a figure appeared in which an unseen wind flapped a milky gown over a female frame. The young woman was a ghost, clothed in dignity and unblemished in the afterlife, who called out in a Canadian accent. "Stop!"

Layla gasped but her lungs froze. Unable to move, she spoke to the apparition within her mind. "Who are you?"

The ghost's black eyes glared. "I am the Maiden of Toronto. The man below you killed me fifty years ago. You must avenge me."

"You mean, I have to kill him."

"Yes."

Knowing she could get away with it by claiming self-defense, Layla had been planning on it. Although being caught in time and talking to a ghost shocked her, she managed to communicate coherent thoughts. "I will."

"Avoid his dagger. Do not touch it."

"But I want it."

"It is cursed. You must wrap it in cloth and deliver it where I tell you, but do not touch it."

"Who the hell are you to tell me what to do?"

The ghost shrieked a haunting response. "You will heed my warning, or you will perish!"

Layla willed the ghost's departure, and the maiden disappeared. She stooped again towards the dagger and grabbed it.

Reality took a sharp turn, and her very essence changed. Although smeared with red sticky fluid, the bronze touching her skin imbued her with purpose and drive. Instantly, she saw a future of wealth and power, an impossible deliverance from her oppressed poverty and hopelessness. Raising the blade to her nose, she fell into its captive trance. "Yes. I see."

The helpless teacher was terrified. "What? What do you see?"

"You'll find out." She flung the rifle's strap over her shoulder and carried the dagger in both hands as she marched across the basement. Reaching her fallen rescuer, she probed the corpse's vest for handcuffs. She found the restraints, returned to the beast, and then cuffed his good arm to the leg of a workbench.

"What are you doing?"

As she ripped off his loafers, she begat a howl when she agitated his broken foot. She unbuckled his slacks and pulled them to his feet, and then she followed with his underwear. Although she'd been forced to become familiar with her step-father's nakedness, she found men's genitalia ugly.

With his sensitive parts exposed, the beast grew horrified. "No! Whatever you're doing, don't!"

She then unbuttoned her jeans and stripped below the waist.

"What? I don't understand. You want to have sex with me?"

Glaring at him, she straddled his hips and grabbed his penis. "I will take a son from you."

"What? Why? What are you doing? I won't let you!"

Despite his protests, he proved her suspicions of his perversion when his body complied with her desires. As he succumbed to her will, she sensed more of his thoughts. An unseen source gifted her memory with his Swiss bank account numbers and passwords, and they were so vivid she knew she'd remember them forever. A fortune awaited her, if she could inflict the justice upon him he deserved.

With her new dagger in her hand, she mounted him. The knife invoked a power over her, over them, like the force of an intelligent will. Within moments, she coaxed his seed.

He groaned at the ceiling. When he regained himself, he gave her a quizzical stare. "I don't understand."

With a newborn ability to grasp supernatural prophecy, she

knew she'd bear his offspring. "I've taken my son from you, and he'll inherit the power of the dagger."

"No. That's impossible."

She dismounted him and put on her pants. "I don't care what you believe. It's your turn to fear death now."

He smirked. "Well, if you're really having my kid, you wouldn't kill the father of your child, would you?"

In a swift and decisive move, she lowered the rifle to her hip and sent a three-round burst into his torso. As he collapsed, she finished the job by ramming the blade into his heart, yanking it out, and then wiping her victim's blood off her knife with his shirt.

"Yes, I would." Led by her dagger, she dragged his body to the pyre under her former perch. Using the nearest candle as a catalyst, she ignited the kindling wood. As the flames caught, she tucked the bronze blade into a belt loop of her jeans and trotted towards the stairs and her freedom.

Freedom from her dead captor, freedom from a molesting step-father, and freedom from a life of oppression, anger, and despair.

CHAPTER 2

Seven years later, Layla watched her son during his karate practice. Expecting him to become a powerful man, she'd enrolled him in martial arts to learn to dominate.

Amir nodded at his mother and then popped a jab towards his opponent's face. Taller, the sparring partner leaned away from the punch, but Layla's son advanced with a snap kick to the jaw. With his victim disoriented, he sent a punishing heel into the stomach. Even wearing a protective vest, the hurt boy fell to a knee.

Amir halted his attack and looked towards his mother for approval.

She stared with scorn and slowly shook her head.

After her son's practice, Layla waited in her Porsche Cayenne. When Amir climbed into the passenger seat, she slapped his face. "Never show mercy. Do you hear me?"

He glared at her and seemed to wrestle with a complaint, but he remained silent for fear that a protest would beget another strike.

Having pilfered the teacher-beast's bank accounts after her son's conception, Layla had committed to generous spending in his upbringing, and she demanded every ounce of effort and discipline from him. "I'm not pouring all this money into your classes for you to be weak. What do you have to say for yourself?"

"The instructor was going to stop me. I saw him stepping in."

She curtailed her reaction to slap his cheek again, instead pointing at his nose. "First, you don't give me backtalk. Second, I don't care what anyone else does. You do what I tell you, and I never taught you to show mercy to anyone."

The boy lowered his head. "Yes, ma'am."

Unsure how or when the dagger would empower her son, she knew he'd grow strong like the spirit within the weapon had promised, and she'd protect him from weakness and victimhood. "I'm tough on you for your own good. You'd better learn to appreciate what I do for you."

Two years later, Layla watched her nine-year-old son send a roundhouse kick to his sparring partner's protective headgear. His arms dropping, the stunned victim stood in a helpless daze.

Sending a knowing leer towards his mother, Amir jumped, spun, and aimed a staggering blow into his opponent's padded vest. The boy fell into a fetal position, gasping for breath.

When her son looked up for praise, Layla gave a neutral stare. To drive him, she refused to relax the pressure on him with an approving gesture.

After practice, the karate instructor stepped in front of her. "May I speak to you in private?"

"No. If you have something to say, just say it."

"Amir's become too aggressive. I can't teach him anymore."

"Are you kicking him out of your class?"

"I've warned you several times. You leave me no choice."

Her temper flared. "Screw you, asshole. I'll take him across town. I'm sure someone else will be happy to take my money."

"I've already talked to Master Davis and Master Nakamura. Neither of them wants him, and nobody else in the area has a dojo worth going to. You have to stop pushing the boy to violate the tenets that are taught as part of the art."

She glared at him. "Then we'll move to a town with better karate instructors."

Five years later, Layla drove her Mercedes sedan by a park. Since she had several cocktails in her system, she blinked several times to verify her vision and then glared at the group of middle school children gathered around park benches.

Facing a baseball field's fenced backstop, her fourteen-year-old son was kissing a girl.

Layla swung her car through four lanes of traffic, sending an oncoming car onto the shoulder. Tires screeched as she whipped her vehicle into the park's asphalt lot. Leaving the engine running and her door open, she marched onto the grass. When she reached her son, she smacked the back of his head. "What the hell do you think you're doing?"

Flushed with surprise and anger, he faced her. "What the hell?"

"Don't talk back to me."

Hormones gave him courage. "I can do what I want."

She backhanded his face. "I'm keeping you from impregnating some young slut and ruining your life."

The girl her son had been kissing ran towards the group of children who shuffled from Layla.

Amir glared at her, but as his hormones subsided, his expression yielded to her dominance. "Sorry, Mom."

"Shut up and get your ass in the car."

Three years later, the toned body of a seventeen-year-old man stood before Layla. "Three As and two Bs. That's not bad for the hard classes I was taking."

Expecting perfection, she launched a backhand towards his jaw.

With a simple, strong motion, he blocked her. "No."

Her wrist throbbing from the block, she aimed her finger at his face. "How dare you!"

His eyes darkened with defiance, marking the end of his childhood. "You'll never slap me again, woman."

Rage blinding her, she clawed for his eyes, but a burst of her son's overpowering skill brought her to her knees in a wrist lock. "That hurts!"

With one hand, he retained the pressure on her joint. "Not enough for what you've done to me."

As her son rebelled, her world crumbled. "I gave you the best of everything."

"You never loved me." He released her, turned, and walked towards the foyer of her oversized suburban mansion.

Shock and anger holding her on the floor, she rubbed her wrist and yelled. "Where are you going?"

"Away. Forever."

"No. You can't!"

He grabbed car keys from a hook. "I can, and I am. I knew you'd freak out with my grades, and my bag's already in the car."

She sought any argument to keep him with her and under her control. "I'll report the car stolen."

"It's in my name."

"You'll be back when you run out of money!"

"I took what I needed to live forever from your accounts."

"How?"

"I set up a camera in your office to watch you type in your passwords."

"You bastard!"

He stopped walking and smirked. "I am a bastard. You denied me a father."

"I gave you life!"

"And you tried to ruin it. I'm too smart and too strong for you, and you're not going to screw with me anymore. Oh, and that dagger you kept in the safe? I know it's mine, even though you hid it from me. So, I took it last night. It's in my bag."

"No! You're not ready!"

"Really? When do you think I'll be ready, genius?"

"I'm your mother. I'll know!"

"Newsflash. I'm ready. Good bye." He walked out the door and shut it.

Alone, she collapsed on the floor and howled in anger and pain. Tears blurred her sight, and as she looked up at a woman floating over her hardwood planks, she doubted her vision.

An unseen wind flapping a milky gown over her frame, the ghost called out in a Canadian accent. "You failed to heed my warning."

Within her vision, Layla recalled her seventeen-year-old encounter with the apparition. Unable to move, she spoke through telepathy. "You? The Maiden of Toronto."

The maiden's black eyes glared. "I told you the dagger was cursed. Now, you suffer for ignoring me."

"If I had obeyed you, I wouldn't have my son."

"But you have lost him, and you may never regain him."

"Shut up!"

"I bring you a new warning. You must retrieve the dagger from your son."

"Don't tell me what to do."

The ghost's eyes grew large as she groaned a deep, resonating response. "You will heed my warning, or you will perish."

Layla screamed, leapt from the floor, and lashed out, but the maiden disappeared before she could strike her. Alone again, she gnashed her teeth and punched a hole in a wall.

CHAPTER 3

Eight years later, Diane sat in the waiting room outside the order's inner sanctum. She stared at the temporary plywood doors to the courtroom which reminded her of the battle against her third wraith, which had ended in his capture weeks ago. Her patience for the private proceedings waned. "Come on!"

In the armchair opposite her, Emma, the German empath, twisted her neck to see the doors. "No kidding. This is taking so long. You must be going crazy."

The Chaldean empath agreed. "How long can it possibly take to read through a bunch of rules?"

Emma shrugged. "Old men. Ancient rules. I don't think they know how to make quick decisions."

"But people's lives are at stake." Diane felt selfish after speaking. The council protected people targeted for assassination, and their present discussion about her desire to marry the young hunter was a less important matter than serial killers and homicides. But to her, it was everything. She stood and paced.

"Stop. You're making me nervous."

The Chaldean empath returned to her seat. "I'm having trouble just sitting here."

"I know. But worrying won't help."

Diane snapped. "Easy for you to say! Your soulmate isn't a royal slave!"

The German empath smirked. "Did you just call him your soulmate?"

Diane's face warmed with blood. "Yeah, I guess I did. Whatever he is, I wish he'd hurry."

"You're letting your fears destroy you. Try to let your emotions flow without making yourself panic."

"Now you sound like an empath."

Emma winked. "I'm not as good as you, but I've got a good mentor."

"Right. I'll try to chill."

Her wait ended as the plywood swung open and the young hunter stepped from the room. "Can we talk? In private?"

Emma took the hint and walked away. "Excuse me. I need to use the ladies' room."

Dizzy with anxiety, Diane stood and faced the young hunter. "Well?"

Liam sounded fatigued from the hearing. "It's just like my father said. There has to be fewer wraiths than hunting lines for me, or any hunter for that matter, to get married."

Her heart sank. "When's the next wraith supposed to be killing?"

"Twenty-five years. All three are twenty-five years away."

She had hoped for one sooner. "Are you serious?"

"All seven wraiths work on fifty-year cycles, except for the one who got pushed to the blood-moon cycle. The first two we killed were in cycle this year. The German hunters killed another one, centuries ago, on the same timing. The last three are all out of phase by exactly twenty-five years."

Diane swallowed. "Does that mean we have to wait twenty-five years before we can even hope to get married?"

"It might. Sort of."

"What do you mean 'sort of'?"

"It's a complex thing with lots of moving parts."

She knew there had to be a better answer. "Let me talk to Friar Lucio. I'm not waiting that long."

As she stormed towards the sanctum, the vice grip of Liam's hand enveloped her upper arm. "Don't."

His grip immobilizing her, she stopped and glared at him. "If you won't you fight for us, I will!"

"I have fought. You didn't let me finish. It's not all bad." He released her.

"What's not so bad?"

"It may not be much, but Friar Lucio assigned Father and me to the second wraith. Starting now, we have a mission to stop him."

Though poor at math outside of transcendent visions, Diane found the numbers easy. "Connor would have to still be hunting when he's a hundred for that to work."

"I know. But don't put it beyond the old codger yet, though."

"Get serious! I'm not waiting twenty-five years."

"Well, that's good because we'll know in fifteen. Friar Lucio only guaranteed me the right to marry if any of the three remaining wraiths is retired in fifteen years. After that, I'll be forty, and he'll look to the new sons from the other lines if the opportunity arises."

If he considered that good news, she wondered if she'd be better off without him. "Seriously? How does that help?"

"Consider if we can find him off his cycle. There's no rule that says I have to hunt a wraith on his cycle. It's just easiest to do it when he's leaving a trail of bodies."

"You got a plan, then?"

"Yeah. Sort of." He seemed hesitant to share.

"Well?"

"I know two empaths, each with her own enchanted dagger, and I have access to a living wraith who wants to help."

Emma had taken the enchanted dagger as her own after the team had retired their third wraith, Ethan, the one who'd sought redemption and surrendered. Diane hadn't yet taught her to use the bronze blade, but she was concerned that her would-be husband concluded the German empath was ready. "You think we can all just hold hands and summon this next wraith to invite us over for dinner?"

"No."

She buried an earnest stare into his eyes. "Then what are you thinking?"

He raised his voice. "Fine, damn it. Yes. That's what I was thinking. You'll need to try using your powers with Emma and maybe even with Ethan to find our new wraith."

"Oh, he's 'Ethan' now? Your new drinking buddy?"

"Maybe he was a monster for a thousand years, but he was a different man by the time we encountered him."

"He tried to kill us all!"

"No, he didn't. A demon made him do it."

Having heard enough, she walked away and flopped into the couch. She tried to calm herself. "So, I have to solve this?"

He crouched by her side. "We'll get through this."

She looked away. "If we don't get through this, there won't be an 'us' anymore."

"I know. I don't like it any more than you do."

Tears blurred her vision, and she wiped her eyes. She wanted to appear stronger to him and to herself, but she needed to indulge in a selfish moment. Aiming her jaw at him, she pleaded. "Forget them all. Let's run away. For crying out loud, we've killed three wraiths. Most of your kind don't even get to fight one. You've paid your dues over and over."

He sighed. "I'd love to, but I can't."

"Why not?"

"It's in my blood. It's divine rules I don't understand, but I know I can't disobey them. I was born to serve a power greater than myself."

"Our love is a power greater than yourself." She couldn't believe she'd said something so sentimental, but he ignored it.

He frowned. "You think it's so easy? Why don't you tell me the name of the hunter you met in the sanctum?"

She remembered him vividly, the hunter from Senegal, but a supernatural force prevented her from mentioning anything about him. "Okay, fine. I can't."

"Why not?"

"I just can't. Divine forces, or whatever."

"And that's why I can't walk away from the order. It'll always be part of me, and I need to follow its guidance if I'm ever going to be free to pursue a life with you."

Accepting her only escape from heartache as the defeat of another wraith, she turned her mind to the task. "Where was his last kill?"

"That's actually not quite the right question. His last kill was in Toronto seventy-five years ago. But his last attempt was in

Chicago twenty-five years ago. He killed both hunters in a Chicago suburb, but he died, too."

"What?"

"Yeah, he died. Hunters and wraith, all three. But his dagger was never found. So, we assume that a new wraith picked it up."

The update frustrated her. "What if the dagger was lost? There may not even be a wraith."

"The council says there is, and I believe them."

"What? They're empaths now?"

"No. But they have their ways."

She remembered Friar Lucio leading the council in summoning an angel in the sanctum to break one of her telepathic links. The act made her question how much she had yet to learn about the paranormal. "Let's say they're right. Then we need to get moving."

"To Chicago?"

"Not yet. I want to try some things here with Emma and, like you said, maybe with the guy we captured." She couldn't say the imprisoned wraith's name yet.

"Okay. So, no need to panic and get upset. I know I've been the guy in the hurry in the past, but that's only because we were racing clocks over weeks and days. This time, we can get it right without any real time pressure."

She shrugged. "Maybe there's no clock on the wraith, but there's a clock on my patience on waiting for you to propose. I'm not waiting forever."

CHAPTER 4

Liam gathered the small team in a conference room. In addition to inviting the two empaths, he'd brought his father and Diane's family members to update everyone together. He removed the cap from a marker, wrinkled his nose at its toxic scent, and then wrote on a whiteboard. "Let's share what we know, starting with the wraith."

Defying his seventy-five years of aging, Connor sounded perky. "Why not? Let us continue our streak of victories. Damn the odds!" He sipped from a coffee cup and lowered it to a table.

Attributing the elder hunter's spryness to caffeine, Liam challenged the odds. "Right, Father. Damn the odds, whatever they are. Historically, you could say that it's hopeless until he enters his killing cycle, but that was before we had empaths. Let's review our assets and possible tactics before judging our chances."

"That's what I meant, lad. And to echo your point, they're not just empaths, they're also targeted sacrifices who overcame their wraiths. That must be significant."

Liam agreed. "I believe there's something in their selection as a sacrificial target that gives them special power on top of their empathic abilities." He glanced at Diane and Emma, wondered about the unknown reaches of their skills, and then continued. "But before we dive into what they're capable of, let's talk about the second wraith." He wrote two dates on the board.

Diane canted her head. "September twenty-ninth, twenty-forty-two and September nineteenth, twenty-forty-three... that spread between dates looks kind of familiar."

"The first date is when he's scheduled to start his next killing cycle. He's on the same sort of calendar as the one who held you captive, but he's on an autumn cycle and twenty-five years off. One tribute under each full moon for a year starting in September, then a sacrifice under the full moon the subsequent September."

His father crossed his legs and smirked. "I'm blessed with

good health, but I can't promise you that I'll be breathing, much less in fighting shape, when I'm one hundred years old."

Seated next to Connor in an office chair behind a table of laminated wood, the Chaldean psychic empath folder her arms. "And I already told you, I'm not waiting for you that long."

On the table's opposite site, Diane's grandmother flicked her wrist. "No. She can't wait. I want to live to see my great-grand-children."

With his emotions exposed and his formerly impossible love life taking shape under the scrutiny of two stubborn Iraqi women, the young hunter grew frustrated. "I didn't say I planned on waiting until then. None of us wants to wait, and we're not going to. We're going to find him long before then."

"Any idea how long?" Diane seemed detached, like she considered a successful hunt impossible.

Liam feared that the rules standing between him and marrying Diane were driving her away. "That depends on what we learn." He spoke while writing the word 'cursed dagger' below the dates on the whiteboard. "We assume he's got a dagger, since the council assured us of it, but that's not going to help us much."

Connor interrupted his son's presentation. "I hate to be a downer, but it's not going to help us at all. His dagger's only useful for tracking him during his killing cycle."

"Of course, Father. That's why we're figuring this out. Let's move on to what our dagger does, in absence of a wraith using his."

The elder hunter sipped coffee and then lowered his cup. "In absence of him using his dagger, ours will only point to the site of his last kill. But we already know where that is, and it wasn't even his kill. It was that of his predecessor."

Liam wrote 'Chicago' and 'Missing Sacrifice' as his last bullet points about the wraith. "Right. His predecessor last killed in Toronto, seventy-five years ago and then died trying to kill a sacrifice in Chicago twenty-five years ago. Dental remains from the fire identified both hunters, and DNA identified the third set of remains as a male we assume was the predecessor wraith, but there were no other bodies found."

His father challenged the text. "What do you mean by a missing sacrifice?"

"We didn't find her. So, we have to ask ourselves, where did she go? The whole reason three men converged on that house was to kill her or to save her, but there's no sign of her ever being there."

Connor plopped his cup to the table. "The primary theory is that the wraith was making preparations for his sacrifice when the hunters caught up to him. Then a fire broke out during their combat, all three men died, and thus began our mystery. The wraith was planning to capture his sacrifice and bring her to the house before the hunters foiled his plan. Of course, this is merely conjecture, and there are other theories, but the council considers this one the most likely, as do I."

Liam placed his marker on the board. "That theory sucks."

"Easy, lad. Explain yourself. Do you mean you disagree with it, or that you just don't like it?"

"I don't like it. It doesn't produce a new wraith."

"Many people could have come by the house and found the dagger. A neighbor, a passerby, a first responder, and that's only if he had it with him when he died. He could've kept it anywhere, which means anyone could have it."

Liam's scientific mind kicked into gear. "That's a ton of random possibilities that would take a lot of detective work to chase down. I prefer to consider the simpler cases first, such as the possibility that the sacrifice was already in the house during the gunfight."

Connor shot a glance into the ceiling while pondering it. "That would implicate her as falling short of her civic duty. At the very least, she would've witnessed three homicides without telling anyone. Sacrifices are usually ladies of virtue."

Liam smirked at the two empaths. "Not all of them are perfect angels."

Diane rolled her eyes. "Well, that can be debated."

The young hunter continued. "So, nobody went to the police. Three men died, plenty of bullet shells were scattered around the basement, and a fire burned the house to the ground. It looks like a beginning of a fledgling wraith's career that has zero useful clues. But, hang with me on this... what if the sacrifice took the dagger?"

Connor frowned. "Why would she? There's no point. There's never been a female wraith."

"I'm guessing, but maybe she had a boyfriend or a brother or some other close male friend or relative, and she gave it to him. That would've turned him into a wraith on the spot."

Connor scoffed. "In that case, he'd have been in his kill cycle, standing under a full moon next to his girlfriend, or his sister, who happens to be a sacrifice. What would have prevented him from killing her?"

"She was a targeted sacrifice for the predecessor wraith, not necessarily for him."

The elder hunter waved his hand. "Bah. We're speculating. We can only unravel the mystery so far."

"But we haven't gotten to the best part yet." Liam faced the empaths. "We know what Diane can do, which may be enough on its own. But we don't know yet what Emma can do, and we don't know what they can do together, each with a dagger, with two hunters and maybe even a wraith at their disposal."

Diane shook her head. "He's not a friend. He's not an ally. He's a prisoner, and he's still possessed by an evil spirit."

Suspecting a powerful demon and a man of weakened will, Liam expected months of repeated sessions to exorcise the spirit from the captured wraith. "He won't be possessed forever. Friar Lucio will take care of it, and while he's working on it, there'll be times where Ethan's free to help us."

Connor raised a finger. "Beware that he could pretend to be free of the demon's influence at any moment while lying to us as the demon lies through him."

Liam nodded. "Agreed, and I'll trust Friar Lucio to guide us. Regardless, the best options are with our empaths. So, ladies, let's review what we know about your special skills."

Emma shrugged. "I just got my knife yesterday, and I've been afraid to touch it. I still want to learn more from Diane before I try it on my own." She'd received the enchanted twin to Ethan's cursed dagger in the prior day's ceremony. Grateful to her hunting team for having saved her from a wraith, the German empath had volunteered to help solve the riddle of the next wraith.

Liam appreciated her participation and hoped she could help Diane, and he considered her cautious instincts good, as those of an empathic psychic should be. "You're wise to wait. Following Diane's a good idea. She's learned under pressure."

The Chaldean psychic rattled off her talents. "I can experience the world through someone else's senses, and I can even make people do things, if I have my dagger and depending how much they resist."

Recalling her attempt to make him pick his nose, Liam stopped her. "Is it how much they resist, or is it something else, like how much they know about you?"

"I don't know what causes it, but from my perspective it's resistance. You had a hard enough time resisting me when you were right across the table from me watching me do it."

"It wasn't that hard."

"Whatever. I didn't try getting into the last wraith's head until it was a team effort, and the wraith before that made me watch him kill someone before kicking me out. So, the resistance varies."

Liam had anticipated the empath's answer, but he'd hoped by explaining it, she'd uncover an insight. No luck. He moved on. "You've seen visions of the past and future, too, using your dagger."

"Yeah, I did with the wraith in Istanbul. And with help from combinations of you guys, I can aim a dagger at a targeted sacrifice and sometimes summon a ghost maiden, but the ghosts pretty much show up whenever they want."

The conversation reached where Liam had anticipated.

"We've got a lot of possibilities. The empath skills at our disposal aren't entirely predictable, but there's a hierarchy in effort and resources, like using more daggers or more people. I say we start out with the simplest effort."

Diane folded her arms. "Don't you think that I should be deciding which efforts to use for myself?"

Liam shook his head. "Nope. You'll be deciding for you and Emma, both. Since we're going deep into uncharted empath waters, I want you to go with a buddy and to start out slow. I'm not waiting years, but we've got time for you to train her to help."

CHAPTER 5

Layla tipped back her vodka and cranberry cocktail, lowered the crystal glass, and then answered her phone. Her empathic awareness clawed at her, and she braced for bad news. "What'd you find?"

Her private investigator sounded grim. "I found him, but I don't think you'll like what I found."

Adrenaline and alcohol coursed through her veins. Her detective had lost track of Amir six months ago after her son had left his prior home in Las Vegas, and she needed to know about her child. "Is he stronger? Is he more powerful?"

"I can only assume so. I did some digging, and he's set up a company that's trading international currencies. He's a smart and capable man. I've watched him build a fortune."

His growing strength fed her need. "Where is he?"

"Phoenix."

"What's his address?"

"We can come to that later. I need to tell you how I found him. There's a young lady who's recently been murdered in the area under the same circumstances I've seen surrounding your son. That's the news that drew me to look for him in Phoenix."

She raised her voice. "You've proven nothing about the circumstances surrounding my son."

He sighed. "Only because you're not paying me to. But the evidence is there. I just happen to be looking the other way."

Without bothering to mute her phone, she yelled for her housekeeper to refill her drink.

An attentive servant marched into the room, grabbed the empty glass, and darted away.

The detective continued his report. "The young lady in the Phoenix area went missing under a full moon shortly after the time I assume your son moved into the valley. She was in her early twenties. A deeply religious person. A sloppy and hasty job with her body found in a dumpster."

Layla snapped. "How do you know she's religious?"

"Was religious. She's dead."

"Answer the damned question!"

"Her church is holding a candlelight prayer session."

Deep within her subconscious awareness, she knew her son had grown into a killer, but she refused to accept it. "That could just be a token gesture."

"The articles about her disappearance include a lot of description about her having an active church life."

"So what? I'm not paying you to tell me about coincidences and conjectures."

"No. You're paying me to follow your son across the country. I've been doing that for years, but I can't anymore. I know too much. I'm resigning."

"You son of a bitch."

"I found him in Phoenix because I assumed he was a serial killer. You can't expect me in good conscience to keep looking the other way."

That's what she'd been paying him to do, and her voice became icy. "If you want your last paycheck, text me his address, and text me his alias. Then go to hell." She hung up and tossed her phone onto the desk.

The housekeeper placed the drink by her side.

Layla grabbed the crystal, gulped half of it, and held the glass by her cheek. "Get me another one."

The servant departed.

As her phone chimed with a message, Layla downed the remainder of her cocktail. After reading the text containing her son's business address and his assumed name, she bought a plane ticket to Phoenix.

She swore as she burned her hand on the rental Cadillac's seatbelt. Nothing had prepared her for the blistering heat of Arizona's low desert. "Damn it."

With the Escalade's air conditioner blowing at full capacity, she drove towards the wealthy suburb of Scottsdale. Congested movement on Route 202 tested her patience, and as nausea consumed her stomach, she knew her discomfort came from more than temperature and traffic.

As with her prior six attempts to approach her son, supernatural forces sickened her. Her psychic discernment told her a truth she tried to ignore. The closer she got to Amir, the sicker she became.

Slowing with worsening traffic, she recalled her attempt to meet him three years earlier in Utah. On that day, she'd pushed through a third bout of dry heaves, vomiting her stomach acids onto a street of disgusted onlookers. But she'd pursued him on the busy sidewalk despite having been dizzy, queasy, and dehydrated. When she'd reached within distance to call him, her voice had failed. Then she'd passed out and collapsed.

Refusing to let the past deter her, she exited Route 202 in Scottsdale. All the way to the suburb's commercial district, lines of cars covered the squared grid roads, and her nausea worsened with each stop-and-go mile.

When she reached her son's work address, she parked across the street at a diner. As she walked out of the vehicle, the brutal August sun smacked her in the face and baked her exposed skin. She hurried through the door into the air-conditioned space and then sat in a booth by a window facing her son's building.

At the corner facing the restaurant, tannish brown stone walls blended the structure with the surrounding architecture and with the underlying dessert. Standing four-stories tall, it rose above the lines of yucca trees planted in front of it. A glass door at its main entrance opened, but she knew before seeing the occupant pass into the punishing heat that it wasn't her son.

"Hi there. Can I get you something to drink, or are you ready to order?" An older woman with hard lines carved into her face by decades of sun worship held a scratchpad and pen.

Layla chose food she knew would quell her stomach. "Dry toast and Coke."

"Is that all?"

"Yes."

"I'll put it right in. It'll be right up."

Knowing her son was working in his building, Layla watched the structure in hopes of seeing him, but her empathic sense said he would remain inside while she ate.

The waitress returned and plopped the toast and drink on the table. "Let me know if I can get you anything else."

"Nothing." Layla nibbled on the bread, and when it landed in her stomach, it eased her queasiness. As the carbonated sugar water diluted acids, leveling out her nausea, she reached into her purse, pulled out a ten-dollar bill, and tossed it on the table. But after she swallowed the final bite of toast, a toxic chill consumed her, and she looked through the window.

Wearing a long sleeve white cotton dress shirt, a fit young man carried a beige jacket over his shoulder. Sunglasses protected his eyes from the harsh sun beating down on his tanned face. He walked towards a red Maserati GranTurismo Sport parked in a reserved spot.

Layla held her breath and stared. Though the distance and sunglasses complicated her view, she knew he was her son. She raised her fingers towards the diner's window. "Amir."

As if hearing her, he stood with his hand on the opened door to his car and stared in her direction.

Her nausea worsened, and she cringed to hold down bile. As she looked up again, she saw a new image.

Instead of a handsome, successful man, a disgusting demon looked at her, his face a twisted aberration of sagging and torn skins. Fangs protruded from the slimy mouth under a long, crooked nose. His clothes were invisible, revealing a body of scarred and blighted leather, and at its extreme ends, horns, a pointed tail, and cloven hooves.

She turned her head. "No." Looking up again, she saw the unblemished version of her human son. Fighting against a growing illness, she stood from her seat and strode towards the restaurant's exit hoping to run to him before he drove away.

Blocking her path, the ghost appeared, and time entered its drastic halt as the figure wearing a milky gown blown by an unseen wind called out. "Stop!"

Layla gasped but her lungs froze. Unable to move, she spoke to the apparition within her mind. "Not you again."

The ghost's black eyes glared. "I am the Maiden of Toronto. Heed my warning. You must recover the dagger from your son."

"Get out of my way!"

"You grow sick as you approach him."

"It's a coincidence."

"Your sickness arises from a lack of love. You seek your son from a desire to control. Yield your need for dominion. Find love, and find your son. Love is the power of the empath."

"Go away, bitch!" Expecting the apparition to disappear, Layla urged her legs forward, but time lingered in its transcendental trap.

Undaunted, the misty maiden remained in place, and her eyes grew large as she shrieked a haunting response. "You will heed my warning, or you will perish!"

Layla's lucid memories of her supernatural episodes replayed in her mind. "What the hell do you care? Didn't I avenge you when I killed the history teacher? You told me to kill him twenty-five years ago, and I did. Leave me alone!"

"You avenged me, but you did not redeem me. You must free me."

"How can I get rid of you forever?"

The ghost's eyes softened. "Take your son's dagger and give it to the hunters."

"What hunters?"

"They will find you. They are coming."

CHAPTER 6

With her dagger in her purse, Diane listened to Friar Lucio's soothing voice. She considered him a wise and calming factor.

"The enchanted dagger may once have been the property of the order, but after you captured Ethan, its ownership transferred to Emma, just the way you received your dagger after you survived your wraith."

Diane glanced at Emma. "See? There's no need to be afraid."

All of Emma's knuckles were white on the lacquered wooden box. "I'm not afraid. I'm just cautious."

"You young ladies are wise to be cautious. Never before have we been blessed with such talent, but also never before have we attempted to thwart a wraith off cycle. But I expect you'll be safe running your experiments in the center of the sanctum. It's our most sacred location." He pushed open the temporary plywood door. "I'll be right outside. Good luck, my young empaths."

Diane led Emma down the aisle and stopped at the arced bench. She took off the backpack she'd borrowed from Liam and withdrew the young hunter's laptop. She aimed it towards the center of the semicircle, checked the view of its camera, and started the video.

"We're going to record this?"

"That's what Liam wanted, and it makes sense. You'll want to watch yourself later. It's a weird feeling when you do, but it's worth it." Diane moved to the focal point of the council's semicircular bench. Looking at her feet, she verified she stood in the center of the floor's carved compass. Facing east, she lowered her purse by her foot. "Face me."

Emma placed her wooden box by her foot and placed her back to the east. "Now what?"

Seeking to define a proper sequence of experiments, Diane had rehearsed scenarios in her mind but arrived at nothing. She instead opted to obey her instincts as they unfolded while she stood on the compass. Reaching her decision, she stooped, grabbed the wooden box, and opened it towards the German empath. "Grab it and see what happens."

Emma followed the advice and reached out with both hands. She took and lifted the knife. "I like it."

"I knew you would. But you don't feel anything special?"

"Special, yeah. I love it." The dagger captivated Emma. For a solid minute, only her breathing and the veins pulsating on her neck proved she remained in sidereal time.

Diane coached her student. "Try to see if you can invite Connor to come down here."

Emma ignored her.

"Hello?"

"Huh?"

Realizing that a telepathic link with the elder hunter was beyond her student's present skills, Diane backed out of the test. "Um, just put your dagger back in the box."

"No. I like holding it."

The refusal set off Diane's psychic alarms, but she remained calm and treated the German empath like her autistic brother. "Can you please put your dagger away, Emma?"

"I don't want to."

"Can you do it as a favor for me, Emma?"

No answer.

"Emma, can you please do a favor for me? I'm your friend."

"What is it?"

"Can you please put your dagger in the box for a little while?"

The German empath lowered the knife.

"Very good, Emma. Now let go of it, please."

Emma pouted. "Why? Do I have to?"

"You're doing something nice for me. I'm your friend. We do nice things for each other."

"Okay." She released the weapon.

Diane yanked away the box and tucked it under her arm.

Groggy, Emma extended a hand. "I want it back."

"Not yet."

Recovering her senses, the German psychic blinked and

scowled. "Why do I want it back so badly?"

"That's sort of what happened to me. It's a bit of shock to your system, but in a good way. You get used to it after a while."

"I think we should stop for today. I really want to hold it again, which is why I shouldn't be near it."

Diane appreciated her new friend's wisdom. "That's good self-control. Just to make sure, I'm going to give it to Friar Lucio to hold during my turn." She trotted up the aisle and tripped, but her free hand slapped against the back of a bench and stabilized her.

Emma's voice echoed in the empty space. "Are you okay?"

"Fine. I just tripped."

"Over what?"

"Myself." With her empathic sister's dagger enclosed in the box under her arm, she left the courtroom.

Friar Lucio paced outside the plywood doors. "Any luck?"

"Not really. She tried holding her dagger and sort of fell in love with it."

"Is that a concern?"

"Not really. It happened to me. But she was smart enough to know better than to try again today. Can you hold this for her?"

"If you insist." He accepted the box.

Diane spun back towards the plywood and strode into the sanctum. When she reached her partner, she announced her intention. "My turn now."

"What should I do?"

"Just stand there." Diane crouched and lifted the dagger from her purse. She waited for whatever phenomenon the paranormal world divined for her.

"Is anything happening?"

"Well, since we're talking, no." Diane felt anxiety probing her. "Wait. I've got something." She generated her own feelings of worry to connect with the incoming emotion, and then she slipped into a link.

The young hunter's voice rolled within her mind. "Diane?"

"Liam! What are you doing?"

"What do you mean? You just entered my head. You're supposed to be looking for a wraith."

"I am, but I can't do it when you're suffocating me."

"Huh? I'm not doing anything."

"I'm holding my dagger, and the first signal I got was you worrying about me."

"I can't help that!"

"Maybe a little confidence? If I'm going to be your wife, you need to show a little trust."

"I trust you implicitly. That doesn't mean I'm not going to worry. I'm only human."

She agreed. "Can't you think of something else?"

"Like what?"

"I don't know. What do boys think of when they're not thinking of girls? Baseball?"

"I don't know a baseball from a handball."

"Think of something."

"There's a soccer World Cup quarterfinal match tomorrow. That'll be a nice distraction."

"I'm not waiting until tomorrow."

"I'll run off and read something. Give me a moment."

"Fine. Bye."

Time returned to normal, and Diane slid her dagger into her purse.

Emma furrowed her brow. "Did you just slip away?"

"Yeah. I had a link with Liam."

"Why Liam? What's wrong?"

"Nothing's wrong except that he's crowding me. He's worried about me, and his anxiety was blocking me."

"Maybe you should put some food in front of him. That would take care of it."

Picturing the young hunter with a turkey leg hanging from his mouth, Diane chuckled. "I don't need to get that drastic yet. He said he's going to read something. Let's try that first." She bent over and fished her phone from her purse. "I'm calling him." After dialing, she listened for his voice.

"Yes, Diane."

"Are you reading yet?"

"I just opened my computer. Give me a second."

"I'll wait."

"You're bossy."

"Get used to it."

"Okay. I'm reading an article. I'm not worrying about you."

She put her phone in her purse, picked up her dagger, and repeated her attempt. Anxiety tickled her telepathic antenna, and she locked onto it. It was Liam again. "You're still worrying about me!"

"I'm sorry. I can't help it."

"You're throwing a wet blanket over this whole thing."

"I don't know what to do."

She was an empath. She knew. "Think of kittens."

"What?"

"You like kittens. In fact, you like cats. A lot!"

"How'd you know? We've never talked about it, but I adore cats. All of them. I can name every species–ocelots, jaguarundis, servals, caracals... all the weird ones. I'm a feline fanatic."

Although she hated to digress, she had to probe a level deeper. "I know you like cats because I'm an empath, and I've got you in a telepathic link. Sometimes, I get random info like that. But isn't that weird for guys? Don't guys like dogs?"

"Dogs are cool. Each one is descended from a wolf. But wolves hunt in a pack within a hierarchy. Every cat is its own master and a natural hunting carnivore. If that's not cool, I don't know what is."

"Okay. I can respect that. But set aside the idea of hunting and think of kittens for a minute."

"Kittens doing what?"

"I don't know! Sleeping. Playing with a ball of yarn. Wrestling with each other. Flip through stupid cat videos on YouTube until you find one you like."

"Great thinking! I'll watch stupid cat tricks."

She cast him away, and as his stifling anxiety waned, she

credited him with following her advice. Time recommenced, and she saw Emma looking at her. "It was Liam again, but I think we finally took care of it."

"That's good. You looked like you slipped away again."

"I did, but now I'm free to search. Here goes." Tuning herself to the emotions a fledgling wraith might have–arrogance, haughtiness, hatred–she sought her quarry, but nothing surfaced. Although she'd expected to come up empty, she was disappointed to verify that she'd need better targeting information. "Dang it. I'm not feeling anything."

"So, what do we do next?"

Diane walked to the bench and stopped the video on Liam's spare laptop. "Nothing. We wait. You need to get accustomed to your dagger, and I need to squeeze better info out of Liam. Let's get some lunch. I'm starved."

"Yeah. Me, too, now that you mention it."

"This work takes a lot of energy. It would be a great diet plan if we could bottle it and sell it."

Emma grinned. "But we'd be less special if everybody were an empath."

"Good point. I like being special, too. Let's go. I want to splurge on Connor's credit card and get some good food."

CHAPTER 7

While his father played golf with a group of friars, Liam worked on the mystery. With three computers and stacks of folders, he ransacked the archives about the last known episode in the wraith's lineage–his predecessor's failed attempt to murder a sacrifice on September 30th, 1993. "Bloody hell." From the corner of his eye, he sought a response.

Seated at a table within the small reading room, which adjoined the order's library, Josh kept his nose aimed at a tablet.

Liam groped again for a reaction. "I mean, think about how close the hunters got to ending this. If only one of them had survived, we'd have retired the dagger."

Silently, Josh ran his finger across his tablet's screen.

"Then I'd already be engaged to your sister."

Hearing the personal angle, Josh cast a glance to the room's upper corner, pondered a thought that would remain a secret buried within his complex mind, and then aimed his nose back to his tablet.

Liam appreciated his peculiar assistant. Though quirky and quiet, Diane's brother was a thorough researcher. While the young hunter read about the fire, he had his companion reading about the predecessor wraith's last successful sacrifice in Toronto.

Josh cleared his throat.

"Did you find something, Josh?"

"No."

Giving up on small talk, Liam refocused his eyes on the nearest screen. The hunters had tracked their prey to his three-story greystone house in the Chicago suburb of Evanston. Though neighboring residences crowded its walls, the home provided adequate privacy with its large basement.

Josh lifted his phone to his cheek. "Hello... yes... okay. Liam, Diane says she's going to lunch with Nana and Emma. Do we want to come?"

"No, thanks. I'm going to order a sandwich. I'll get one for you, too, if you want."

"He says he's going to order a sandwich... No. I want to stay with Liam... I love you, too. Bye." Josh put his phone on his desk and returned his attention to his reading.

The hunter reviewed a report about the fire. Having started in the back of the basement with kindling wood and accelerant, it had risen into the ground floor's boards and consumed the structure. Large masses of the stone walls had crumbled as the mortar had failed, and the house had fallen in on itself. Three bodies had been found, all male, two of them the hunters. The third remained unidentified, and attempts to find the tenant had led to false names and untraceable bank accounts. "Even if we could identify the body, he's a dead end. This whole fire's just a random starting point for a new wraith."

"What would you do without a wraith to hunt?"

The autistic man's question surprised Liam. "Well, hell, buddy. I'll worry about that when it happens."

"If you're going to marry Diane, you'll need to make a living."

Liam lobbed the first silly idea he thought of. "Maybe I'd learn to cook and be a house husband. She wants a career in marketing, doesn't she?"

"No, not anymore."

"Are you sure?"

"I can tell. She's too excited about what she's doing now."

"But you're right. We can't hunt wraiths forever."

"There will always be bad people she can help hunt."

"I'm not sure she can make a living doing that. I guess if we ever do get married, I'll need to get a real job."

"She said you wanted to be an engineer."

"I have half my credits towards a degree. I'd be done already if I weren't putting all my time into... this."

"This is important."

As his companion became silent, Liam returned to reading about the last confrontation with his enemy. To its credit, the order had employed a local consultant to help an Evanston police detective identify the hunters and to gather private information. "The nine-one-one call came from a neighbor across the street. Four minutes later, the first responders arrived. But the fire was already out of control by the time they got there."

Josh ignored him.

Liam analyzed the reports for witnesses and neighbors, whom he considered suspects to have taken the dagger. A check of the elderly retiree who'd called the fire department led to an obituary eight years later. Neighbors on one side had been female coeds attending Northwestern University, and the inhabitants on the burned house's other side had been exchange students who'd returned to China. The ladies could not be wraiths, and the Chinese nationals could not be found on any search, since they were beyond the young hunter's ability to probe via Internet.

Frustrated, Liam stared at a printout, discolored with age, summarizing a mystery with a murky beginning and an unseen end. When his patience died, he closed the manila folder's flap and flicked the report across the table with his middle finger.

As his pessimism worsened, he entertained thoughts of contacting the other hunting lines. Reflecting upon his successes taking down three wraiths, he asked himself if the council could call upon the other two lines to accelerate their hunts.

Then he remembered.

They lacked an empath.

Giving up on natural means to find his prey, he accepted Diane as his only chance. Whatever mystical powers dwelled within her, he hoped her desire to marry him would inspire her rapid mastery. But then he recalled her recent aloofness and feared she'd recognized their mission's futility. Was she abandoning their short and bizarre courtship to seek more opportune companionship? He needed to find out. "Hey, Josh?"

The young man grunted.

"You like the idea of me and your sister getting married, right?"

"Uh huh."

"Do you think she still, you know, likes me."

41

"Uh huh."

"I mean, do you still think she wants to get married?"

"Uh huh."

"Well, if I asked you how sure you are, could you tell me?"

"Uh huh."

Losing patience, Liam raised his voice. "Josh!"

"What?"

"How sure are you?"

"About Diane?"

"Yes. How sure are you that she still wants to marry me?"

His companion looked at the ceiling.

"I'm sorry, Josh. I didn't mean to be so rude."

Josh returned his gaze at his tablet. "I'm one hundred percent sure that she wants to marry you."

"Well, um. That's good." Liam wanted to inquire further about how he could be certain, but he stopped himself. He'd prodded enough. Hungry, he scanned a local sandwich shop's menu.

"A group of cats is called a clowder."

"Huh? What's that?" The young hunter eyed his companion.

Josh frowned. "Weren't you listening?"

"No, I'm sorry, Josh. I was getting ready to order lunch. What was that about cats?"

"A group of cats is called a clowder."

"I knew that... Wait. No, I didn't."

"A group of kittens is called a kindle."

"Seriously? That's cool, I guess. But why are cats on your mind? I thought you were doing research."

"The research isn't helping."

"Yeah, I just concluded the same thing."

A feeble smile crept across Josh's face. "You said you know everything about cats, but then I thought about the clowder, and you didn't know."

Liam snorted. "Yup. You got me there."

Josh swiped his finger across his screen, probably looking for a new book to read.

Something bit at Liam's subconscious. A vague concept swirled within him, identified itself as a logical disconnect, and then landed in his awareness. "I never told you I liked cats, at least I don't think I did. But I sure as hell never told you that I knew everything about them."

Josh shrugged. "I don't know."

"Maybe I did tell you." Liam recalled his telepathic link with Diane in which she'd discerned his feline affinities. Since she'd headed straight for lunch after their transcendental communication, Josh must have learned about their ethereal conversation from his own special link to his sister. The young hunter flagged the phenomenon for future reference.

Again, Josh looked to the ceiling. "Liam?"

"Yes. What's on your mind, Josh?"

"Promise you won't get mad."

"It'll take a lot for me to get mad at you."

"You have to promise."

"Okay. I promise I won't get mad."

"You're being stupid."

Liam frowned and recalled the one theory he'd voiced that differed from the common opinion. "Why? Because I think the lady the wraith was going to kill was in the house during the gun fight?"

"No. That's smart."

The young hunter made a mental note to revisit the compliment after resolving the insult. The empath's brother was feeding him a healthy dose of opinions and insights. "At least I'm doing something right. But what am I doing that makes me stupid?"

"You're ignoring Ethan."

"I don't know that I'm ignoring him. I'm not sure what good he is for us yet, though. I wouldn't know what to ask him."

Josh's hands trembled with frustration, and he sounded irritated. "Oh, it's so obvious!"

Liam shook his head. "I'm sorry, Josh. Sometimes people around you have trouble understanding things that you to see.

You have special vision."

The compliment reduced Josh's visible annoyance. "You need to ask him how a wraith learns to kill before his first tribute. Whatever Ethan did a thousand years ago is how you'll find the new one."

CHAPTER 8

In the lounge of the Four Seasons Resort in Scottsdale, Layla slurped her vodka and cranberry cocktail. Her latest encounter with her son weighed on her, and she wrestled to grasp what he'd become.

An attentive steward strode across the floor and then stopped before the chaise lounge upon which she reclined. "Would you like another drink, ma'am?"

"Yeah. Same thing." She waved him away.

"Right away, ma'am." The server marched off.

When Layla was alone, she looked at one of the televisions to watch the reality show that held the attention of other resort guests, but the misty white ghost appeared, blocking her view.

The ornate lounge slipped into slow motion as the figure wearing a milky gown blown by an unseen wind looked upon her. "Heed me, or die a failed empath."

Petrified in trickling time, Layla spoke within her mind to the apparition. "Stay out of my life."

The ghost's black eyes grew large. "You must recover the dagger from your son."

"I'm not deaf. I heard you the first umpteen times."

"You must recover it for your sake and his."

"The dagger's my son's. I survived. I overcame a madman, and it was mine to give."

"He was not yours to conceive."

Layla's ethereal voice hit the supernatural stratosphere. "Go to hell! He's my son. He was always my son. He will always be my son. There's not a damned thing you can do to change that."

The Maiden of Toronto furrowed her brow and dug a cold stare into the empath. "If I had wielded the power, I would have prevented this. But now I can only counsel you to undo what you have done."

"Go away."

"If you continue to ignore me, more will die."

"Shut up."

"He will kill under the full moon tonight."

"I don't care what he does."

"That is why you fail as an empath."

"You're lying anyway. Get out of here!"

The ghost vanished as the waiter brought a fresh cocktail and lowered it to the table beside the haunted empath. "A Ketel One with cranberry juice."

Layla gulped the drink in her hand and then extended the empty glass to her server.

He placed the container on a tray and headed to the kitchen.

The haunted empath powered down her new drink and then acted upon an idea. She walked through the hotel's lobby and into the punishing afternoon heat. She had a valet retrieve her Cadillac SUV, and then she drove to a Best Buy.

Inside the electronics store, she browsed GPS trackers and picked the most expensive model. After checking out, she returned to the Escalade and drove to the restaurant across the street from her son's office building.

As she lingered within the proximity of her child, the sickness rose within her. She selected toast and Coke again, and when a server brought her order, Layla slapped a one-hundred-dollar bill on the table. "This is yours if you put a GPS tracker on that Maserati GranTurismo Sport." She pointed at her son's car across the street.

The young lady eyed the cash like a discovered treasure. "How do you expect me to do that?"

The haunted psychic had anticipated the question. "Walk up the street a block. Then walk back by the car. Pull out your phone and take a picture and pretend to admire it. Drop your phone, and when you pick it up, put this under the passenger side door."

"I don't get it. Why do you want me to do it? Why not do it yourself?"

Expecting this second challenge, Layla leaned towards the waitress and lowered her voice. "It's my husband's car. He's cheating on me, and I need to catch him in the act so I don't get screwed in the divorce. He'd obviously get suspicious if he saw me hanging out near his car."

The young server looked out the window. "A guy with a car like that must be super-rich."

Layla reached into her purse, pulled out a second one-hundred-dollar bill, and dropped it on first. "Think you can handle it?"

"Show me the tracker."

The haunted empath pulled the product from her purse and slid it to her waitress. "Take it. Take the cash. Get it done."

With a rapid nod, the server took the GPS device and the money.

After watching the waitress complete the task, Layla drove to her hotel to escape her proximity-based nausea. An hour after she downed another vodka and cranberry cocktail, the tracking application showed her son driving towards Tucson.

She retrieved her Cadillac and pursued him southbound on Interstate 10. Staying ten miles behind him, she avoided sickness. Her imagination played tricks on her as she pondered her son's possible agendas, but her ignorance about his affairs made her helpless to speculate.

Ninety minutes later, she glanced at her phone, and the tracking application showed that Amir had exited the highway. In a Tucson suburb, he navigated backstreets and then stopped. Ten minutes behind him, she stopped at a gas station near the highway interchange and watched her application for movement while refilling her tank.

With the sun slipping below the horizon, she examined icons on her screen showing the businesses near her child's parked car. A Baptist church stood diagonally opposite his Maserati's location. Her former detective's accusation of churchgoers being victims of her son, the supposed serial killer, flickered in her memory and then faded as she denied the possibility.

The nozzle clicked, and she returned it to the gas pump. As she returned to the driver's seat, she saw the icon of her son's car in motion again. She moved the Escalade into a parking spot beside the convenience store and watched the Maserati moving towards sparsely populated foothills.

Curious, she drove a loose intercept path, attempting to predict his route and approach him without suffering her proximity-based nausea. As the elevation increased, the air thinned, and the density of artificial lights aligning the roadside dissipated with the increasing acreage of the large home plots and the unowned land between them.

While looking to her phone on a climbing curve, a pair of headlights surprised her. A honking horn startled her, and a Ford sedan whipped around the Cadillac in the darkness. As she recovered her bearings, she steered from the opposing lane back into hers.

As if supernatural guidance governed her timing, she glanced at her phone again and noticed the Maserati had stopped. Having learned from her near fatal collision, she pulled over to investigate Amir's stationary location. Even against the backdrop of rural foothills, it was remote.

As quickly as he'd stopped his car, her son turned around.

Realizing he'd doubled back towards her, she accelerated into an abrupt U-turn and sped down the hill to avoid him. The tracking map showed a new subdivision with streets extending several miles from the main road, and she angled her Cadillac into the rural bedroom community.

She sought a street far from her son's passage and parked beside a wooden fence separating huge yards of dirt. As her tracker showed the Maserati at its closest point, bile rose in her stomach but then subsided as Amir opened distance towards the highway.

Freed from her risk of illness, she steered the Cadillac up the mountain. As she slowed near the spot where her son had parked, she scanned the environs and saw moonlit sagebrush and cacti ranging from tall saguaros to fat barrels and flat prickly pears.

She stopped where Amir had been, and she stepped from the car. The high desert's nighttime coolness surprised her. Startling her, a cactus wren flew low with its silhouette streaking across a starry backdrop. She withdrew her phone and illuminated its flashlight, which cast a circle of white onto the hard dirt. Seeing nothing of interest, she turned back to her SUV.

A coyote howled, and she spun to face the sound. The scavenging hunter crept down the foothill and stopped under a mesquite tree. Overcoming her innate fear of the predator, she started towards it, scanning the desert floor for snakes and scorpions.

With unnatural courage, she stopped under the tree's leaves, heard the animal's slurping and chewing, and stared down the coyote's silhouette. Its eyes glimmered in the light of the full moon as it looked up from its dinner, and then it growled.

Layla slid her phone into her pocket, folded her arms, and aimed the angry daggers of her eyes at her adversary. Feeling a supernatural power flowing through her, she spoke with an icy tone. "Leave."

With a submissive whimper, the beast cowered and ran.

The haunted empath called upon her flashlight to identify the departed animal's meal. As she stepped forward, sandals and bare human legs came into view.

Gasping, Layla ran her light over the body of a young woman who stared at the sky with lifeless eyes. A gash in her abdomen showed the coyote's attempt to scavenge food, but a deep wound on her forehead revealed her cause of death.

The concept of her son's guilt as the murderer rose within Layla's subconscious mind, collided with her pride and denial, and then diffused into oblivion. She shook her head. "No."

A final glimpse of the corpse revealed a church group tee shirt with blood stains from the head wound.

Layla retraced her steps to the Escalade and sped away from a truth she rejected.

CHAPTER 9

Diane stood atop the compassed floor in the inner sanctum, facing the German empath. "Now relax and chill. It's yours."

"I think I liked life better when I was volunteering."

"Look at this as another form of volunteering."

"You make it sound like I could say 'no'. But I can't. I need to hold it."

Glancing at the laptop on the council's desk to verify it recorded the session, Diane extended the case. "*Yulla*. Take it."

With both hands, Emma held her inherited talisman. "I like it more than last time. I didn't think it was possible." As the dagger captivated her, only her breathing and the veins pulsating on her neck proved she hadn't slipped into a time-altering trance.

Diane prodded her. "Now see if you can get into Connor's head and have him come down here."

The German psychic showed improved attentiveness versus her prior training session. "You told me how to do this, didn't you?"

"Yes. Do you remember?"

"I... I love my dagger."

"That's not what I asked."

"Connor?"

"Yes. Call for him."

Emma's voice was weak and lazy. "Connor! Come here."

Diane refocused her colleague. "No. In your mind. You appreciate him saving your life. He's a sweet old man. He was willing to die to protect you. There are strong emotions there to grab onto and use."

"Okay." The German empath closed her eyes. When she reopened them, she dropped her jaw. "I think it worked."

"Really?"

"Unless I dreamt it all."

Diane hadn't noticed any stoppage of time, but her colleague's success would have marked the team's first telepathic link without the Chaldean empath's involvement. It was the first time Diane had to observe from the outside. "Wow! Did he say he was coming?"

"Yes. I think so."

"Can you put your dagger away until he gets here?"

"But I like holding it."

As Diane extended the open box, she treated her colleague like her brother. "Can you please put your dagger away, Emma?"

Requiring less coaxing than during the prior session, the German empath dropped the knife into the case.

Diane yanked away the box and tucked it under her arm.

"When can I have it back?"

"Soon. We'll run another experiment after Connor gets here."

The German psychic blinked and frowned. "I can't get over how badly I keep wanting it back. Will this ever get any better?"

"Yeah. I imagine it's like having a child. You never want to let go until you learn to trust that it'll come back. Did Connor say how far away he was?"

"He was in the study with Liam and your brother. Not long."

A minute later, a temporary knob on the sanctum's plywood door clicked, and Connor stuck his head in the room. "I believe I've been telepathically summoned."

Diane squeaked. "Sweet! It worked. You did it!"

Emma shrugged. "I guess I did."

The hunter walked down the aisle. "There's no question in my mind, unless I've been tricked." He reached the compass. "So, that's impressive. Emma called for me all by herself."

"She did."

"I can only imagine what two empaths can do together as her power grows."

Diane also could only speculate. "There's one way to find out. Let's see if you and Emma can link with me."

"Shall I hold her hand?"

"Yeah."

"Does that mean I get only one hand to hold my dagger?"

"Yeah. It doesn't matter, at least not that I've noticed. I've never seen a difference whether I hold it in my left or right. Now buddy up and hold hands, you two."

Emma and Connor followed instructions.

Diane extended the box, Emma lifted the dagger, and time receded into a glacial lethargy.

Emma's voice was distant and tentative. "Diane?"

"Emma? I hear you. Is Connor with you?"

Caught in near-motionlessness, the hunter sounded confident. "I'm here. Speak up, Emma. Don't be shy."

The German empath's voice boomed. "I'm here. Diane. Can you hear me?"

"Loud and clear. Too loud. Tone it down."

Emma's voice became natural. "Sorry. How's this?"

"Much better. Just like that."

"Why's this so much different than when you hold your dagger?"

Diane speculated. "The whole telepathic link must take on attributes of the personality and the mood of whoever's starting it with a dagger."

"I do feel like I'm in charge, like this link is an extension of me."

"Try ending it all by yourself. Don't warn us. Don't say goodbye. Just end it." Time recommenced its normal cadence.

"I did it!"

"You sure did. That was as good as any links I've ever done. Are you ready to try the big experiment?"

Connor interrupted. "Should I leave the room?"

Diane blurted her concern. "No! God knows what's going to happen. Stick around."

"Of course. What's the big experiment?"

"Two empaths, two daggers, holding hands."

Emma opened her eyes wide. "I don't know if I'm ready for that."

Diane lowered Emma's box to the floor and then strode to the council's bench where she grabbed the case with her dagger. "We'll never know until we try." She returned to her spot in front of her colleague and set her weapon's box beside that of the German empath and then opened both cases. While crouched, she slid Emma's box across the compass.

"What now?"

Diane stood. "We'll grab our daggers on the count of three. Nothing should happen. Then we'll hold hands, and I'll lead us into a link. Ready?"

"Sure. I guess."

"One. Two. Three." Diane bent her knees and grabbed her dagger. As she stood, she saw Emma in the same posture. "Connor?"

"Still here, breathing like normal."

Emma accepted the Chaldean psychic's extended hand.

Diane clasped her colleague's sweaty palm. "Still no trance. You're still with is in the real world, right, Connor?"

"Yes, young lady."

"Good. Okay. Here we go." Joining her empathic sister in a telepathic link was trivial, and with the slightest thought of their union, Diane stopped time around her and her colleague. She spoke with her mind. "Emma?"

"I'm here. I'm here. I'm here. I'm here. I'm here. I'm here." The German empath's voice echoed like amplified reverberation without signs of abating.

"Quiet!"

"I'm here. I'm here. I can't stop it. I can't stop it. I'm here. I'm here. I can't stop it. I can't stop it."

The German empath's reverberating voice hammered Diane's head. "Crap. Connor!" The Chaldean empath thought of the elder hunter and the fatherly love she had for him. Love is the tool of the empath. "Say something, Connor. Emma, just listen. Don't talk."

"Hello, young ladies." The German empath's painful echo subsided into silence.

"What happened?" Emma's voice was normal.

"I think our link's so powerful that it's... what's the word I'm looking for, Connor? It gets stuck in a loop."

"Oscillating?"

"Yeah. That's it. It's oscillating, unless we focus on a third person. That's why I brought Connor in."

Connor sounded optimistic. "If I had to guess, both of you were overly excited. You each reflected and added to the energy of the other and then back again in an unstable cycle."

Emma interrupted him. "Yes. It was like Diane's voice was echoing in my head really loudly."

"Same thing for me."

"I bet if you were both to whisper and make an effort to absorb each other's voices, you'd be able to control it."

Diane pondered the advice aloud. "I'm not sure how we'd do that."

"Try it out now. Try to bring all our voices down to a whisper as you hear them. Start with my voice, for example."

"I've never done that, but, um, I guess."

"I'll yammer on, and you see if you can lower my volume. Ready?"

Diane considered the idea silly but humored him. "Sure. Go ahead."

"I'll recite a poem by William Butler Yeats. It's one of my favorites, although I don't recall the title. Here goes. I went out to the hazel wood. Because a fire was in my head."

Diane envisioned herself as an energy sponge, absorbing the ethereal sound of the elder hunter's voice as he continued his recitation. Her complete lack of interest in his poem helped her dial down his volume.

"And cut and peeled a hazel wand. And hooked a berry to a thread; And when white moths were on the wing." His voice faded into an unnatural distance.

"It's working for me. How about you, Emma?"

"Yes! He can be very boring when he tries."

"Trust me. He doesn't have to try."

"And moth-like stars were flickering out. I dropped the berry in a stream. And caught a little silver trout." His last words tapered to silence.

"It worked! Is he still talking?"

Emma's voice remained at normal volume. "I can't hear him, and if we can't hear him, how can we tell?"

"We can't. That's enough for this session." Diane willed the link severed, and she released Emma's hand when time returned to normal.

"Were you able to absorb my energy?"

"I was. I think Emma could to."

The German empath nodded.

"I think you're ready to try it again without me. See if you can control how you absorb and reflect each other's energy. Then see if you can harness your energies together to explore whatever realms your consciousnesses can find."

Diane lifted her arm. "Ready?"

Emma accepted her hand.

With a simple thought, Diane invoked the link with her psychic sister, and time slogged to a crawl. She gave a weak mental whisper. "Emma?"

No response.

She boosted her whisper's volume. "Emma?"

"I can barely hear you." The energy from the German empath's voice was overbearing.

Instead of resisting, Diane let the supernatural sound flow through her, and the conversation succumbed to her control. "Great. I can hear you." She risked speaking at normal volume. "How's this."

"A bit loud, but it's fine if I flow with it."

"I guess we figured it out. Flow with it. That's sort of what Connor meant, I guess."

"So, now what? You're going to have to walk me through this."

Diane was excited to explore an idea she'd had days earlier. "I want to see if we can find another sister." As she finished her telepathic statement, she sensed her colleague's trepidation.

"Really? Isn't that one possibility Liam mentioned as a way we might find our wraith?"

"Liam was overthinking it like always, and now you are, too. Let's just see what we find."

"You're the mentor. How do we proceed?"

"Think about what you like about having me as your sister, and I'll do the same. We'll see if anyone wants to join the group hug."

"Sure. Now?"

"Yup. Here we go." Diane called upon feelings of kinship, of having someone who implicitly understood her, and she received a surprise visit.

"Hello? Diane? And Emma, too?"

Diane mentally giggled. "Josh? Sorry, we called you by mistake. Can you distract yourself somewhere else for a few minutes?"

"I want to go back to reading about Ethan's life. Friar Lucio's writing his biography. It's cool."

"Okay. Yeah. Go read and try to ignore me if you sense me."

Her brother's spirit disappeared.

Diane tried again. This time, she sensed Emma, and only Emma. They connected without words, their transcendent link burrowing deeper into subconscious caverns where emotions riveted meaning upon minds with such force that words lacked meaning.

The material world, caught in its lethargic near-timelessness, slipped into a vapid void. Connor, his face frozen in a goofy position as he drew breath to utter a thought, evaporated along with the walls, benches, and floor of the courtroom.

Although deprived of conventional language, Diane shared a perfect understanding with her German colleague. They were fused into one being, a super-empath, and as a symbiotic entity, they floated in the center of a blackness.

But stars backlit the incomplete blackness.

Not stars.

Entities like them. Empaths. Psychics. Sisters.

With an unspoken effort, the Diane-Emma tandem harkened to the brightest star, a light with an angelic azure aura. The world then took form, and time marched with normalcy by the shore of a river in a rain forest. Diane felt sweat on her arms and warm humidity. She–they–were inside the mind and body of a sister.

"Who's there? In my head?"

Together, Diane-Emma offered their wordless answer. They were kindred spirits of empathy.

"I somehow know... I can trust you."

In a flash, Diane knew everything about their sister.

Her name was Jimena, and she lived on the Amazon River in Peru. People in her village considered her advice divinely inspired. "You're like me. There's more than one of me? I thought I was the only one. But you're... more powerful than me. How?"

The Diane-Emma being expressed their affinity for their daggers.

"You have a charm. More than one. There's more than one of you."

As the Peruvian empath uttered her mental sentiment, Diane sensed other bright lights gravitating towards her and Emma. The empathic duo had become a telepathic magnet to those attuned to their frequency.

Diane felt a sensory overload and willed a retreat.

Emma caught the hint and did the same.

But before all links were severed, Diane noticed several darker light forms emitting blood red and harsh purples while trying to remain hidden behind the bright auras. She knew they were problematic lives, and she recognized their colors as warnings. Instead of getting scared, she tucked the off-spectrum stars in the back of her mind and embraced her German student-partner in a victorious hug.

CHAPTER 10

Liam's pulse quickened as he followed his father and Friar Lucio down a subterranean corridor. He'd avoided the imprisoned wraith since his capture, letting the friar exorcise the demon and letting himself recover from the mortal fear of his former enemy.

At a security door, the friar tapped a code. "We had to convert a restroom into his jail cell. Otherwise, bodily necessities would have made for a poor prison."

As they passed into a space Liam had last seen during his initial building tour, he recognized it as a waiting room converted into a guard shack. A lone sentry wearing business casual attire stayed seated where he watched a video feed from the jail cell.

The friar approached him from behind the desk and pointed at the computer. "Mister Smith doesn't do much but brood all day."

Liam looked at the screen and saw the captured wraith sitting on a cot with his head in the mitts of his hands, which hard casts covered. The young hunter scratched his upper arm which a hard plastic brace had covered as he'd healed from bullet wounds. Compared to the miserable and broken man he watched, Liam considered his injuries trivial. "Does he do anything other than mope around?"

"We've offered him reading material, but he declines. I believe he's in a self-imposed torture through boredom. You can ask him yourself, if you'd like." Friar Lucio tapped a code into the final barrier, which opened to an alcove which had been designed to give access to opposing restrooms for men and women.

As Liam followed his father and the friar into the small space, he peeked inside the former ladies' room. A temporary hose and nozzle arrangement had been rigged to allow the prisoner to take showers when released from his pen, which a door of iron bars defined at the entrance to the former men's room.

The friar tapped the ring on his finger against a bar. "Mister

Smith, you have visitors."

Lifting his head from his casts, Ethan glanced out his jail cell. "I was wondering when you'd come."

Unsure how to address the captive, Liam let his father lead. Connor took charge with a probing question. "Were you wondering or hoping?"

"A little of both. If you've come to condemn me, I welcome it. I deserve nothing less."

"You would be dead if my son and I had no use for you."

"I would welcome that, but I linger here as a just punishment for my wretched life." As Ethan twisted his torso and waved his bandaged arm, the overhead lights illuminated the deep cuts on his face.

"I offer you the chance to help us capture one of your kind. Perhaps between you and whatever maker you acknowledge, that can earn you a measure of redemption."

The prisoner looked up with hope. "I had considered myself beyond redemption until you just mentioned it."

"It's not mine to give, but if you help us, you may open yourself up to the possibility."

"How could I possibly help you?"

"Answer truthfully when asked."

"My road to redemption may be impassable, but I'm willing to try."

Friar Lucio preempted Connor's response. "Before we enter a meaningful dialogue, I must be assured that Mister Smith speaks without demonic influence."

Ethan rose to his feet, reached for a plastic chair, and shoved it across the floor with his casts. Lumbering to the front of his cage, he obeyed the friar from memory as he sat facing his exorcist with his hands on his lap.

From his cloak, the friar withdrew a bottle of clear liquid and recited a prayer to Saint Michael the Archangel in Latin while sprinkling holy water through the bars.

As droplets hit the prisoner's face, he brushed them away with the bandages of his arms. "No demons, friar. I'm clean."

"I'll be the judge of that. Get your cup."

The prisoner stood, reached for a drinking cup by the sink, and pressed it between his muffed hands. He returned to his seat and extended the vessel.

The friar poured a small quantify of holy water into it.

From memorized orders, Ethan lifted the cup and swallowed its contents. Then he returned it to the sink and sat back down.

Friar Lucio stepped aside. "He's all yours, gentlemen."

Connor looked to his son. "Perhaps it's best that you take the lead."

Liam studied his father's face. The lines of age seemed more pronounced than at the beginning of their first wraith hunt. He leaned into the elder hunter's ear and whispered. "Why?"

His father whispered back. "This is your hunt more so than mine. I fear I'm approaching the end of my usefulness as a hunter."

"Don't be silly."

"I can't defy age forever."

"But it's your fate to hunt."

"If we can find our quarry soon, yes. Otherwise, well, I don't expect to be strong into my eighties."

Knowing he'd expend Diane's patience long before then, Liam let the conversation end. He gathered his thoughts and turned towards the prison bars. "I understand you've been cooperating with Friar Lucio in writing your biography."

"Yes. I never meant to become what I am. It's part of my penance to relive it."

"Penance may not be the right word. It implies repentance. Are you repentant or just feeling guilty because you were caught?"

"I see no reason to mince words. I know I was a monster for a millennium. I may still be. But I want to do whatever I can to earn passage to the next world with a shred of dignity."

"Dignity? Like you gave to the thousands of women you killed?"

Connor clasped his hand on his son's shoulder.

Liam recognized the warning to ease up and nodded.

His father lowered his arm.

"I'm going start asking real questions. Father, can you film this?"

The elder hunter frowned while fumbling for his phone. "Well, I... I'm sure it's possible. Just give me a moment. It's been a while since I've done this."

Liam took his phone, started recording video, and extended it to his father. "Just watch it to make sure you're aiming it right. I've already got it running."

The elder hunter pointed the lens at the prisoner. "Go ahead."

Liam began his inquiry. "What do you know about the one we're hunting now?"

Behind the bars, the prisoner retained his respectful tone. "Friar Lucio told me there's a wraith on a fifty-year cycle he wants you and your father to kill."

"Do you remember your fifty-year cycle? Can you remember back that far?"

Ethan looked up and to his right. "If there would be any reason to keep me alive, it would be to study my memory–other than helping you, of course–"

Although impressed with his interview subject's eye movements to the right suggesting the reconstruction of a true memory, Liam minimized Ethan's leeway. "Don't pander. Answer the question."

"I can remember a thousand years ago like it was last week. I wouldn't believe it myself if I weren't living it. There's a trick I've played of remembering when I last remembered something. For example, there's an important episode I want to never forget when they, um, excuse me... when your predecessor cut me."

Liam had braced himself for the history of battles running close to his heritage. "I know what they did... what you did. Go on."

"The last time I remembered that episode was less than a month ago. I was lying in my cot in the volunteer's dormitory on Lesbos, and I ran through my full visualization. It takes about five minutes to replay every important detail, including the pain, which I never want to forget. I've been doing this every year on the anniversary of my wound, incurred on the fourteenth day of July in the year of our Lord, one thousand two hundred and ninety-nine."

"You know no lord but the one who dominated you."

"He still dominates me. I cooperate with Friar Lucio, but I'm still subject to my former Master's wicked control."

Friar Lucio interjected his exorcism knowledge. "The rite may need to be repeated for a couple years or longer, depending how tenacious the demon is and how pious the energumen can become."

Liam scoffed. "Him? Pious?"

"We must hold out hope of redemption for everyone. Even him. I will continue the sessions as long as I can divinely discern that it's the proper thing to do."

The young hunter recommenced his questioning. "First he has to help us." He looked to his subject. "We're hunting a new wraith. I call him a fledgling wraith. What can you tell me about a fledgling wraith who hasn't started his first killing cycle yet?"

Again, Ethan looked up to his right, and then he dropped his gaze to the floor. "I picked up my dagger from a dying predecessor in the woods. It was the day after he'd killed a sacrifice. So, I had to wait forty-nine years before my killing year started. I remember it well."

"Tell me everything about your behavior that could leave a trail of evidence. Did you kill? Did you injure? Did you kidnap?"

The prisoner raised his voice. "All of it! It was like a training session to get ready for a lifetime of obeying a demanding Master's commands. He made me kill small animals first–birds, squirrels, rabbits, by stabbing their beating hearts. It wasn't terribly traumatic for me since I'd butchered enough animals on a farm, but attacking a beating heart required getting used to."

"And now it's easy."

"It unfortunately is, or was. My former Master's devious and wise in his ways. He forced me through incremental steps. After the animal slaughters, he made me kidnap young children, since they're gullible and weak. To avoid persecution, I'd always set them free and then move to another town. Then I moved on to kidnapping young adults." The prisoner pursed his lips.

Liam anticipated the next step. "Then what? Go on."

"My first murder. You'd think it'd be easy, after slaughtering animals and building confidence in holding people as helpless captives, but when you're getting ready to snuff a life from another human, the anxiety is crippling."

"But you managed."

"I had to! I was under his complete control, or if I wasn't yet, I was damned close to it. Maybe I'm exaggerating and making lame excuses, but that's what it felt like."

"Calm down. We're not judging what you are. We've already done that. We're understanding how you operated."

"On that first murder, very sloppily. My former Master gave no instructions other than to kill her however I wished and then to burn down the house. I remember being too afraid to draw her blood, and I didn't want her to suffer. I wanted it to be over fast. So, I clubbed her in the head, and she was unconscious while I kept beating her. I cracked her skull open to be sure I finished it, and then there was so much blood anyway. It was a disaster."

Considering the pre-killing-cycle murder a useful trait for finding his new wraith, Liam continued. "How many did you kill?"

"Many. Too many. I got better at it quickly, as I imagine all serial killers do. I remember it being only several per year, always under a full moon, of course, until I finally took my first human life by slipping a knife through a beating heart."

"Was there a pattern? Did it become less blunt trauma and more sharp-edge-based over time?"

Ethan nodded. "I honestly don't remember all of them. I was sloppy back then, even as I improved by accident, and I still wasn't sure at the time if I'd really earn my so-called reward of long life."

The comment spurred Liam's insightful question. "But you weren't ageing yet, were you?"

"I was, but slowly. I was seventeen when I found the dagger. People say I look anywhere from twenty-eight to thirty-five now. That's how much I aged in the first fifty years."

"So, ageing is retarded, and there's a pattern of killing. Good. Tell me how fast you progressed on this pattern. We have an idea of when this fledgling wraith found his dagger. I need to know what to look for in his mode of operation."

"It just progressed."

"Linearly? Like an equation? Should I guess at when you moved from a club to a spear to a sword and then to a dagger?"

"I'm sorry. I can't remember."

"Was there anything special about the victims? All female? All virgins? Anything special that your Master dictated."

"I said I can't remember!"

Liam turned to the friar. "We're done here for today. I want him to think about this and see if he can delve deeper into his memories the next time."

Friar Lucio gestured for the hunters to leave the alcove.

Ethan sprang to his feet and pressed his casts against the bars. Tears welled in his horrified eyes. "Wait! You made me remember. God, no. It can't be."

The young hunter studied the man. "What can't be?"

"No. How could I have repressed a memory for so long? It can't be true. No, it's fading. I'm forgetting."

Liam impressed himself with his authority. "Speak!"

The prisoner turned to the young hunter. "Why? Can you help me remember? Are you a hypnosis expert?"

"No, but that's a damned good idea for next time."

Releasing the bars, the captured wraith sat and lowered his head into his broken hands. "Don't bother. I remember. You made me remember!" He sobbed.

"Spit it out, man."

Between heaves of labored breath, the crying man spat his

anger and sadness. "The first murder victim with my knife was my mother!"

CHAPTER 11

Layla awoke in her resort suite to the sight of the ghost hovering over her bed. "What do you want?"

Her vague brow line tilted upward, the milky white apparition seemed anxious. "You must run."

Without witnesses to the ethereal visit, the haunted empath was able to move her physical body. She rolled out of bed and turned her back to her ethereal visitor.

But the Maiden of Toronto instantiated herself before her. "You must not run from me, but from him."

"Why are you harassing me? Leave me alone."

"He will not leave you alone. He is coming."

Layla doubted her suspicions that the ghost spoke of her child. "Who?"

"Your son."

She defied the maiden. "Good. I want to see him."

"You misunderstand. He seeks to kill you."

Finding the claim preposterous, Layla shook her head and marched towards the ghost. "Get the hell out of my way."

The floating sacrifice screamed with multiple voices, a deep baritone underlying a howling screech. "Stop!"

Layla fell back on her haunches, and the room shook.

Rising above the fallen empath, the apparition looked down upon her. "He wants to take you prisoner today. He wants to kill you under the next full moon."

"He's not a killer."

"You saw his victim in the Tucson foothills."

"I didn't see anything but a coincidence."

"If you remain in denial, I cannot help you."

"You've never helped me. All you do is harass me."

"I need to help you to help me pass from this realm."

"That sounds like a load of crap."

As the ghost calmed her demeanor, she floated to the room's center. "I understand your resistance, but what does your heart tell you?"

Layla propped her torso on her arms. "Nothing. My heart was broken long ago."

"That is the first truth you have admitted."

"If you knew anything about me, it was obvious."

"I know you better than you credit me. We are sisters."

Layla opened herself to the astral visitor in hopes that a few minutes of conversational candor would entice her harasser to leave her alone–forever. "I guess you'd be the older sister, the one who harasses the younger one?"

"Yes. And I beg you to heed my warning."

"If you're a big sister, give me something I can use. Don't just tell me the sky's falling."

"Will you believe that your son is a killer?"

"No. And stop it with that horrible accusation."

"Will you believe that his presence sickens you?"

Layla reflected upon her history of pursing him. "I admit that I feel bad when I get near him, but it's just my nerves. If he actually wanted to see me and came for me, I'd be fine. I know it."

"No. You would suffer."

"How can you be so sure?"

"While trapped in this realm, I am gifted with insight. If you would embrace your true self, you would also know."

Layla tucked her feet under her buttocks, stood, and then sat on the edge of the bed. "I want what's best for my son. What's wrong with that?"

"Every mother wants that. But even before conceiving him, your anger blinded you."

"I had every right to be angry. Life was taking a huge dump on my head until I found my son's dagger."

"I understand your anger."

"The hell you do! Nobody knows what it's like."

"Did you forget that the man who sired your son had sacrificed me fifty years before you killed him?"

The memory lurked in a cavern deep within Layla's mind. "So, maybe you do know something about being a victim."

Silent, the levitating presence looked upward while Layla assumed she tapped into whatever divine lord governed the rules of her corporeal communications. Endowed with her replenishment of divine wisdom, the ghost aimed her black eyes at the empath. "I can help you avoid further victimhood, but you must trust me."

"What do you want me to do?"

"You must leave."

"And if I agree, where would I go?"

"Far away. You must keep moving. You must stay ahead of him."

"How long? Forever?"

"Until you retrieve his dagger."

"It's his. It's my son's destiny to be powerful."

"Do you believe the dagger gives him power?"

The bronze blade had been everything to Layla since first touching it. It had gifted her a son and had promised his bright future. "Yes, of course. Isn't it obvious?"

"It is true, but you misunderstand the nature of his power."

Layla recalled the agony of her abusive childhood, which ended the moment her divine weapon rescued her. "I don't care about the nature of his power! Power is power. If you're so smart, you know the hell my life was when I was weak. Now, I have money, and look how I'm living." She swept her arm across the luxurious three-room suite. "I took my money from a monster who abducted me and tried to kill me, and it's mine. I'm not giving it back. My son has power. He made himself successful with the dagger's help. I'm not giving it back, either."

"You mistake possessions for power and power for justice."

"What the hell does that mean? I'm tired of your doubletalk."

"The dagger is evil. It is true that it gives your son power, but it is a wicked power that will destroy him and many innocent victims, including his mother."

"Stop it. You're lying."

"Am I? Do you not feel ill now?"

Layla shifted her awareness to her stomach and admitted a

rising queasiness. "So what? You're making me sick."

"You can no longer deny it. He is coming."

"You're lying."

"Check your phone."

The failed psychic reached for her nightstand and invoked the GPS tracking app. Her son's Maserati was on Route 101 heading north into Scottsdale. A pang of anxiety shot through her, but she fought it. "He's driving in this general direction, but he could be going anywhere."

"The dagger guides him towards you, not with love but with malice. He intends to kidnap you, imprison you, and kill you."

"Why the hell would he do that?"

"Because he must. The dagger drives him."

"You're insane. He's my son."

"You admit that his presence sickens you."

The nausea worsened as she focused on it. "Maybe."

"Get in your car. If I am wrong, you will have lost nothing. If I am right, you will live."

"Fine, then. I'll do that. Get out of my way." Layla stood and strode towards the bathroom to hurry through her morning routine. The room became silent as she brushed her teeth, and she stuck her head through the doorway.

The ghost had departed.

Watching the clock on her phone, Layla powered through a quick shower and then dressed herself. Doubting her ethereal visitor, she refused to pack anything but her purse, which she threw over her shoulder on the way out the door.

After taking an elevator to the lobby and walking to the valet, she flopped into the driver's seat of her Escalade. She drove to a corner of the resort's lot and watched her phone, which showed her son eight miles away.

While her nausea worsened, she rehearsed phrases in her mind about what she would say to him. Why had he been so audacious to run away? Why was he defying her by staying out of her life? How could he be so brash?

As the icon on her phone crept onto the square grid of

Scottsdale's main thoroughfares, Layla's pulse quickened, and she wiped sweat from her brow. She rolled up the Cadillac's windows, cranked the engine, and maximized the air conditioner.

When her son reached three miles away, she swallowed hard to bite back bile. At two-miles distance, she heaved, but an empty stomach from having skipped breakfast prevented her vomiting.

Twisting her misty neck towards the failed empath, the ghost appeared in the passenger seat. The apparition's seated posture portrayed her as a companion instead of as an enemy. "You must flee."

"Damn it." Layla snapped the SUV into gear and escaped towards the north. "Why's this happening?"

"The sickness is your natural defense against him."

"I don't understand."

"It compels you to flee."

"Why?"

"As long as he wields the dagger, he is your enemy."

"That's impossible! I gave him life. I loved him."

"No. You passed your anger and bitterness to him."

Processing the accusation, Layla navigated Scottsdale's streets. Nothing made sense. "If it's true and he's really my enemy, why now? Why not earlier? Why'd he leave me at all?"

"He is of age. It is the first full moon after the twenty-fifth anniversary of his conception in your womb."

The realization was unbearable, but Layla's survival instincts kept her focus on driving. As she turned towards the highway, she glanced at her paranormal companion, half expecting she'd left.

But the ghost remained. "Keep running until I tell you to stop. He hunts you."

CHAPTER 12

During the morning's training session in the sanctum, Diane smirked. "Can you handle it?"

"No. I can't do it."

"Come on. It'll be fun."

"No!"

"I've done it before. He won't care. If anything, he'll think it's funny. And if he doesn't, he can get over it."

"If you say so. I'll try it."

"Good." Diane extended the open case.

Emma grabbed her dagger. "Here goes."

As Diane became familiar with her role as a mentor, she was able to observe the gentle telepathic shift as time slowed and then accelerated to its normal pace. "Did you connect with him?"

The German empath covered her mouth to hide her giggle. "Oh my God. I did it."

"All of it?'

"Well, no. I couldn't do everything, but I was able to see through his eyes and hear through his ears."

Diane extended the case. "Did you really try to manipulate him?"

Emma deposited her dagger in the box. "I tried, but by the time I got around to it, he knew it was coming."

"You still should've tried, but you do that next time." The Chaldean psychic placed the shut case by her foot. As she looked up, the plywood door opened.

With a grin covering his face, Liam stormed into the courtroom. "If there were ever a proper textbook written on how to train an empath, it wouldn't include anything about trying to make a wraith hunter pick his own nose!"

Diane shrugged while rising to her feet. "Can't blame a girl for trying."

"I think Emma had too much maturity to try."

"Oh! So, does that make me immature for trying in Istanbul?"

"By comparison, yes!"

Diane flicked her wrist at him.

"Dismiss me if you want, but I'm here to help. Emma's learning fast. She was able to sense the world through my senses, and we were talking like we were standing next to each other."

"Are you ready to join us?"

"Yup. Emma asked me to come down here."

"Since that experiment went so well, let's do the next one. Are you both ready?"

The German empath nodded. "I am."

Liam looked around his location between the forward benches. "What do I do? Just stand here?"

"Yeah. Just do what I tell you."

"Obeying your orders is becoming a theme in my life."

Diane bent down and reached for the case with her enchanted knife. She picked it up and connected with Emma. Time slowed to near nothingness, and she spoke within her companion's mind. "How are you feeling?"

"Fine."

"Here we go. I'll connect with him." The Chaldean empath created a telepathic link with the young hunter and pulled him into the shared trance with Emma.

"Good morning, ladies."

Diane skipped the pleasantries and jumped into the test. "Everyone try to walk forward." As she willed time to march forward, she was able to shift her eyes to one companion and then the other.

Liam handled the unnatural acceleration of time from hardening concrete to molasses with the silent brute force of a warrior's will.

But a look of horror rose on the German empath's face.

"Are you okay, Emma?"

"This is weird."

"But you're getting the hang of it, right?"

Emma grimaced as she lifted her foot. "I am, I guess." In a flash, the German psychic burst to twice normal speed, and she speed-walked across the floor.

Diane broke the link and raised her hand to brace her colleague as she bumped into her at normal speed. "Careful!"

Emma steadied herself. "I tried too hard."

"Right. Let's do it again. Get back in place."

The German empath returned to her spot and faced Diane. "Does including Liam make this easier or harder?"

"I'm not sure, but it's important that you can do this with normal people."

The young hunter scoffed. "So, I'm just normal now?"

"That's what we call non-empaths." Diane kicked the weapons case to her female colleague's feet. "Go ahead and use your dagger this time. It's probably easier for you to learn while you're in control."

Emma stooped and lifted her blade, and then she brought Diane into a telepathic link with Liam. The German empath sounded calm. "This is better. I feel like I'm in control."

"From what I've figured out, the easiest way to let time move forward is to relax your control."

"I'm relaxing."

Diane wiggled her fingers to verify her freedom, and then she stepped towards her colleague. "When I've done these links, I haven't been moving much myself. It's more about letting other people move while you dedicate your energy to holding the link."

"I think I've got it."

"You're doing great so far."

Liam walked towards the ladies. "I feel normal. Good job, Emma. You're a fast learner."

"She is. Now, try seeing through my eyes." After giving her command, Diane felt her colleague's spirit rummaging through her head.

"I see myself!"

"Good. Now through Liam's eyes."

"I see you and me. Now I'm coming back into myself." Emma lifted her eyes slowly from her dagger to the Chaldean empath.

"If someone else walks in the room, they'll see all of us, and we'll all be in the same timeframe, right?"

"That's right. But you'd control it. The funny thing is, it takes more energy to link up with time stopped, but that's the natural way that links start. Does that make sense?"

"It does."

"Ready for some more fun?"

"Sure."

"I'm going to throw my shoe in the air, and you see if you can stop it and start it again."

Liam raised his voice. "No! Not with your clumsiness. I'll do it."

"Fine. Go ahead."

The young hunter balanced on one leg while pulling off his sneaker. He then lobbed his shoe upward, and it froze at its apex.

Diane noticed her body had gone rigid, and she spoke in Emma's mind. "Good. Now let it drop."

The shoe accelerated towards the floor like it had been subjected to Jupiter's gravity, and then it stopped short of landing.

Emma cringed. "Sorry."

"No, that's fine. It's no worse than I did when I was learning on my own. You can break the link now."

Time returned to normalcy, and then Emma put away her dagger.

"That wasn't perfect, but it was a good first attempt." With her skillful apprentice, Diane was ready to reach farther beyond her comfort zone. "Are you ready to contact some sisters?"

Liam preempted Emma's response. "Wait. Why?"

Diane scowled. "To see what's out there."

"Shouldn't you be going after the targeted sacrifice who escaped our wraith's predecessor?"

His pressure bothered Diane. She struggled with the thought of losing the young hunter due to stupid rules the order imposed upon him, and under his challenge in the courtroom, she replayed an argument that had been repeating itself in her head.

She told herself she didn't love him. It was just infatuation.

Their short time together had been a whirlwind of fear and heroism, and anything resembling a courtship had been imagined. Even the scant time they'd spent together in romantic settings had seemed forced and artificial. In her defense, she needed to brace herself to move on.

As part of her bracing, she distracted herself from her dilemma with Liam by befriending and training Emma. The kinship of the divine sisterhood couldn't fill the gap in Diane's heart from her failing romance, but it helped ease the pain. "Emma and I are exploring our power and our sisterhood."

"I get that, but what about finding the wraith?"

Before she could filter her emotions, Diane blurted her frustrations. "What do you think I'm doing? I'm doing what I can to figure it out, but I don't have any idea how to find your damned wraith!"

Liam's ire rose. "My wraith? Isn't it our wraith?"

Diane blushed. "Yeah. That's what I meant."

"I'm not so sure." The young hunter turned and stormed away.

Alone with Emma, Diane walked to a bench. "I need to sit down."

"Sure. Let's take a break." The German psychic walked to Diane and sat beside her. "What was that all about?"

Diane rolled her cheeks into her palms and mumbled. "I don't know."

"It's the angriest I've ever seen him."

"I don't want to talk about it."

"Not even with your empathic sister?"

Diane's pain was too intense. "Not now. Just let me suffer alone–which is unfortunately the way I'm going to spend the rest of my love life."

CHAPTER 13

Diane finished brooding, excused herself to Emma, and walked up the aisle. Pushing her way through the plywood doors, she questioned if she'd ruined her future with the young hunter. She continued to the ladies' room where she splashed her face over the sink and then wiped it dry with paper towels. Staring at herself in the mirror, she chastised herself. "Stupid Diane." After drying her hands and strolling back to the sanctum, she passed her seated colleague. "I'm ready. You want to try contacting some sisters?"

"Why not? What's the worst that can happen?"

"I have no idea, but I'm fed up with not knowing how to find the wraith. Let's learn what we can from the sisterhood."

Emma stood, walked to her spot on the compass, and faced the Chaldean empath.

"Remember to think about what you like about having me as your sister, and I'll do the same. Let's not bother our Peruvian friend but see who else we can find. Here we go." Diane called upon feelings of kinship and of strong underlying loving bonds. Like the prior time, she stumbled upon an unwanted interruption.

"Hello?"

Diane mentally rolled her eyes. "Josh? We called you by mistake again. I don't know if there's a way to avoid it, but can you distract yourself again?"

"Okay. Bye." Her brother's spirit disappeared.

Diane tried again. This time, she sensed Emma without a distraction. They connected in their deep, subconscious link where emotions supplanted words. The courtroom slipped into glacial near-timelessness and then disappeared into a black void.

As conventional human language receded into meaninglessness and impossibility, Diane fused into one being with Emma and floated in the center of a blackness dotted with the starry souls of their sisters.

With their shared consciousness, the Diane-Emma tandem identified the brightest star, but this time they knew it was someone other than the Peruvian sister they'd previously contacted. With instant understanding, they grasped that the lumens of the angelic azure auras within their community varied from moment to moment. They called to the most radiant of their kind.

The world materialized in normal time in the woods within sight of a major highway. A cool breeze rolled over Diane's exposed arms, which she shared with a newly discovered sister.

Unfazed, the new empath was cool as she responded within her mind. "Identify yourself."

Together, Diane-Emma claimed their wordless kinship.

"I understand. I'd normally welcome you, but I'm busy now. Remember me and contact me later if you need me."

Instantaneously, Diane knew their new sister.

Her name was Rachel, and she lived outside of Boston. A professional psychic, she worked for a police department investigating crimes. The Diane-Emma intrusion was happening while she combed the woods with detectives seeking a missing person's body, and the empathic tandem knew to give her space.

They backed off into the starry darkness and then gravitated towards another bright aura. Within the body of another sister, they reentered the world's reality.

A dozen Vietnamese people of varied ages formed a line on a dirt path to receive their fortune from the empath who sat with her legs crossed under a thatched hut.

The Vietnamese psychic straightened her back, tapped her fingertips to her temple, and greeted her otherworldly visitors. "Someone's in my head. Who? Sisters?"

The Diane-Emma duo shared their love.

"Wonderful. But how? I'm the most powerful I know, but I've never been able to find more like me... like us... not through just the power of my mind."

The duo revealed the power of their daggers.

"Charmed weapons? From where?"

As Diane recalled her traumatic fear during the battles in which she'd captured blades, her anxiety rose and severed the link.

The Vietnamese empath called out while fading. "Why are you leaving?"

Within the void, Diane noticed darker light forms of blood red and harsh purples emerging from behind the bright auras. These problematic empaths sought her and Emma based upon the duo's painful memories of winning their daggers.

A British empath groped for the Diane-Emma tandem and pulled it into her mind. From the slurred wordless thoughts, Diane knew their new host was drunk. "What's this? A couple of psychics running around looking for friendship?"

The Diane-Emma duo validated their host's assumption.

"Not here, you stupid witches. You think being me's a picnic? I see horrible futures for my prophecies. People about to die. People about to suffer pain and loss. Good people. Decent, honest hard-working folk. What am I supposed to tell them? I hate this so-called gift. Stop looking for friends before you go buggers like me."

Returning to the blackness, Diane shared her fear with Emma and urged her to retreat to their bodies.

But another sister dragged them into herself. The Spanish psychic ran a razor over the tender flesh of her forearm. "Pain. Only this self-inflicted cutting pain can distract me from the horror of what I am. Ghosts torment me. The souls of the damned cling to me to bridge them to the real world. Terrifying figures that nobody else can see threaten me in the dark. I just want them to leave me alone. Why are you going out of your way to look for more like us, for more suffering?"

Unsure if she'd subconsciously decided to risk the revelation or if the psychic had coaxed the information, Diane-Emma shared their intention of hunting a killer.

The Spanish empath was unimpressed. "A killer, huh? If you find him, send him to me. Maybe he can put me out of my misery." The psychic's bitterness pushed away the Diane-Emma pair.

Absorbing the negative energy of the embittered empaths, Diane found herself tumbling in the blackness. She willed a hasty retreat to her body, but a powerful life force latched onto the empathic tandem and swallowed them into her mind.

Their angry host displayed her power by hiding her identity, and she gave them a harsh salutation. "I thought I sensed a jokester screwing around with me."

Silently, the Diane-Emma team claimed innocence.

"There's more than one of you."

Two.

"Idiots. What's wrong with you? What the hell are you doing?"

They admitted to having sought companionship before becoming lost.

"Liars. What do you really want? Do you want money? Are you going to try to harass me until I pay you to stop?"

Again, the transcendental travelers denied malicious intent.

"Whatever. Don't bother threatening me. You're not the first unnatural assholes to screw with me, and you won't be the last. But nobody's beating me in this game. I'm nobody's victim. Got it? Now get out!"

After a rapid plunge into the dark abyss, Diane willed herself and Emma out of the netherworld. Her consciousness materialized within her body, and she gasped for air. Before she could express herself, her knife glowed red and rotated in her hand. Remembering a sprained wrist from prior improper dagger handling, she dropped the blade to the floor.

Mimicking her mentor, the German psychic did the same. "What's going on?"

"I don't know. I've never done anything like this."

"Those nasty sisters... I don't understand."

"Me neither. I've never been able to contact them without you. There's something powerful about us being a team, but I still felt helpless against the mean ones."

"Love is the power of the empath, right? They didn't have

any."

"Yeah. I agree, for whatever it's worth." Diane watched the glowing daggers rotate. "This is the first time yours has glowed red for you."

"Should I do anything?"

"No. Just let them do their thing."

Slowly, the daggers twisted towards their final resting orientations. After a minute, they settled in parallel, and their glows receded.

Diane picked up her phone and aimed its camera at the unmoving knives. While walking around the daggers to get pictures at different angles, she commanded her apprentice. "Don't touch them. Don't go near them. Don't even blow on them. I'm going to call Liam. Whatever they're pointing at, it's important."

CHAPTER 14

Excited, Liam barged through the plywood doors, banging one of them against a wall. "Sorry." To his relief, the empaths stood by the council's bench, staying distant from the coppery knives resting on the floor.

Saying nothing, Diane canted her head towards the blades and aimed her palm at them.

Fearing the slightest perturbation would disturb the charmed weapons, Liam crept down the aisle.

Diane called out. "Don't worry. They aren't moving, and they aren't going to."

Liam knew the tenacity of an enchanted dagger to retain its intended orientation. "Right. But there's no need to disturb them, just in case."

"Just in case what?"

"Just in case... I don't know. Just humor me." He reached the compass carved into the stone floor. "You both just dropped them here?"

Diane nodded and shrugged.

"Why?"

"I got scared after our session. I probably overreacted, but I was shaken up, and I remembered my sprained wrist from Lesbos. After I dropped it, Emma was smart enough to drop hers."

"I was shaken up, too. It was scary. I'm not sure we should go back into that space."

"Are you two okay?"

Diane nodded. "We're fine. We can talk about it later. I think we'd better first figure out what this is all about."

"Right." He studied the daggers. "You took a video?"

"Yeah." Diane tapped the phone in her pocket.

"From overhead?"

"Sort of. From about where you're standing."

"Good enough. But just to be sure." He withdrew his phone and walked between the knives. He extended the camera over one dagger and then the other. "Alright. Let's go."

"Huh?"

"Let's go. That's all we can do until I get the equipment."

"You're losing me. What equipment?"

Liam wanted to explain his plan, but he knew it wouldn't make sense until he demonstrated it. "Give me a few hours, and I'll show you."

Half an hour later, he met Friar Lucio in the lobby. Dressed for business outside the order's headquarters, the council's chairman wore a green polo shirt and black slacks. "We got lucky that this is working out on such short notice."

"I thought that if you made a phone call, all of Rome jumped to obey."

The friar smiled. "I have some influence, but sometimes it's just better to have a little help from above. A fellow friar just happened to know the right person with the right equipment you asked for. Come. Our driver's waiting."

A taxi ride to an industrial district brought Liam and the friar to an engineering services shop. The young hunter followed his companion into a rundown visitor lobby where fading pictures of the company's historical products lined the drywall.

Seated behind a window, a receptionist greeted the arrivals in Italian.

Friar Lucio shared his name, and the woman asked him to sit while she summoned the owner.

Before Liam could assess the hazard of sitting on the waiting room's tattered couch, a round man with graying chest hair sticking out the unbuttoned top of his shirt stepped through a doorway.

Friar Lucio greeted the owner, who pressed his palms against the holy man's shoulders and then waved him into the back offices. Liam followed them into a corridor of supervisory offices with windows showing computers and strewn papers covering old wooden desks.

Beyond the offices, a tool and die section covered the area of two tennis courts, and Liam recognized lathes, drill presses,

CNC mills, three-dimensional printers, and machines with names that escaped him. One machinist in goggles clicked a red button, setting a CNC router's cutting edge into motion over sheet metal.

A creaking metal door brought the men into an electronics workshop with antennas sticking up from workbenches covered with digital meters, oscilloscopes, spectrum analyzers, and radio frequency sniffers. A technician who hunched over colored wires clamped a plastic connector to a circuit board and then looked to his oscilloscope as a square-wave trace appeared.

Liam was relieved the owner walked through his employees' work areas without bragging about his wares and abilities, like every other service provider hungry for business. When the young hunter had asked Friar Lucio for rapid help, they'd omitted money from the conversation, leaving him to assume the holy man intended to pay the shop's boss a generous premium in exchange for speed of service.

The owner waddled through a door to a messy space resembling a toddler's playroom with space-age gadgets and computers positioned in random locations around scattered children's toys. In his native language, he explained the disorder. "This room is where we demonstrate the three-dimensional scanners. The clutter shows the full capability of the software."

Friar Lucio queried Liam in English. "Did you understand that?"

Liam nodded. "Enough. But ask him to verify the resolution. He said he had access to the best. This is all about precision."

The holy man nodded. "Of course." He switched to rapid-fire Italian with the boss, conducted a quick exchange, and then confirmed the young hunter's hopes. "He said his best room scanner gets down to one half of one tenth of a millimeter."

"Good. That's the best in the industry, per my research. But ask him if it gets better if I use multiple machines."

During another burst of Italian, the owner shrugged.

"He says he thinks so, with the full software suite that merges the data of the scanners, but he needs his expert to call the scanner company's field engineer to verify how accurate."

Liam waved off the friar. "Don't worry about it. Don't worry about the demo, either. I've seen these types of machines at the university, and I know what they can do. I'm confident this is as good as it gets. I want three of them with the upgraded software."

"I'm sure he'll rent them to us–as long as the order's bank account can withstand it."

In the sanctum, Liam elevated a telescoping tripod two-meters above and between the fallen daggers. He then set up three-legged mounts a meter above and outside each blade. Atop the stabilizing structures, he secured three laser scanners which he connected via USB cables to laptops running on the floor.

Diane clicked open the knob on the temporary plywood and entered the courtroom. "Good lord! You've got a science project going on. Are you sure you're not overdoing this?"

Fearing she'd trip as she came down the aisle, he pointed at the power cables he'd routed into the sanctum from its waiting room. "Watch out for the extension cords."

She stepped around them and moved near him. "I'm not that uncoordinated."

With his mind focused on mastering technology to find answers, he found her sweet voice and alluring scent distracting. "I guess you're right. I haven't seen you trip over yourself for at least a week."

She folder her arms. "You didn't answer my question."

He nodded towards the nearest scanner. "You mean this?"

She shrugged. "Yeah. Why so geeky now when you've just eye-balled it before?"

He walked to a laptop he'd staged on the council's bench as the master of the other computers. "Because we've never had two daggers."

"So what? Aren't they pointing in the same direction?"

Bringing the software on three slave computers to life through a wireless router, he energized the three scanners. "In a few minutes, I hope to prove you mostly right but just a little bit wrong. Stay off the compass floor, please."

She glanced at her feet and then looked back to him. "Sometimes I wonder if you'd be happier if you'd been born as a robot."

He moved his mouse cursor over an icon and clicked. Turning around, he saw the scanners rotating on their mounts and shooting green pulsating lights from their cores. He inhaled deeply to quell his rising excitement. "I'm not sure I can argue that, although, maybe if I were a cyborg..."

"What's a cyborg?"

"Never mind."

"What are they doing?"

"They're shooting millions of laser beams at the world around them. I set up the range really close to them so that I can get tight precision. It's going to be sub-millimeter accuracy."

She shrugged.

"I'll show you pictures when it's done. It'll make sense then."

"Whatever. This is boring."

"You don't understand. That's all."

"How much did all this cost?"

"I don't know. I don't care. The scanners with the software are about a hundred grand each on the retail market, but we're just renting this setup for a while."

"Holy cow! A hundred grand each!"

"Just wait. They're worth it. You'll see." After the machines finished the rotations he'd commanded them to follow, he set the master computer to its computational task. As it crunched hundreds of millions of bits, he tapped his fingers on the bench.

"Is it done yet?"

He flicked his wrist at her. "This chews up serious processing power."

"Ugh. It's getting close to dinner time. I'm hungry."

"Chill, my good lady. And... *voila*! Yes!"

"What's it say?"

"Come take a look."

She walked around the daggers and the industrial engineering gear to reach his side.

He pointed at the image on the screen, which was a three-dimensional digital recreation of the grounded daggers.

"Okay. It looks really cool, but what's it mean?"

"Watch." He grabbed his mouse and highlighted the central elevated spines running down each dagger. Numbers on the screen flickered with their coordinates. He then highlighted the nearest compass line carved on the floor. With the flickering data in his short-term memory, he called up a geography program.

"What are you doing?"

"Mapping the daggers' bearings, as you'd expect."

"Okay. I get it, but I'm not impressed."

"Just wait." With two daggers differing by a tiny fraction of a degree, he drew two lines. Their precision across the globe was horrible, but he knew he could improve it with the proper effort.

"I'm waiting."

"Done. It's seriously blunt, but I have a fix, sort of."

She frowned while glaring at his computer. "I don't get it."

"What's not to get?"

"Why are the lines running into each other?"

"They're not. They're crossing. Even though it's almost useless as close as the daggers are, they're in different locations. And my hunch proved true. They differed by a tiny fraction of a degree. We're into degree minutes."

"You mean, they weren't perfectly parallel."

"Right."

Her face softened with understanding. "I never would've thought of that."

"You're not a geek, like me."

"So, where are they crossing? I can't see it on the map."

"You won't because you and Emma dropped your daggers only two meters apart, and their lines of bearing intersect somewhere around ten thousand kilometers away. That's anywhere from, I'd say, Texas to California."

"That's really cool, but that doesn't help much. That's a lot of ground to cover, and we still don't know what they're pointing to."

Liam had expected the challenge. "I know how to solve the first problem. We experiment to see how far away you can be from Emma while repeating this, and the greater the separation, the tighter this fix becomes."

"That makes sense. Sure. I'll try that."

Content with his day's effort, he put his laptop into sleep mode. "It was about time I used some technology to carry my own weight in our hunt. Now the ball's back in your court. We need to separate you and Emma to get a useful fix and find out where your daggers will take us."

CHAPTER 15

Seeking microexpressions on Ethan's face, Liam studied the video in slow motion. The eye and mouth movements after each interrogation question revealed the captured wraith's truthfulness, and the evidence convinced the young hunter of the prisoner's sincerity to assist his hunt.

Seated beside him in the study, Josh looked up from his tablet. "What are you looking for?"

Liam stopped the video and pointed at Ethan's eye. "Right there. You see how he's looking to the right immediately after I asked him about his fifty-year cycle? It's nowhere near fool-proof, but it suggests that he's saying something from memory. If he was making something up, he'd look the other way."

"Cool."

"And if he was a good liar, he'd look the other way for a fraction of a second before correcting the direction of his eyes. But he wasn't doing anything like that."

"Okay."

"There's more, sort of. I was looking for evidence of him showing an emotion for a fraction of a second and then hiding it, but there was nothing. He wasn't trying to mask his emotions from us."

"What's that mean?"

Liam applied his intuition to the minimal evidence. "It means I believe he really wants to help us."

"We need the help."

The investigative sidekick's certitude surprised him. "Why do you say that?"

"None of the books talk about new wraiths before they start their killing cycle."

"So, we need his advice?"

"Yes."

"He's already helped, then. He said his demon spirit made him kill animals and then people and then even his mother, all before he started his first killing cycle."

Josh looked upward while processing the hunter's report. "It'll be the same for the new wraith."

"Seriously? How can you be so sure?"

His sidekick lowered his gaze to his tablet. "I just am."

"You're not an empath, too, are you?"

"No." In a flash, a greenish aura arose around Josh and then faded.

Startled and mesmerized, Liam stared at his companion. "Hey, Josh? Did you just... notice anything weird?"

"No."

"You didn't feel anything weird?

"No."

"Sure. Okay."

As he often did, Josh flipped the conversation to a random subject of his choosing. "Who's supposed to help you hunt him twenty-five years from now?"

The question stymied the young hunter. "Bloody hell. I can't believe nobody's asked that yet."

"You're supposed to get your son when you turn fifty. That's not going to help with this wraith."

Ashamed he'd ignored the obvious flaw in his new assignment, Liam sent his brain into hyperdrive. "I know. I can't believe I didn't think of it. I was so busy trying to figure out how to catch him as soon as possible that I didn't question the future. But you're right. It doesn't make sense."

"No. It makes sense."

"How?"

"You're either going to hunt him by yourself twenty-five years from now, or you're supposed to find him before then."

Finding the answer simplistic, Liam left it unanswered. Instead of talking, he committed his synapses to understanding. Did Friar Lucio and the council anticipate him finding the wraith now, or did they expect him to hunt the savage alone twenty-five years later? Were they unsure and pressuring him to figure it out? Or worse, was it a game to create the illusion of possibility in his marrying Diane, and, if so, for what reason?

Again, Josh hit Liam with a new subject. "Diane's ready for us."

"Huh?"

"Diane wants us to go to the sanctum."

"How do you know?"

"She told me."

Knowing better than to aggravate Josh, Liam assumed his sister had summoned him telepathically. He closed his laptop and led his peculiar companion to the basement.

In the courtroom, Diane leaned against the council's bench with her dagger resting on the carved compass. "Mine's still pointing the same way."

"What's Emma got?"

"You have to ask Connor. He measured her dagger, but he wants to talk to you."

Liam lifted his phone and called his father.

"Yes, lad. We have a new bearing."

"Are you in the hotel?"

"Safe and sound in Barcelona with Emma. Her dagger's sitting quietly on a table at a bearing of three-one-zero."

"Three-one-zero. Let me map that. Hold on." Liam walked to the laptop on the council's bench, called up his view of the globe, and updated the bearing for the German empath's weapon. It formed an arc that cut through Canada and then crossed with the bearing from Diane's dagger in Arizona. "You still there, Father?"

"Yes."

"It's still blunt in this geometry, but it's starting to clear up. It's aiming at Arizona."

"I may be off a degree either way while eye-balling this."

"I know, but we'll dial this in over time. We'll tighten this easily with better geometry as we move in."

Connor's tone became cautioning. "Let's make sure we're chasing a consistent target. Given what I understand about their last session, our empaths are unsure about whom their daggers have selected as their mark."

"Or even if they're pointing to the same target, but I'm not letting that stop me."

"Nor should you. But let's take the next logical step. Emma's ready."

Liam looked to Diane. "Are you ready to link with her?"

"Sure." She stepped to the center of the compass. "Now?"

"Yeah. Go ahead."

She stooped and lifted her bronze blade.

"Have Emma grab her dagger, Father."

"She is."

"Go ahead, Diane." Whatever effort the psychics made in the ethereal realm happened in a blink of Liam's eye.

Diane's expression became one of anguished frustration as she released her knife and let it clink against the floor.

As Liam lowered his gaze to the weapon, he saw it glowing red and then fading as it settled on its bearing. He looked back to Diane. "Are you okay? That looked painful."

"Whoever we're connecting with is miserable and mean."

"But you connected?"

She walked to the bench, pressed her forearms onto it, and stretched her back above the arced surface.

"I'll take that as a 'yes'. Seriously, are you okay?"

"Fine. Enough. Just give me a minute."

Recalling the phone he held near his ear, he sought the German empath's condition. "Father, how's Emma?"

No response.

"Father... Father?"

"Sorry. I had to help Emma to her seat. She appears moved and fatigued from the effort, but otherwise okay. Her dagger glowed red for a bit but then stopped. It's settled on a bearing now. I'll measure it to be certain, but it appears to be in the same direction."

"Same here with Diane's dagger."

The Chaldean empath straightened her back and attacked with sarcasm. "I'm glad you noticed that my dagger's doing just fine. Your concern for my personal well-being is overwhelming."

"Sorry."

"Stop apologizing when you don't mean it!"

He kept his mouth shut and turned his attention to her blade's orientation. Against the floor's carved compass, it appeared unchanged from her prior experiment. His phone still in hand, he pressed it against his ear. "Is Emma's dagger on the same bearing?"

"Yes. I checked it against the GPS compass. Three-one-zero again."

"That's good. Real good. Consistency."

"Agreed. Shall we take the next step and tighten even further?"

"You're reading my mind, Father. One empath to the north, one to the south." Liam turned back to the global mapping program open on his laptop. "Diane and I will go to... Tucson. You and Emma to Las Vegas."

"Sounds great, lad. Good work. Bring Josh and Nana, too, to keep the family together."

"Is that permission to make plans and spend money?"

"Most assuredly."

"I'll take care of it. Happy travels."

"Same to you, lad. Keep in touch during transit."

Liam slid his phone into his pocket and turned to Diane. "Did you get that?"

"Yeah. Sounds like I'm going to get a tan."

"Sure." He switched subjects. "Your link with Emma was good?"

She shrugged. "It took a little longer to connect, but it was fine."

"Any degradation of signal strength?"

"Come again, Mister Geek."

"I mean, any notable loss of power or fidelity? Any limits?"

"I don't know. We didn't stay connected long. We ran into the same ugly person we ran into last time. So, we made it quick."

"Then that ugly person's your daggers' target?"

"Probably. Your guess is as good as mine."

"One way to find out is to show up."

His face in his tablet, Josh sat in the front row of benches. "Where are we going?"

Turning to address his colleague, Liam had forgotten about the young man's presence. "Tucson Arizona, Josh."

"It's going to be really hot."

The hunter smirked. "That's right, Josh. We missed the hottest season, but it'll still be over a hundred degrees Fahrenheit."

"Don't forget to bring the enchanted twin dagger."

Liam questioned if his thoughts were slow or if his colleague's were abnormally fast. "Great thinking, Josh. I hadn't gotten to that point in my planning yet, but I'll bring it."

"It hasn't moved at all recently, has it?"

"No, Josh. If our wraith's killing now for practice, like Ethan says he should be, the dagger's not catching it."

"Trust me. You need to bring it."

CHAPTER 16

After three days in a motel outside Sedona, Arizona, Layla had exhausted her patience. The stink of the old carpet, the rattling wall-unit air conditioner, and the cramped confines had taken their toll. As she sat on the bedspread, her imagination abused her with the possible sources of stains underneath her buttocks. She called for the ghost who'd abandoned her days ago. "Hello? Maiden of Toronto? I can't take this anymore!"

The ethereal world met her plea with silence.

"I'm leaving. I don't care what you say. This place is disgusting."

Again, silence.

The bed creaking as she stood, Layla looked out the window at the dark two-lane highway as she walked towards the closet. "I mean it. I'm leaving."

More silence.

Demonstrating her resolution to override the ghost's warning of hiding in the motel, she reached for the closet's knob with the intent to retrieve her suitcase. As she slid open the accordion door, the milky white spirit appeared between a small safe and a hanging ironing board. Startled, Layla squealed.

"Where would you go?"

"Did you have to scare me like that?"

"I needed to earn your attention."

"Get out of my way. I'm packing."

"Answer my question, sister."

The spirit's salutation as 'sister' sounded sarcastic, or perhaps doubtful. Her heart pounding from the surprise in the closet, Layla was unsure and confused. "What question?"

The Maiden of Toronto frowned. "Where would you go?"

"A real hotel. Anywhere but this dump."

"How would you pay?"

The question prompted the haunted empath's memory of the ghost having warned her to pay for the motel with cash. "I'd use my damned credit card. What's it matter if he can hunt me down with his dagger, like you say he can?"

"His dagger guides him, but he resists."

The maiden's unpredictable demeanor, terrifying her one day and then placating her the next, bothered the psychic. "Three days ago, you made me run for my life because you said his dagger guided him. He got within only a couple miles of me, and he hasn't come for me since then. Why should I believe you? Maybe he was driving somewhere else?"

"Check the GPS history."

Layla grunted, pulled her phone from her pocket, and ran through the archives of her son's GPS movement. Three days ago, her son had stopped where she'd been. "Fine. He showed up at the resort. But if he can find me whenever he wants, how am I safe in this dump?"

"You are safe because I watch him."

Overwhelmed, Layla shook her head and her hands. "Look. Wait. Would you just get out of the closet?" She walked to the room's armchair and flopped into it.

The ghost appeared, floating over the room's center. "Your son resists the dagger because part of him still loves you."

"Part of him?"

"That man you raised is devolving into the same type of vile creature as your failed murderer."

"How can you expect me to believe you when everything I see is circumstantial? All you do is throw threats in my face."

The levitating presence looked upward while Layla assumed she again tapped into whatever divine lord governed her bodily speaking rules. Reinvigorated with divine wisdom, the ghost aimed her black eyes at the empath. "I will earn your confidence before this night ends."

The haunted empath flicked her wrist and turned her head from the ghost. "Whatever. I'll believe it when I see it. But you didn't answer my question. Why do I have to stay another night in this dump?"

"This is the only safe place for you."

Layla glared at the ghost. "Really? Why? Is there some sort of wizard's spell protecting this place?"

The maiden cocked her head. "He watches for your credit and debit cards. This is the only place you can afford with cash."

The psychic dug her elbows into her knees and rested her head in her hands. "I can't believe a ghost is schooling me in being cheap. I thought you said he was resisting the dagger."

"His will is fallible. The less you tempt him, the better."

"Tempt him? I'm his mother. How can I tempt him to kill me?"

"By attracting him with information. Instead, force him to rely upon only his dagger to find you. Let him focus his resistance upon the dagger and the evil spirit within it. You must live in this room and keep your cards in your pocket."

Layla scoffed. "For how much longer?"

"I do not know the strength of his will, but as the full moon approaches, it will fail."

"Fail? Meaning he'll try to kill me?"

"Yes."

As she started to believe the maiden, Layla recalled her past counsel. "You told me to get his dagger. Not that I agree to it, but if I got it, would that stop him from killing me?"

The ghost's tone was somber. "Yes."

"Why do you sound like the world would end?"

"To take back his dagger, you must be willing to die."

Layla's chest tightened. "You're kidding. Why?"

"He regards the dagger as a part of himself. He will not part with it lightly. To take it, you must risk everything."

"You're not quite impossible to deal with, but you're close."

"I speak the truth. You must act before the full moon."

"When's that?" Keeping her jaw in her hands, she raised her eyes to the maiden.

But the apparition was gone.

"Damn her. Just when I was starting to not hate her." Alone, Layla lifted her phone to her face and tapped its screen in search of the next full moon's date. September 24th popped up, and her stomach fell with the realization that she had two weeks–if her spirit guide had told her the truth.

Tired from the stress, she verified her room's door was locked and then braved another night within the lumpy bed's sheets. She turned off the lamp on the nightstand and slid into the bed. Thoughts swirled in her head until their repetition became fatiguing, and she drifted into sleep.

A recurring nightmare hindered her rest. She hung upon a cross, a madman preparing to stab her. Terrified, she screamed for help, but the gag in her mouth muffled her howl. As the killer approached her in the shadows, her heart pounded in her chest, and as the light of ceremonial candles lit his face, she recognized him as her son.

She awoke and sat back on her arms.

Above her, the maiden's white form shimmered in the moonlight that passed through the curtains of the second-story room. "Nightmares?"

"Are you seriously teasing me?"

The ghost said nothing.

"I thought we were sisters. You're supposed to help me."

"If your subconscious mind warns you, as an empath, you must heed its advice."

"No. My son is no murderer." As she said it, she started to accept the possibility that he was a killer.

"If you deny my warnings and those of your subconscious mind, perhaps you will heed those of the hunters."

"What? I don't understand."

"Look out your window."

Obeying, Layla strode to the curtain, brushed it aside, and saw an object hovering outside her room. She released the curtain and snapped her jaw towards the ghost. "What's that?"

"It is a hovercraft. They are watching you."

Having recovered from her nightmare, Layla's heart pounded again. "Who is?"

"The hunters."

"I got that part. But why are they hunting me?"

"They seek your son."

"Stop them!"

"I cannot. Nor can you."

"What do I do?"

"Make yourself presentable to greet them and pray you can make them your allies. You have three minutes. You cannot escape."

Confused but trusting, Layla brushed her teeth and washed her face. Half-expecting the ghost to have disappeared, she was relieved to see the maiden floating in the room. "Now what?"

"Take a towel, sit, and hold the towel over your face."

"That's weird."

"Do you trust me?"

"Enough." Layla obeyed the ghost, sat in the chair facing the entrance door, and peeked over the top of the white bath towel she held in front of her nose. "Are they coming in through the door or window?"

As Layla noticed the maiden had vanished, the door flew open with a single deep thud of a battering ram. The black cylinder landed on the worn carpet, and two men in body armor burst into the room. The first intruder shot a beam of liquid, and she blocked it with her towel. The second man traversed the carpet in three bounds before flying into her. He smacked down her arms, bearhugged her, and knocked her backwards in her chair.

With his weight on her, she strained to yell her protest. "I'm not resisting. You're crushing me." She heard lighter footsteps near the doorway as someone turned on the overhead lighting, hurting her eyes.

One man clamped his grip around her hand and tightened cold steel around her wrist. With both hands, he yanked her cuffed hand over the neck of the mass weighing upon her, and then he joined her other wrist into the handcuffs. "She's cuffed."

"Thank God." The heavy one lifted himself from her chest. "She attacked me with her towel." He slid down her legs, fumbled through his vest, and pulled out handcuffs. Reaching behind his back, he clamped one cuff to her ankle. He turned the other way and secured her other foot into the shackles.

Seeing the young man's face turning puffy and red, the swelling shutting his eyes, Layla snorted. "What's wrong? Got your own pepper spray in your face, you big dummy?"

"I wasn't expecting... the towel... bloody hell!" Brushing the shoulders of both ladies who'd broken into the room, he darted across the carpet and into the bathroom.

Behind her, the man with the older voice addressed her with a surprisingly polite tone. "I apologize for our rough entrance, but we can't be too careful. I'll lift you up on the count of three. Here we go. One... two... three."

Within her chair, she rotated ninety degrees.

But he kept his arms around hers. "Duct tape, please."

Layla protested. "I'm not resisting. Is that really necessary?"

"Like I said. Can't be too careful."

The ladies, who appeared to be in their mid-twenties, ran lengths of tape around her arms and the chair while the older man stepped in front of her.

Taking off his body armor's helmet, he appeared older than his voice suggested.

She glared at him more out of curiosity than spite. "Who are you?"

His voice became paternal and soothing, like the father she'd always envisioned but never knew. "I'm sorry, young lady. But where are my manners? I am Connor Brady, a bounty hunter of sorts. Depending on the conversation we're about to have, I may be arriving here just in time to help you."

CHAPTER 17

Despite the harsh entrance, Layla found the old man charming, but she suspected he could get violent if pushed. Dazed, she stared at him, failing to recall when a man had been as polite to her without expecting a tip or a paycheck. But he expected something, she knew, and he'd find a way to get it. "You called me a 'young lady'. That's super nice for a guy who just knocked me over and taped me up."

"From my perspective, you're quite young. Again, forgive me for my lack of pleasantries, but by any chance, do you believe yourself to be psychic or empathic?"

"Wow. Just like that? Barge in here, knock me over, tie me up, and ask questions. And you start with a wild one."

"In my line of business, the wild question, as you call it, is rather basic and important to know."

"So, you're a psychic bounty hunter?"

"Not exactly. I'm the bounty hunter. They're the psychics."

Staring at her, the women folded their arms.

Her final captor emerged from the bathroom, his eyes half shut.

"And who's he?"

"That unfortunate soul is my son." He shouted over his shoulder. "Close the door as best you can, lad. Prop it shut with the battering ram."

The young one obeyed his father and then stood behind him and palpated the swollen skin around his eyes. "You'll have to ask the questions, Father. I'm not quite up to it."

"Right. I don't mind. Where were we? Yes. I was letting the young lady ask all the questions, but it's time to do this properly. Let's get things back in order. As I was asking, are you an empath, a psychic, a fortune-teller, or any other sort of person gifted with supernatural abilities?"

Layla's mind buzzed with possible responses. Her assailants seemed like they could become her worst enemies or her new best friends, depending on their agenda. Given the advice of the

Maiden of Toronto, whom she dared to believe after her warning, she hoped they might become helpful. But her defensive instincts compelled her to trust nobody. She shrugged the best she could under the duct tape. "I get feelings and strong intuitions, but so do a lot of people. I'm nothing special."

The old man's politeness lessened. "Would you care to share a bit more about that? Your feelings? Your intuitions?"

"Well, I'm not exactly sure what you mean. Can you give me an example?"

His tone became stern. "Oh, I don't know. Premonitions... paranormal visions... mental telepathy."

The haunted empath's defensive instincts kicked in. "That covers a lot of stuff."

Shifting into complete threatening mode, her interrogator pressed his palms to his knees while stooping forward. "I'll ask nicely one more time, and if you continue to dodge the question, the nice ladies standing here will show you how rough they can be."

The women reached towards their hips where items shimmered with coppery glows.

Halting them, the old man angled his head. "Not yet, ladies. Now, let's try it a final time. Do you have any supernatural abilities?"

Layla's instincts overrode the logical decisions swirling through her mind. "No. I don't believe in any of that crap. Whoever you're looking for, it isn't me."

The old man stood and stepped back. "Very well, then. Ladies, do your thing."

Filling the gap where her interrogator had stood, the blonde stood facing the brunette's back. They each lifted their shimmering metal objects from their right hips, held them beyond Layla's view, and then interlaced the fingers of the blonde's free hand with those of the brunette.

A split second later, Layla's body went numb and the presence of someone or something rummaged through her mind. The invader was familiar, like one she'd cast out multiple times, but this time it latched onto her thoughts tenaciously. "Who are you? Get out!"

With a wordless response, the entity indicated its intent to stay.

"What do you want?"

The presence wanted the truth.

"What truth?"

Her identity. The entity dug into her psyche, unlocking ignored memories, self-delusions, and denials. A torrent of repressed emotions flowed through Layla, drowning her in sorrow, anger, and fear. "Stop!"

The invader was in control and would cease its exploration when it desired. It catalogued her life's strongest emotions, starting with the terror that had surged throughout her flesh while hanging on a cross in an Evanston basement.

Layla relived the sadistic expression of her would-be murderer's face in her mind's eye. "Stop!"

Continuing to tap her archived fears, the intruder called upon an older memory—the first time her stepfather had fondled her.

The stench of alcohol on the man's breath played through her mind, along with the repulsion of his touch. "I'll do anything you want! Just stop!"

No. The assailant was content to devour knowledge while letting Layla suffer the relived effects of her exposure. Running through her past episodes of rage, it unlocked her greatest revenge.

She saw the moment she'd mounted the monster to conceive her son, and then she jabbed a bronze dagger into her enemy's heart. "That's enough."

Ignoring her plea, the entity probed a spike of anger marking another memory. A ghost had visited and had accused her son of being a serial killer.

"Get out. Go away."

The exploration continued, examining her past illnesses as she'd approached within the proximity of her son. The invading entity opened the old wounds.

Nausea and pain overwhelmed her, and she lost the energy to protest. Within herself, her mind blanked in self-defense. From her perspective, she ceased to exist.

When she regained her awareness, she was lying in the back seat of a moving vehicle, and she heard the gentle rumble of the engine and tire vibrations. Her neck ached from holding her head to one side, despite the pillow a captor had placed under her ear. Her cheeks were cool with moisture from tears she didn't recall shedding. "What happened? Where am I?"

From the passenger seat, the young man looked back at her. "You passed out."

"I get that part. I mean after that."

"I carried you into our car. Don't worry, I grabbed all your stuff from your motel. It's in the back."

Her hands and feet remained shackled, but she was free to sit. As she gained her bearings, she saw that she was inside an SUV with the old man and his son. Elsewhere were the ladies–the attackers she realized had somehow assaulted her mind and had unlocked a lifetime of pain. "Where are the women?"

The old one kept his eyes forward while answering. "They're in the car behind us."

Layla looked through the rear window at the headlights following them. Then she turned back to the young one. "They're not alone."

She knew she'd discerned correctly as the young one looked to her and his voice became defensive. "What makes you say that?"

"I'm psychic, remember?"

The young one looked back to the road. "The grandmother and brother of one of our empaths is with them."

As her defensive instincts again overcame her, she made her desperate act. With a quick motion, she shot her cuffed hands over the passenger's head and then yanked her handcuff's chain across his neck. She pulled with all her weight. "Take me somewhere public. Now!"

Amazing her, the young one stayed calm as he raised both his hands to her right wrist. Despite her tugging, he overpowered her enough to speak. "Don't worry, Father. Just keep driving."

The old man shot a glance at his son. "You're sure?"

"No problem. She's pulling with everything she's got, but I can handle it. It was a nice try, but shame on me if I didn't know how to defend against it. She doesn't have the strength."

Layla relaxed. "Shit. Can I have my hands back?"

The young one released his grip. "Stop fighting us. If we wanted to hurt you, we already would have."

She put her hands in her lap. "What do you want from me?"

The young one spoke while the older one kept his eyes on the curving road. "I'd say information, but our empaths already got it out of you, if you remember."

"Unfortunately, I do. Some of it, anyway."

"So, we have the information we want from you, and you're still alive. What's that tell you?"

Feeling better about her chances of survival, she found his condescending tone demeaning. "I don't know. Maybe you're taking me somewhere to kill me without witnesses."

"Don't be dense. I carried you to this car over my shoulder wrapped in a blanket. Don't you think the perfect opportunity to kill you in your motel room has already come and gone?"

"Fine. But where are you taking me?"

"Someplace safe."

After the assault on her mind, the truth seemed clearer. Painful as it was, she admitted to herself her son's intent. "How can you know what's safe? I... someone's hunting me."

"We know. Your son."

The ease with which he spoke the revelation astonished her. "Did they really figure that out by getting into my head?"

"That and more. But don't worry. We've handled guys like him before. He's a kitten compared to the guys we've faced."

The old man kept his eyes forward where high beam headlights illuminated pine trees covering hills of red stone. "Tone down the bravado, lad."

"Sorry, Father, but I want her to be confident in our abilities so she can trust us."

"I understand that, but take care how you speak. Her son is still her son, despite being what he is."

Layla was unsure if she could trust even herself, and the influx of thoughts and emotions threatened to incapacitate her. She drew several breaths to calm herself. "And what is he?"

The young one retook the conversation. "We call him a wraith."

"That's horrible."

"I'm sorry, but he is horrible. You know that he's already killed, and that's not even what a wraith does. That's just his training. It gets uglier and messier in twenty-five years if we don't stop him."

Tears welled in her eyes. "All this... you know from my mind?"

"From your mind and from our work in similar cases."

"Is that it? Am I just another case for you?"

"We risk our lives to protect those of others. At the moment, you're the one we're protecting. If you can't see that, it's going to be hard to protect you."

"I see."

"We've rented a secluded cabin in the woods where we can hide you from your son and protect you. We know what he's capable of and how to stop him."

"Don't hurt him! You're not going to hurt him, are you?"

The young man turned and looked her in the eye. "That depends. Our empaths were able to learn everything you know. But you haven't yet figured out what outcome you want for him. Once you figure that out, we can make plans."

CHAPTER 18

Inside the rented cabin, Diane glanced out the windows. Roof-mounted spotlights illuminated pine trees and reddish earth, which Sedona, Arizona's sandstone painted a unique color.

As Connor walked around the living room closing blinds, he snuffed the view.

Diane turned her jaw towards their seated and shackled captive. "That was therapeutic for you, wasn't it?"

Her prisoner's swarthy skin, brown eyes, and dark shoulder-length hair reminded Diane of herself. "What? Being kidnapped?"

"No. Exposing the truth from within you."

The detainee shrugged. "Maybe."

"I know it was painful. I didn't feel it as badly as you did, but I felt it. So did Emma. I'd apologize, but we had to do it."

"Are you seeking my forgiveness, or are you trying to forgive yourself?"

"You talk like an empath. That's good. Now you need to think like one."

"What's that supposed to mean?"

Surprised to hear herself speaking with the authority of an expert psychic, Diane reminded herself of the intensity of her trials. She'd learned under fire as fast as anyone could expect. "Embrace the truth. You see things other people can't, and it can get uncomfortable. I can't imagine how it feels knowing your son's a killer, but you can't hide from it."

Tears welled in the prisoner's eyes. "Do you have to remind me?"

"Yes. It's going to be the topic of conversation until we resolve it. You have to make some tough decisions."

"Like what?"

Anxiety rose within Diane as she prepared to lay out the brutal choices.

Startling her, Connor clasped her shoulder and intercepted the question. "You must decide now if you want your son to live or die. There's unfortunately no time to delay. We need your answer."

The captive lowered her head into her manacled hands and wept.

"Liam! Fetch Miss Jazani some tissues, will you, lad?"

The young hunter darted to the powder room, emerged with a small box, and presented the tissues to the crying psychic.

Knowing her captive's history, Diane pitied her, the psychic empath she identified as Layla Jazani. But she considered pity a potential virus threatening her goal of stopping the wraith. She drove forward for the required decision. "When you calm down, you have to make a choice."

"To kill my son?"

"Or not. We have ways of stopping him while sparing his life, but it's more dangerous and complicated that way. You probably noticed that we have bags of weapons and lots of ammo. Bullets solve the problem a lot more easily than being merciful."

"My son's a problem?"

"You need to accept that."

The detainee clenched her eyes shut. "Okay! Okay! I get it. He's dangerous. But he's my son. Of course, I want to spare his life. Do you even need to ask?"

"Yes, because you'll need to risk your life to spare his."

"How can you know that?"

Diane's memory of Layla's memory, one of many she and Emma had witnessed within the captured empath's mind, was a murky rendition of a visitation from a milky white supernatural visitor. But the Chaldean psychic had discerned the apparition's message and accepted it as truth. "A ghost told you. A sister ghost, a maiden."

The captive looked up with widening eyes. "The Maiden of Toronto."

"I didn't catch her name from your memories, but that makes sense."

"She's been bothering me a lot."

Having felt the detainee's emotions from within, the Chaldean empath understood the resistance. Layla was bitter, angry, and sad for reasons with which Diane empathized. The prisoner's early life had been traumatic, but Diane considered rising from victimhood a personal responsibility at which the fledgling wraith's mother had failed. "She's not bothering you. She's warning you."

"Now you sound like her."

"I should sound like her. We're sisters. We're all of the same lineage."

"I have no family other than my son. Can we get back to talking about him? How can I save his life?"

"You know that you have to be willing to risk your life for him?"

"Yes. The ghost said that, and apparently you heard her say it in my memory. So, I believe her."

"Well?"

"Well what?"

"Are you willing to risk your life for him?"

The captive lowered her cheeks into her palms. "I don't know."

Diane sensed the response's veracity. "Good answer. I believe that you're telling the truth, but we still need to verify it." She turned and waved to Emma, who was sitting on a cloth couch.

The detainee looked up again. "What are you going to do?"

"The same thing we did last time."

Layla rose to her feet. "No! That hurt!"

"We need to know how far you're willing to go."

Connor and Liam moved to opposing sides of their prisoner and ushered her into her seat.

Despite her hesitation, Diane allowed herself an iota of pity, labeling it in her reckoning as compassion to rationalize it. "If you don't resist, it'll go faster."

Emma stopped behind the Chaldean empath, faced her, and lifted her dagger from her hip. She raised her free hand towards the detainee.

Keeping her back to the German psychic, Diane grabbed the dagger from her belt loop and then pushed the knuckles of her free hand into Emma's palm.

The world slipped into a lethargic time flow and then melted into a black void. Diane merged her awareness with that of her German colleague, again becoming the super-empath, floating in darkness.

Within the starry night of the ether, the life forces of sister-empaths dotted the canvas around them, and a dark star burned with a powerful sanguine purple before them. The Diane-Emma tandem slid into the consciousness of their distressed sister.

Emotions rose and fell around them as they navigated deeper into their subject's essence. The memories with the strongest combinations of feelings drew their attention, but the symbiotic empathic invader's keen mental recollection from their prior exploration tagged those remembered episodes of Layla's life as being previously digested. Burrowing farther, they sought something new.

The power and recentness of the desired memory brought it to the forefront. When forced to consider her son's life, the sentiments that had overcome Layla left a footprint of her answer. Stopping to investigate the memory, the Diane-Emma tandem ingested it with the truthfulness of their subject's answer. Unsurprised that Layla wanted her son to live, they sought the next memory, the controversial issue of her willingness to risk her life.

The hunted memory surfaced behind the prior one, and the symbiotic psychic probed it. In response, the captured empath's mind revealed its exposed core.

Layla's spoken answer had been accurate. She was unsure if she could risk her life for her child.

Diane withdrew the empathic tandem from their prisoner, reentered reality, and released Emma's hand. "She told the truth."

Connor released the seated psychic. "I had expected a mother to instinctively be willing to risk her life for a child."

Diane frowned. "She's not the average mother. She's troubled."

"Yes. I see." Connor stroked his chin. "This complicates matters. We'll need to draft a plan that accounts for her uncertainty."

With his hands rising from the prisoner, Liam countered. "I'm not sure how we'd do that."

The elder hunter shot a glance at his son. "We're learning a lot quickly, but we'll take the time we need to assess our options."

Liam pressed further. "The full moon's only two weeks away. He's going to come for her when he can't resist the urge anymore. He's already come for her once at her hotel. He could snap again any minute."

"We have three empaths, lad. I don't think he'll be surprising us."

Deferring to his father, Liam clenched his jaw.

Connor rallied the team to its next step. "Thank you again, Diane and Emma for uncovering what we need to know. It's now time to discuss our shared knowledge and begin planning. We'll leave our guest under Nana's guard."

Diane scanned the cabin's ground floor. From her perspective, the empty kitchen abutted the brick wall that framed an unused central fireplace. To the other side of the masonry, she saw the entrance to an illuminated but empty hallway. "Where are Josh and Nana?"

Connor marched towards the entryway. "They were walking outside." As the elder hunter opened the main door, a cool evening breeze flowed through the living room. He stuck his head through the doorway and yelled. "Nana?"

A moment later, Diane's grandmother waddled against her orthopedic injuries as she entered the cabin. Behind her, Josh held his hands in his pockets.

Connor reached into his vest and withdrew a pistol. "Enjoying the lovely evening?"

Nana nodded. "I wanted Josh to see this beautiful place. You know. Some time without his computer in his face."

"What a lovely idea." Connor clasped his weapon's barrel and extended the handle towards the grandmother.

"What do I do with this?"

"You remember how to shoot one, don't you?"

"Yes. But I like the rifles better."

Connor smirked. "I know. You're quite good with them, but the long barrel is hard to use indoors."

"Okay." Nana accepted the pistol.

Connor walked to Layla. "Stand up, young lady."

The detainee obeyed.

Facing the grandmother, Connor's tone suggested his question was a command. "Nana, while the rest of us are making plans, will you and Josh please escort our guest upstairs into the nearest bedroom and lock the windows?"

"Of course."

The elder hunter pointed to the prisoner's abdomen. "If she tries to leave the room through the door or a window, shoot her here." He then pointed to her lower back. "Or here, depending on your perspective when you pull the trigger. And keep shooting until she falls to the floor."

As Connor had trained her, Nana slid back the bolt, aimed the weapon towards a light, and verified the empty chamber. She then lifted the bolt and let it slam home the first round. "Shoot her in the belly or the back. Got it. No problem."

CHAPTER 19

Liam paced beside the edge of the coffee table situated between the couches. "I don't like it. Not one bit."

Seated beside her empathic colleague, Diane protested. "What's wrong? I thought that went great."

He needed more convincing. "I'm not so sure about that. A mother that doesn't know if she's willing to risk her life for her son? Not to necessarily die for him, but only to risk it."

"You asked me to get the truth, and I did."

Emma cleared her throat.

Diane turned to her colleague. "Sorry. We did. You're doing great, actually. I couldn't do this without you."

Liam's patience thinned. "I hate to destroy the empathic group hug, but remember us hunters. That's what we're ultimately here for, and I don't know how to lure our prey to a decoy who could bail out when she gets scared."

Diane frowned. "Scared of what?"

"That's the problem! Is she more afraid of dying or of seeing her son die? I don't know. She doesn't even know. She's so conflicted that she's liable to run at the worst time."

Connor grunted and then sat on the couch opposite the empaths. "I understand your concern, lad. A day ago, we weren't sure if we'd find the wraith or his next target at the end of their daggers, and now we have an influx of data. It may not offer us a clear path yet, but let's analyze it."

His father's calming tone focused Liam, but his doubts remained. "Sure. Let's give it a go." He wanted to sit, but the best he could achieve was walking around the couch and resting his palms on its back beside the elder hunter. "Before we dive in, we need someone to take notes."

Emma reached for one of the laptops on the coffee table. "I'll do it. I type pretty fast."

"Thanks." The contrast and comparisons with prior efforts rose to the front of Liam's thoughts. "Let's start with similarities to our past missions. We've got a wraith with one dagger going after one target, and it's happening under a full moon."

Diane interrupted him. "But she's also his mother. That's a huge difference."

Liam nodded. "Sure. Emma, start a list of differences, too. For example, he's a fledgling wraith, which means he's still learning how to use his dagger. That reminds me… Emma, start another list of questions for Friar Lucio to ask Ethan. I want him to share everything about… what was his name, this new wraith?"

Emma looked up from the laptop. "Amir."

"Right. Amir. Share everything we know about him and get Ethan's assessment of how skilled Amir is in killing."

"Okay, I've started the lists."

As the German empath typed, Liam noticed the elder hunter stirring. "What's wrong, Father?"

"What if wraiths have some sort of telepathic connection? Ethan could warn Amir."

In unison, the empaths blurted their assessments. "They don't."

"Impressive, young ladies, how you denounce the theory so quickly and together. Why so quick?"

The psychics shared a glance before Diane explained. "Love is the power of the empath. It's what connects us to each other and the world. Wraiths lack love. It's what makes them wraiths. It's why they're such loners."

"I can't argue with the logic, and I'm far too old–and wise–to argue with two empaths."

"Thanks, Father. I think we'll find out that when Ethan attacked his mother, it was desperate and sloppy. I expect the same thing from Amir."

Connor lifted his jaw over his shoulder towards his son. "But we can't bank on his sloppiness as a requirement for our success."

"No. But we need to be ready for it. Without a ritual, without a need to bind her to a cross, or stab her in the heart, he can move a lot faster than one who needs to be careful."

"Fair enough, lad. What else for Friar Lucio?"

"I'd like to know what he can do with his knife. Does it already have supernatural abilities? Will it obey his will or his Master's, despite the laws of physics? Can he throw it with wicked accuracy and push it through steel? Can he block bullets?"

"We shouldn't need bullets."

"But the time to find out is now, not in battle."

Connor lowered his gaze to the empaths. "Agreed. I'll make sure to ask the friar."

As Emma typed, Diane added another distinction. "He's also fighting it. Part of him doesn't want to kill his mother."

Liam shrugged. "Sure. Tactically, that could work in our favor, and unlike our wraith in Rome, it might actually slow him down. Ethan didn't want to kill Emma, but his demon drove him. I don't think the spirit, demon, or whatever's imbued in his dagger has a complete hold on a fledgling wraith before his first sacrifice."

Connor nodded. "Emma, please add that to the list of questions for me to bring to Ethan through Friar Lucio."

"Okay." Emma typed, looked up, and then added her first thoughts. "I know I wasn't with you for the first two wraiths, but I understand that you had to attack them. This time, he has to attack us, like in Rome."

The young hunter noted a key distinction. "And we'll have warning like we did in Rome, but it'll be much different. He won't know that we expect him. He won't know of us at all. We'll completely surprise him."

Diane voiced an angle Liam had missed. "Technically, we surprised Ethan, too, at the last minute. Your electronic mist trap's what got him."

Liam wiggled his finger at the Chaldean psychic. "That's true. The more we can bank on surprise, the less we'll need violence. I admit, I was going to ask you and Emma to engage him with your daggers to keep him busy while I shot a net gun at him."

"What? Emma's never used her dagger like that."

"But you have, and you could teach her. I'm not sure she even needs teaching, with the dagger practically handling itself."

"That's not the point. The point is to avoid violence, and a knife fight with magical daggers can get pretty violent."

"Well, I'm not setting up another electronic mist trap. That nearly killed Ethan."

Diane waved dismissive fingers at him. "You're the hunter. You think of something."

Many concepts flickered through Liam's mind. "I've got a bunch of ideas. Tasers, bean bag rounds, pepper spray... too many possibilities, really."

Diane looked at him. "You're forgetting one big thing."

"What's that?"

"She's an empath, and she already has a dagger."

Liam recalled the encased enchanted blade, the blessed twin of the cursed one in the fledgling wraith's possession. "Well, yeah. You're right, except that she doesn't. We do."

"You know what I meant. Just give it to her."

The idea irked him. "Isn't that overkill? We've already got two empaths with daggers."

"But I told you she always gets sick when he's near her. She hasn't gotten within half a mile of him since he left her house. For all we know, she could die if they're in the same room."

Liam shrugged. "Fine. So, we track him farther out and nab him before he gets within half a mile. You said she put a GPS tracker on his car."

"So what? Even if he brings his own car to a murder, what makes you think you'll stop it before he gets too close to... um–"

"That's the problem. We don't know what happens. Does she just keep getting sicker? We could live with that. Hell, it could solve everything. We lock her in a room and let her barf all she needs to while we nab her son."

Diane folded her arms. "It's not going to work."

"Why not?"

"Haven't you been paying attention? The ghost told her she needs to be willing to sacrifice herself. That's what ghosts told me before, too. She needs to be involved. She needs to face him."

To calm himself, Liam inhaled through his nostrils. "I understand that's part of your sister code, but I'm not bound by your rules."

The comment propelled Diane to her feet. "Oh, really?" She strode across the floor where she crouched next to the canvas equipment bags.

"What are you doing?"

She flicked her fingers, silencing him as she rummaged through their wares. After withdrawing a weapons case from a bag, she stood and walked to the coffee table. She plunked the case to the flat surface and then opened it. Thinking better of touching the bronze blade with her skin, she untucked her shirt and used it as a glove to remove the dagger, which she placed on the table.

As Liam watched it, the knife rotated towards him, but then it rotated towards the standing psychic. "What the hell."

Diane shrugged.

With four pairs of eyes burning on it, the enchanted knife stopped and shook.

Liam walked towards it and crouched near it. "I've never seen one wiggle and vibrate like that. I think it's confused."

Diane stooped beside him. "Yeah. I've got an idea. Emma, close your eyes while I close mine."

Avoiding the temptation to examine his father's face for a re-action, Liam kept his gaze on the dagger as it rotated and then stopped. To record a blunt bearing, he grabbed a spare laptop and paralleled its edge with the blade, and then he took a picture with his camera. "I'll check it against a compass, but I bet that's about zero six zero. Toronto."

"That makes sense with our eyes on it. Let's close them and let the ladies have a turn."

Liam shut his eyes and let the empaths look. "Anything yet?"

Diane sounded fascinated. "It's still moving. Be patient."

"Sure."

"Okay. It stopped."

"Get a picture."

"I don't think we need to. I got a good idea about where it's pointing. What do you think, Emma?"

"I think I've figured it out, too."

Liam had to know. "Are you going to keep us in suspense?"

"Nope. I just pointed upstairs, and Emma nodded. We think it's pointing at Layla. It knows who it belongs to."

CHAPTER 20

Feeling like an inmate of a makeshift prison that doubled as an insane asylum, Layla followed the young man down the stairs into the short hallway leading to the living room.

The old man descended the stairs behind her. "Remember to thank your sisters for the gift you're about to receive. Liam and I aren't sure it's a good idea to give it to you, but I deferred to the ladies' judgment."

She hesitated to accept his definition of a gift. "What is it?"

The young man's voice echoed off drywall as he passed the fireplace's brick edge into the space in which the cabin's other four occupants sat. "You'll see." He continued into the room and motioned for her to sit in the central armchair.

Lowering herself into the cushion, she sat with a rigid back, anticipating an unwelcomed surprise.

The young man obliged by stretching duct tape over her ribs. "Scoot all the way back."

Tight pressure constricted her breaths. "Can you try not to suffocate me?"

He whispered. "There are worse ways to die." After he bound her torso to the chair, he retreated behind a couch and folded his arms in apparent defiance of her promised present.

Holding coppery knives, the ladies stood in front of her chair, one empath near each of her arms.

Their possessions caught Layla's gaze, and she lifted her shackled hands to cover her mouth while gasping. "What are those?"

Carrying a square case, Connor stepped between the women and stopped before her. "They're bronze daggers. I understand that you've seen one much like them."

Memories of her life's shift from victim to survivor flooded her mind. She was sixteen again, driven by a madness imbued within her newfound dagger as she mounted a maniac to conceive her son. Then she was thrusting the cursed blade into the savage's beating heart. "Yes."

"Well, these young ladies assure me that you're the rightful owner of this one." He pulled back the case's lid, exposing a replica of the knife her son had taken when abandoning her.

Subconsciously, she extended her handcuffed hands towards him.

"Make sure you know what you're about to do."

His warning snapped her from her daze. "What's that?"

"You're about to accept powers countering those of your son."

"What sort of powers?"

"Think of this dagger as a supercharging of your inherent abilities. Isn't that right, ladies?"

The women on either side of the old man nodded.

"I don't know what abilities I have."

"But you have them, and you'll become quite familiar with them once you take this from me. Are you ready?"

"No. Wait. What will this do to Amir?"

The old man glanced at one psychic and then then other. "I'll trust the experts to correct me if I'm wrong, but I believe it'll do nothing to him that you don't already truly desire." As the women beside him remained silent, he extended the box.

Reflecting electric lighting, the dagger shimmered as she reached for it. As her fingers touched it, a flash of awareness shot through her, and she yelped while recoiling.

Across the room, the young man was sarcastic. "Well, that worked out nicely."

Layla wanted to challenge his sarcasm as profound truths spread throughout her cells, but the trauma of instant awareness silenced her. Doubts evaporated. Knowledge solidified. Her son was worse than a killer—he was a monster with a horrific destiny. An evil entity within the dagger she'd found twenty-five years ago had made her conceive a beast, and its influence over her mothering had molded her son into a savage.

As she swooned, the old man stepped forward and stabilized her. "Are you okay?"

Finding her voice, Layla uttered gibberish. "True. Horrible.

Me." Tears streamed down her cheeks as she lost consciousness.

When she awoke, she lifted her head and saw everyone standing where she remembered them. "How long was I out?"

The old man had closed the case. "Not long. Perhaps ten to fifteen seconds." He lifted tissues to her face and wiped away the moisture she'd cried out.

"What's happening to me?"

He tossed the tissues onto the table behind him. "You're learning what you are."

"Yeah. I'm a cursed dumbass and a shitty mother!"

He grunted. "I don't think so. That may be the past, but it's not your destiny. Care to try again?" Holding the weapon's case in his palm, he flipped it open with his free fingers.

Scared and exhilarated, Layla heard her heart pumping while her hands moved forward. Thoughtless, she reacted to a need and grabbed the knife.

Within her grasp, the handle became warm with its intrinsic life. The truths it had solidified during its first connection to Layla had formed a foundation for the dagger's dominating will. Transforming her, the knife exposed her abilities and enhanced them.

While she pulled it towards herself, its power merged with and amplified her empathic abilities. Emotions swirled within her, fighting for priority, until a forerunner emerged–fear. Overwhelmed, she succumbed to the heightened dread of being imprisoned by her kidnappers, targeted for death, and forced to face a child who intended to kill her. As she tried to hold back the bronze blade's influence, it trembled.

The old man challenged her. "Layla?"

She kept her gaze on her gift. But as her fear and her new knife's power fused into a rising energy, she became helpless to her instincts. With the dagger's enchanted speed, she whipped it towards herself and then downward, severing the steel links between her wrists. Faster than she could understand, she lifted her bound feet and whipped her magical knife through the chains. Astonished, she continued freeing herself by yanking the tip upward through her constricting lines of duct tape.

From the corner of her eye, she saw the young man lift and aim something black. As a sheet of gray issued from his hands, she thought of Spider-Man reduced to using a non-lethal shotgun for spinning his webs.

Her head snapped back and her arms became heavy. Before she understood the nature of her trap, the knife contorted her wrist while slicing through the net. Unsure if her dagger worked for or against her, it fought with a frenzy to free itself.

As the netting binding her arms yielded to the blade's slicing, she saw the old man aiming a thick pistol. A stream of liquid glistened while arcing from his weapon towards her face. The last thing she saw before her eyes swelled in defense against the pepper spray was the arms of her empathic prison guards lowering their daggers upon hers. Blinded, struggling to breathe, and incapacitated, she felt her new possession continuing to struggle while keeping her unaware if it resisted on her behalf or for its own hidden agenda.

Imbued with supernatural power, it sought the uncut lengths of her net trap, but two daggers of equal power in the hands of talented and trained sisters clamped her weapon against her ribs. Wise enough to recognize defeat, her knife ceased resisting.

Despite the failed escape attempt, the old man sounded calm. "You've got her?"

The psychic to the left, the brunette she'd heard addressed as 'Diane', answered. "We've got her, but we need to put her dagger away. That's enough for today's lessons."

Layla opened her mouth to agree but again issued gibberish. "Take. Control. Can't."

While one empath pressed her dagger into Layla's new possession, the other wedged her sharp blade under her fingers. One of her guards tugged her knife from her.

Layla relinquished her blade, lost consciousness, and fell into a deep dreamless sleep.

CHAPTER 21

Liam slung the net gun over his shoulder and walked to the prisoner. "I'm dying to hear how anyone can call that a success. I told you all to keep that thing away from her."

Stooped over the unconscious detainee, Connor aimed his voice over his shoulder. "Easy, lad. Now's not the time to gloat."

"I'm just trying to figure out what we all want to accomplish. We're empowering her when she's not ready for it. I say we just keep her tied up and let her puke her guts out while we take down her son."

Diane scowled. "Don't you care about her at all?"

Sensing himself being boxed in as the team's warmonger, Liam thought through his response before speaking. "Of course, I care about her. But I also care about the hundreds of victims her son'll kill if we don't stop him."

The Chaldean psychic was unappeased. "You sound like you're dedicated to a mission but don't care about anyone at all."

"I don't think that's fair."

Diane softened her tone. "Okay. Maybe we can all agree if I share what I just learned." She shot a glance at the German empath.

Emma shrugged. "I'm not sure what you mean. I got some strange feelings when all our daggers touched, but I'm still trying to understand them."

"Good. It hit me when my dagger touched hers, too. It was like a premonition from her dagger to ours, and I've already made sense of it. If Amir gets within sight of her with his dagger while she doesn't have hers, she'll die."

Liam found the statement dubious. "It's weird talking about these knives like they're people, but is there a chance they're... miscommunicating among themselves?"

"You mean lying?"

"I'm afraid to accuse something so powerful of lying. So, let's stick with the miscommunication angle."

Diane brandished her blade. "This one doesn't lie, and it's smart enough to know if another one's lying to it."

Emma corroborated her colleague's testimony. "That's kind of how I saw it. It makes sense. I don't see it as clearly as Diane, though."

"I've seen you, both of you now, do amazing things with those daggers. So, I'll believe you. It's hard to do, but I'll do it."

Diane frowned. "Why do sound like you doubt it?"

The inconsistency hit him. "I just thought of why. Ethan killed his mother, but he did it with his knife, which means she was alive within his sight."

"But his mother was never a targeted sacrifice, and I'd bet you anything that she wasn't an empath."

Placated, the young hunter agreed. "Okay. Fine. But it still doesn't mean she needs her dagger. It's possible to trap Amir without letting him get close to her."

"You're overcomplicating things."

After a long day of travel followed by finding, kidnapping, and interrogating the wraith's mother, Liam showed his emotions. "I get it that I look like the bad guy, but I don't want to hurt anyone if I can help it. I'm trying to make sure we don't screw this up by trying too hard to protect her. This is a slam dunk if we stick to our principles."

"Whose principles?"

"Since we're thinking about getting married, I was hoping they were our principles."

Connor cut the rising tension. "Perhaps now's a good time to break into our watch sections."

"Sure. But what about her?" Liam pointed to Layla, whose face long strands of dark hair covered while she lay slumped over to one side.

"We'll take her upstairs and chain her hands around a headboard. I believe the bed in the nearest room on the left had a headboard sturdy enough. As an extra precautionary measure, I'll sleep on a mattress on the floor next to her."

Liam assumed his father intended to pair himself with the

German empath as one watch team to allow him time alone with Diane in the other pairing. "You could have Emma sleep in there, too, to have her awareness and dagger right there."

Connor looked to Emma, who nodded.

"Okay, then. Diane and I have the first watch. Say, from now to three o'clock?"

"So be it." Defying his age yet again, the elder hunter scooped Layla into his arms and lifted her. Without a further word, he carried her towards the bedrooms.

Taking the hint, everyone else except Diane followed Connor towards their chambers.

Alone with his potential fiancée, Liam was unsure what to say.

She took the lead. "You believe me, don't you?"

"Don't be silly."

"That doesn't sound too convincing."

He considered the proof–or lack of it. The expected death of Layla in her son's presence if caught without her dagger hinged upon Diane's witness and Emma's questionable corroboration. Far from forensic, the evidence of empathic testimony passed his sanity test. "I believe you."

"Then why are you still fighting to keep her dagger from her?"

"You saw the same things I saw. It's too much for her."

"She'll get used to it fast. I'll teach her."

He shook his head. "It's not worth the risk. I'm sure I can trap Amir while keeping him away from her."

Diane narrowed her eyes. "You do realize that you can't be in two places at the same time, don't you?"

"Huh?"

"You can't hunt Amir while you protect Layla, unless they're in the same place."

His heart sank. "Oh, shit. I... uh... technically, that's not true. Father and I could split up, as could you and Emma." His rationalization sounded stupid as he replayed it in his head.

"Liam!"

"Okay, fine. Shit. You got me. Splitting up would be dumb. I admit I hadn't thought it through. She can have her stupid dagger."

"Did you ever think it's not even yours to give? Connor's in charge, and he doesn't need your permission."

He shrugged. "Yeah, but he respects my opinion. It's best that we're all in agreement."

"It doesn't matter, now. We all agree."

"Yeah. She can try again tomorrow, which is what I'm sure Father wants. But let's first make sure we don't get ambushed tonight. You want to go for a walk?"

"I'll get my jacket."

"Let's get some body armor, too. Just in case."

Outside, the terrain's high elevation cooled the midnight September air. As they walked over pine needles, he wrapped his arm around her and guided her to a broad tree trunk. "Stand here."

"Why so close to the tree?"

"To hide." He ducked and lifted night vision goggles to his face. He scanned the darkness beyond the cabin's floodlights, verifying their solitude from his location to the nearest resort homes. One reason he'd selected his cabin was the exposed approaches in all directions. He returned the optics to his vest. "All clear. Let's keep going." With his arm around her, he guided her around the back of their resort.

"You know this isn't very romantic, don't you?"

"I wasn't hoping to earn credit for romance tonight. It's nice out here, though."

"True, but you're not talking."

"I'm patrolling. Sorry. Maybe bringing you along was a bad idea."

"Nah. It's okay. I'll enjoy the view." She looked up through the break between the branches and the cabin's roof.

With his naked eye, he watched the open ground between the adjacent properties for motion. At another large tree, he stopped her.

"Again?"

"Yup." He crouched and scanned the darkness with night vision. "All clear. Let's keep going."

"How often are we going to do this?"

"Two to three times an hour, randomly spaced."

"I guess that's not too crazy."

He ushered her to a final stop behind a tree and verified their security with his optics. "All clear. That's a complete three-sixty view. We can take our time heading back inside."

"What then? You'll be pacing around the house looking through windows all night."

"Well, yeah."

"Why'd we bother doing this together? We're not talking."

"I need to look out for our safety."

"I know. Just don't try to start any deep conversations with me. Do what you've got to do."

Liam asked what he needed to know. "I'll jump to it, then. If we get through all this, do you still want to get married?"

She moved close to him and kissed his cheek. "What do you think, dummy?"

The next morning, Liam awoke after a half night of sleep. Rubbing sleep from his eyes, he rushed through his morning routine and then barreled down the stairs in search of the breakfast he hoped Nana and Josh had fetched.

Instead, he found the cabin's other occupants gathered around their seated prisoner. His father stood between Diane and Emma, facing their duct-taped detainee. "And there's my son. Just in time. I was about to wake you."

"I see that we're not wasting any time. When did she recover?"

The detainee lifted her jaw. "I'll answer for myself. I woke up in the middle of the night. I don't know what time it was, and I have no idea how long I was out."

Liam walked around the room to his preferred spot behind the couch. Lacking a spare net warhead for his gun, he realized he needed a new tool to restrain Layla if needed again. Resigning himself to a Taser, he continued walking to an equipment bag. After clipping his body armor vest over his chest, he stood. With the electronic weapon in hand, he moved behind the couch. "I'm ready."

His father extended the enchanted dagger's case towards Layla.

She grabbed it, and nothing happened.

But something happened.

Liam needed the psychics to reveal it.

Diane extended her free hand. "Hurry! Help me stop her!"

Emma interlaced her fingers.

Again, nothing happened.

But something happened.

Layla gasped and dropped her knife. "Oh, God!"

Connor challenged her. "What?"

"I couldn't help myself."

"What did you do?"

Tears of anguish formed in her eyes. "I'm so sorry. I didn't mean to do it. I couldn't help it. I just did it. It was an accident."

"Spit it out, young lady!"

"I contacted my son. I warned him about you all."

CHAPTER 22

Ten minutes later, Liam sat on a couch with his cheeks in his palms and his elbows on his knees. The other six people in the living room moped in similar postures. He cast a glance at the prisoner.

Layla's downcast gaze revealed her shame. She seemed genuinely mortified for having betrayed her captors.

Liam believed the emotions he read on her face. "Diane? Emma? Forgive me for asking again, but I need to be sure."

Diane preempted his asking the full question. "Yes, I'm sure she contacted him. Please don't ask again."

Emma nodded. "Yeah. Me too. We couldn't stop her."

Layla was still fighting to hold back tears. "I said I was sorry. I don't know what else to say."

Mustering the motivation to stand, Liam rose, unclipped the combat knife from his vest, and walked towards his captive. "Don't say anything."

As the detainee looked up, her tone shifted from shame to fear. "What are you doing?"

Liam aimed his jaw towards his father for approval. "I'm untying you. You've done the worst you could do."

In a rare revelation of vexation, Connor lowered his forehead into the palm of the arm he propped on the couch's armrest. "This is indeed rock bottom. You may as well remove her bonds."

The young hunter stooped before the captive and lifted his combat knife upwards through lines of duct tape. In the back of his mind, he vented his frustration by pretending he was eviscerating her. As the last piece of tape yielded, he chastised himself for fantasizing about a violent response to the empath's mistake.

She kept her eyes away from him while he worked.

He sheathed the knife and then palpated his pockets for keys. When he found them, he released the cuffs from her hands and feet and then slid the shackles into his vest. "You're free now, but you'd be an idiot to face him on your own, given the new situation."

"I'm not leaving, if you'll let me stay."

"That's my father's decision."

"Of course, she stays. Let's not make a bad situation worse." Connor's phone chimed, and he pulled it from his pocket. "Excuse me. It's Friar Lucio." He placed the device to his cheek. "Hello. Yes. Really? Oh, Dear God. That may be related to what just happened here. I believe it was an accident, but Layla just warned her son of our plans to trap him. It does. We will."

"What, Father?"

Connor tucked his phone into his pocket. "Friar Lucio says the demon has overtaken Ethan again."

Liam dared to state his desperate hope. "Maybe it's just a coincidence?"

The elder hunter shook his head. "No, lad. Impossible. The demon is demanding an audience with the empath."

Any doubt of Layla's mistake vanished from Liam's mind. She'd done something terrible, and the repercussions were in motion. "Which empath?"

"He didn't say, and Friar Lucio knew better than to engage the demon with clarifying questions. So, we'll all head back to Rome. We'll bring him all three."

"That depends if all three are coming." Liam turned towards Layla. "Are you with us?"

"I have nowhere else to go. I can't face him alone."

Diane answered the question before Liam could ask her. "She's telling the truth."

Connor stood. "Make haste, everyone. We leave in thirty minutes. Friar Lucio is arranging for a private jet. Rental cars and this cabin will all be handled. There's no time to delay."

Eighteen hours later, Liam entered the sanctum and saw a striking sight. Half seated, half reclining, Ethan rested in a medical gurney with thick nylon restraints. Clad in black robes, two friars the young hunter didn't recognize were praying over and guarding the captured wraith. Following Friar Lucio, Liam walked down the aisle to the possessed man.

His eyes shut, Ethan appeared caught somewhere between life and death.

On the friar's opposite side, Connor gestured to the empaths and Diane's family. "Perhaps they should remain behind him, out of his sight, at least while we begin."

The private aircraft had provided for adequate napping, but Liam's body suffered from jet lag. Unsure of the time of day, he kept his mouth closed while listening to the friar-exorcist.

Friar Lucio, a stole over his cloak, raised his voice. "Let the empaths stand ready behind him. As for Josh and Nana, I leave it to them if they wish to remain. This could become a frightening battle. I suspect I know this demon, and he is the worst type."

Without hesitation, the grandmother moved into a pew and ushered her grandson to join her. "We stay."

"Very well. Connor and Liam Brady, hold down his arms."

Before he could filter his protest, the young hunter blurted his response. "But he's restrained."

"Do you understand the power of an energumen possessed by a demon of this type? He's at least a fallen cherub, possibly a fallen seraph."

Liam recognized the classifications of the most powerful angels—and their demonic counterparts. As his father obeyed the friar and scowled at him, the young hunter stepped to Ethan's side and pressed his palms into his forearm. "I'm sorry. If you say it's necessary, I'll trust you."

"I will prepare to wake him." Friar Lucio reached into his cloak.

The subject stirred and glared at him. He spoke with multiple voices, all low groans. "No need, Holy Liar, I've taken care of it." The beast within Ethan turned the man's head left and then right. As he stared at Liam, he revealed dilated pupils. "I see you've given me an audience. Where's my empath?"

Ignoring the demon's request, Friar Lucio was businesslike in his commencement of the Rite of Exorcism. He went to the bench behind him, lifted a tome, and returned to the center of the semicircle. He opened the book and read from it.

From memory, Liam joined the friar in reciting the Lord's Prayer and the Hail Mary, but he stopped praying when he forgot the words to the longer Athanasian Creed.

The friar returned the tome to the bench and then came back to the energumen. He touched the subject's neck with the hem of his stole while pressing his palm on Ethan's head. He followed with a series of requests to saints for intercession to set the tone for the exorcism.

Through Ethan, the demon interrupted. "Blah blah blah. Spare me the boredom and do what I told you."

Refusing to acknowledge the enemy's command, Friar Lucio issued commands of his own. "In the name of Jesus Christ, tell me your name." He pulled a vial of holy water from his garments and sprinkled the subject.

The prisoner grimaced as water hit his face. "Shame on you if you don't know who I am. And you're stupider than you look if you think I'll say my name."

"In the name of Jesus Christ, tell me if you are held in him by necromancy, by evil signs or amulets."

"I'm held in him by these bonds. They're quite efficient at restraining demons. You've outdone yourself." The energumen chuckled.

"In the name of Jesus Christ, tell me the sign of your departure, so that I'll know when you have left God's servant."

Ethan snorted. "Haven't you read Revelation? Pick a sign or wonder from that rubbish."

"In the name of Jesus Christ, tell me your number."

"You can't count that high."

"In the name of Jesus Christ, tell me why you entered God's servant."

The beast rolled the energumen's eyes. "I might consider answering one of your questions if you'd pose a worthy one."

"In the name of Jesus Christ, tell me when you entered God's servant?"

"Blah blah blah."

"In the name of Jesus Christ, tell me how you gained access to God's servant."

"Now we're getting to something interesting. Where is she? The one with a talisman that you idiots believe connects her with my useful servant?"

Baited, Liam glanced over his shoulder.

But Friar Lucio stopped him by clearing his throat.

"Don't be so rude to the boy. I know she's here. Don't you know that weaker demons serve me and inform me?"

Lucio shifted his gaze to Liam and then Connor. "Ignore him." He lowered his gaze to Ethan. "In the name of Jesus Christ, tell me your name."

"We've already been through this. You know what I want."

"In the name of Jesus Christ, tell me if you are held in him by necromancy, by evil signs or amulets."

"Bring me the empath."

"In the name of Jesus Christ, tell me the sign of your departure, so that I'll know when you have left God's servant."

"Bring me the empath."

"In the name of Jesus Christ, tell me your number."

"Bring me the damned empath."

"In the name of Jesus Christ, tell me why you entered God's servant."

The beast's voice split into deep baritones and high screeches. "I will have my audience with the empath!"

Behind the friar, the long bronze staff capped with the order's eight-pointed cross rose from its hole in the semicircular floor and floated towards the ceiling. Suspecting a demonic cause, Liam watched it rise without visible human impetus. He anticipated its wicked strike and jumped to the friar's side in time to catch the rod before the heavy point clubbed the exorcist's skull.

The demon snorted. "Impressive reaction time, hunter."

Liam glared into the energumen's eyes and saw pure evil red irises. "Your powers are limited on holy ground, jackass!"

Unfazed by his near brush with a head wound, Friar Lucio raised his hand in front of the young hunter's nose. "Thank you for protecting me, but do not engage this beast. Hold him down."

Liam returned to Ethan's arm.

"In the name of Jesus Christ, tell me when you entered God's servant?"

Silent, Ethan writhed in a reptilian rhythm.

"In the name of Jesus Christ, tell me how you gained access to God's servant."

Again, the energumen ignored the friar.

From the corner of his eye, Liam saw Josh rise from his seat. The friar lifted his gaze to the young man but said nothing.

As the room remained quiet, Josh walked behind Connor, turned, and stood next to Friar Lucio.

The friar frowned and glared at the young man, but then he gave a slow, understanding nod. "So be it."

With a focus Liam had considered impossible for his autistic friend, Josh burned his eyes, which radiated a subtle but impossible green glow, into Ethan.

Startling the young hunter and begetting gasps from all in the room, the energumen looked to the new participant. "You? No."

Josh spoke with a clear and powerful voice. "Continue."

Friar Lucio began the third litany of commands. "In the name of Jesus Christ, tell me your name."

"Not in front of him." Referring to Josh, the demon seemed to be yielding. "You know my name. Yes. Yes. You know it." He looked to Josh. "He knows it. The name you suspect is true."

"In the name of Jesus Christ, tell me if you are held in him by necromancy, by evil signs or amulets."

"There is no outside force. I stay because I wish."

"In the name of Jesus Christ, tell me the sign of your departure, so that I'll know when you have left God's servant."

"The lights above you will fail, the doors to this room will open, and my former servant will die."

"In the name of Jesus Christ, tell me your number."

Grimacing and writhing, Ethan seemed to suffer, as did the demon within him. "We are eight."

"In the name of Jesus Christ, tell me why you entered God's servant."

"I took him as my servant to administer my rage."

"In the name of Jesus Christ, tell me when you entered God's servant?"

"The date my servant told you is true."

"In the name of Jesus Christ, tell me how you gained access to God's servant."

"The dagger, the one you say is cursed which is now under guard in this very room."

"I know your name, servant of darkness. In the name of Jesus Christ, I command you to depart from God's servant."

Ethan's head snapped back, the lights went out, and the temporary plywood doors flew open.

Liam heard a distant howl that reminded him of a large predator suffering horrible pain. He lifted his cell phone from his pocket to bring light to the room as the assistant friars lit candles.

Hovering over the prisoner, Connor pressed his finger against his neck. "His pulse is weak. He's fading."

Friar Lucio moved close to Ethan. "You are free of the demon."

The captive surveyed his surroundings. "Where am I? I don't know this room."

"It's a holy place. It's a safe place. Is there anything I can do for you, to save your soul?"

"No. You've already helped. Whatever mercy a monster like me can receive will be mine. Thank you. All of you." His head flopped to the side, and he stopped breathing.

Connor checked his pulse. "He's gone."

Liam considered trying to revive him, but a voice within his heart told him to let the man's spirit pass. Among the shadowy faces in the room, he saw mixed emotions, but nobody urged the attempt to bring Ethan back to this world. But something odd caught the young hunter's attention.

Beside Nana, Josh lowered himself into his seat and buried his nose in his tablet computer.

CHAPTER 23

In the sanctum's waiting room, Diane knelt in front of her brother. "Josh? Can I have your attention please, Josh?"

He looked away.

Standing behind her, Liam offered to help. "Maybe he'll talk to me. We've been spending some quality time together."

Diane looked over her shoulder and with her eyes told the young hunter to shut up.

"Got it." Liam retreated to the opposite couch and sat.

She returned her attention to her brother. "Can we talk, Josh?"

"No."

"Please, Josh. It's very important."

Silence.

"Are you scared, Josh? It's okay. We're all a little scared."

"You want to know why I stood up."

"Yes! I was very impressed, Josh. You did so well. I would appreciate it if you could tell me why."

Silence.

"Can you tell me why you stood up and walked next to Friar Lucio, Josh?"

"No."

"Don't you want to tell me?"

Silence.

"Will you tell me if we're alone, Josh?"

"I don't want to talk about it!"

Sensing the inquiry's limit, Diane stood and addressed the team of curious onlookers. "That's all we're getting from my brother about it for now."

Staying seated, Liam challenged her. "Don't you two have a special bond? What do you think happened?"

She was clueless and shaken. "We just saw an exorcism and a death. Can we just chill for while?"

The young hunter lay back into the cushions. "Maybe. It depends what this demon does next. Is he going to bring Amir here to try attacking us like Ethan did? Is he going to have Amir kill someone else under the next full moon instead of Layla? Either of those scenarios gives us thirteen days."

Josh stood. "I want to leave."

Diane rose next to him and placed her hand on his shoulder. "Sure, Josh. You can go. Just don't leave the building. It may not be safe out there."

"I'm going to read." He marched away.

Struggling to reach her feet, Nana stood and followed her grandson. "I go with him to be sure."

Lucio stuck his head through the courtroom's doorway. "We're bringing Ethan's body through now. He's covered under a sheet, but it's still a disturbing sight. Anyone who's squeamish should look away." He stepped forward and waved the mystery friars into the waiting room with the wheeled gurney.

Diane watched them follow the walls to the hallway leading out. As Friar Lucio tapped a code to open the reinforced door, she wondered about the afterlife and Ethan's destiny within it.

Surprising her, Friar Lucio remained behind the gurney and held open the door. He faced the psychics and hunters. "I expect that you all found that display peculiar. I'm rather certain I know what happened, but by divine edict, I cannot share my knowledge. However, it appears that Josh has adequate understanding to guide you forward. When he's ready to speak, you must listen."

The news worried Diane. "What if he won't talk?"

"You'll have to do your best to coax guidance from him, but you must also wait until he's sure of what he's learned."

"I will. That was my plan."

Appearing to contemplate his next move, the friar looked to the floor and then let the door shut. "There's something I can share. I suspect that a demon oppresses Miss Jazani."

The declaration alarmed Diane. "What's that mean, and why do you only suspect?"

"Demonic oppression is far more common than possessions, but it's impossible to diagnose with certitude. It's impossible to discern if someone's suffering under the will of a demon or if a life of hardship and setbacks results from random events. But I suspect Miss Jazani's oppression due to her precarious position between her son and his Master. It practically begs a demon's harassment."

"What can we do?"

"In the short term, very little, unfortunately." The friar stepped towards the group. "Miss Jazani, do you happen to have an amulet like the ones Miss Yousif and Miss Zeigler have?"

"I don't know what they have, but I don't have anything I'd call an amulet."

Diane walked to Layla and showed her the pendant on her neck, which was a disk of silver holding a milky iridescent ovular moonstone, which lacey, gothic metal twists surrounded with a sharp point at the bottom. The silvery structure and the stone's setting within it suggested a dagger underneath a full moon. "Emma has one just like it from her family."

Studying it, Layla held the jewelry. "I've never seen anything like it."

"The reason I ask is that escaping demonic oppression requires a long-term and continued regimen of prayer and ritual. There's no time to achieve this before the next full moon. However, an amulet would provide you instant protection."

Layla released the pendant and looked at Diane. "You said you and Emma got this from your families?"

Diane recalled the data-mining she'd achieved with Emma while inside their new sister's head. "Yeah. I see the problem now. You were adopted."

"Right."

"And nobody bothered to retain any heirlooms for you from your birthmother."

"I got nothing."

Friar Lucio clasped his hands together. "You won't be able to face your son without some manner of protection. We'll either have to work on a long-term regiment of sanctification, or you'll have to try to contact your birthmother for the amulet."

Diane added her thought. "And for a book of family knowledge, too."

Layla squirmed on the couch. "Hold on! I've written off that... that... well, I'm not going to say what she is. But if she didn't want to keep me, she's nothing to me."

The Chaldean empath felt her colleague's suffering. "I can't imagine. Were you separated at birth?"

"Immediately at birth. No bonding. No love. No nothing. Straight to foster care and then adopted two months later."

"Ouch. I've read that a baby needs at least six months with her mother to understand that she's a separate person from her mother. But I'm too far away from this to even to pretend to understand."

Friar Lucio confirmed the theory. "I've studied this and have counseled many adopted people. Diane's right. The separation at birth creates a foundation of sadness, anger, and fear in the child and makes healthy bonding with other people over her lifetime quite difficult. I believe this challenge can be overcome with extensive nurturing by the adopting parent or parents, but it appears that Miss Jazani lacked such support."

Layla shrugged. "Story of my life, but I'm not asking for excuses."

"No excuses, but these are factors that make you susceptible to demonic oppression. Finding your amulet, if it exists and can be retrieved, will accelerate your defenses greatly–probably instantly and enough to face your son. And Diane's right to inquire about a book, too. If you're as strong an empath as the evidence suggests, these things will have been retained in your lineage."

"I can't just hunt down my birth mother and order her to give me a bunch of family heirlooms."

Liam stood. "But I can. I imagine this will take time, though. Paperwork back and forth with signatures. We need to get started."

The friar raised his palm at the young hunter. "Normally, I'd say you're right. But we have avenues to accelerate such bureaucracies. If Miss Jazani agrees, I can take this as far as it can be taken, and quickly."

Liam frowned. "Really? You can bang through this?"

"As far as the birthmother has requested from her end. If she's reached out to the agencies to find Layla, we can move quickly."

"I've already resigned myself to a life without her. Now you're saying I need to contact her. This isn't easy. Can I say no?"

In his caring tone, the friar handled Layla's anxiety. "You could say no, but delays in facing your son will lead to needless death. I know it seems terrifying to contact your birthmother, but I know you have the courage."

Agitated, Layla tapped her fingers on her knees. "Maybe."

"Think about it while I make a phone call to understand the particular process of the agency I need to contact. Can you tell me what county you were adopted in?"

"Cook County, Illinois."

"I'll get started. Excuse me." The friar nodded and departed through the security door.

With her fellow psychics and the hunters, Diane flopped into the couch. "Should we all stay here and wait?"

Layla snorted. "Wait for what? For me to get the guts to meet the woman who gave me up?"

Nobody spoke for a few minutes until Liam broke an awkward silence. "Is anyone else getting hungry?"

"Good question, lad. I am. Perhaps we should get some food and bring it back for everyone else."

Diane nodded. "Yeah. Get the usual sandwiches. We need some girl time."

When the men left, Diane and Emma huddled around Layla, who let down her guard in the hunters' absence. "I can't do this!"

Diane sat beside her. "It's nerve-racking. I'm getting scared, and it's not even about me."

Emma sat on the adopted empath's other side. "I agree. I can't believe how anxious I am already."

Layla shrugged. "Am I supposed to be ready for Friar Lucio to come back down here and say he's got my birthmother on the phone? This is crazy."

"Knowing how the men around here operate, I wouldn't

be surprised." Diane reflected upon the situation. "But maybe there's a better way."

Layla wiped away her latest tears. "Like what?"

"We're empaths, and there's three of us with our daggers. We can contact you birthmother our way."

"Ugh. The last time I held mine, I screwed up everything."

"I don't know about that. You don't have to listen to everything Connor and Liam say. They're always complicating things. And forget the past. We need to figure out how to use our daggers together. This is as good a place to start as any."

"I'm still scared."

"We'll be together." Diane thought it was creepy to seek the ground where Ethan had died, but it was the safest place to experiment and train a new psychic. "Let's get your dagger and get back onto the compass."

"Connor stuck it in one of his equipment bags right after he took it from me."

Diane smirked. "He never said I couldn't rummage through his bags. I'll head upstairs and grab it, and then I'll be right down. Let's meet in the sanctum in ten minutes."

Ten minutes later, Diane stood in an equilateral triangle with her empathic sisters in the center of the carved compass. "Let's do some practice, first." She kicked the weapons case to Layla. "Grab it and try to contact me in a telepathic link."

"I can't. I..."

"*Yulla*. We don't have all day. Emma, grab yours and get ready in case she gets out of control."

Layla stood and grabbed her dagger. "It's not so overpowering. Is that because we're in the sanctum?"

"I think so. I learned the hard way with people trying to kill me. So, when I got here, I was already used to my dagger."

"And I learned the easy way. Diane taught me down here. So, I knew how to handle it before I got into the real world."

"What do I do?"

"Concentrate on getting into my head. You can use what you

know about me, and you can use my emotions. I'm edgy, a bit anxious about this whole thing of meeting your mother."

"I'll try."

Diane slipped into a trance and saw Emma's face frozen in slow time. "Hello?"

"It's Layla. I did it!"

"Good job. We're moving fast through your training. Now see if you can bring Emma into it."

"How can I tell her apart from you while I'm... wherever this is?"

Diane considered the distinction between herself and her German colleague. "I've been through harder times than her, financially and for personal safety. I guess I'm rougher than her. But she's been volunteering all her adult life. She may be more compassionate."

"I'll try it. Here goes."

Emma entered the link. "Hi. It worked! Our bodies are still paralyzed, though. Are we going to hold a link while we move?"

"No, we don't need that skill for contacting her mom."

The link broke, time started, and Layla staggered backwards. "I couldn't hold it. That's harder than I thought."

Diane adapted to her role of mentoring her newest student. "That's normal. You were holding three of us together. Now, if we all hold hands, Emma and I can hold the link between us while you reach out for your birthmother."

"Now? Already?" Shaking with fear, Layla stepped forward and became the vertex of the empathic triangle.

"Yes. Now." Diane lifted her arms and held the hand with the German empath's dagger.

Trembling, Layla held the hand holding the Chaldean empath's dagger.

"I'll create the link." Time stopped, and the black starry void surrounded the shared consciousness of the merged psychics. Communicating with wordless meaning, Diane checked on her colleagues. "Call for your birth mother. Or is it our birth mother? It's hard to tell when we're one."

"I think it's just mine. I need to try. But it's so hard."

Certain that the unique bond between separated mother and child held identifiers, Diane coached her apprentices. "Emma, help me calm her. Layla, focus on your mother's emotions with respect to you personally. Loss. Abandonment. Guilt. A lot of guilt."

"I'll try."

"It should be easy. This is a really strong, natural connection, even though you haven't met her since birth."

Within their shared mind, Layla sounded nervous. "Oh my God! I think I found her. We're in."

Fused with her empathic sisters, Diane saw the world through an older woman's eyes. Instantly, she knew–they all knew–they'd reached Layla's birth mother. Diane started crying within her mind, as did the sisters. She felt real tears rolling down the woman's real face. "Keep going. Let her know who we are. Learn everything about Layla's heritage."

The birthmother spoke aloud. "I knew you were alive. I knew you were in trouble. Of course, I'll help. Yes, there's a family book. Yes, there's an amulet just like the one you envision, and it's yours. I will ship them overnight."

"Thank you."

"When can I see you?"

As the leader, Diane sensed her sisters waiting for her to answer. She wondered if a physical meeting prior to facing the wraith would be a distraction, but she feared Layla might die at her son's hands. She had to allow the reunion. "Can you get on a plane tonight? We'll pay for it."

"Yes."

"Bring the heirlooms with you. I'll get you a credit card number, and you can fly out here, first class."

CHAPTER 24

In the wee hours of the next morning, Layla awoke to continuing jet lag and an enduring anxiety. She checked her surroundings and noticed she reclined on a cot in a courtroom within the secret underground labyrinth of a public building. After rolling her torso forward, she rubbed her eyes.

On either side of her, flanking her like protective sentries, her new empathic sisters slept in cots. Behind her, Diane's brother and grandmother slept, while farther up the floor gentle snores issued from the old man who seemed to shift personas between a gentle patriarch and a threatening interrogator.

Banished for insufferable snoring, the young hunter slept beyond Layla's view in the waiting room.

A debate caught fire within her skull. How badly had she screwed up her life to need the protection of these former strangers? Then again, her new companions seemed like good people. How would she get out of this without killing herself or her son? Then again, the hunters and empaths knew how to protect lives. How could she trust anyone she'd met scant days ago? Then again, telepathic links and fusions of consciousness had brought her closer to Emma and Diane than she'd been to anyone else—including her son.

Connor rolled to his side, and his soft snoring subsided.

The burning debate also subsided within Layla's mind as she accepted her fate. Her captives-turned-colleagues were her team, her birthmother was part of her life, and she would challenge her son with the outcome determining the fates of many. Bizarre as her recent history had been, it made sense, and she fell back into a deep sleep.

When she awoke again, she was alone and hungry. Checking her phone, she gasped when she realized she'd slept away the morning. She sat on the cot's edge, planted her feet on the floor, and rubbed her eyes. Barefooted, she walked up the aisle, passed through the temporary plywood, and stood while her pupils adjusted to the waiting room's bright light. Wondering where her colleagues had scattered, she accepted her solitude and strolled to the ladies' room.

The shower's heat helped pump the fatigue of the time zone shift and transatlantic travel from her system. As her mind kicked into gear, she remembered her day's challenge–she would meet her birthmother in person. A quick pang of anxiety hit her stomach but dissipated as she recalled having already met her via a telepathic link.

While changing into jeans and a tee shirt, she saw a text on her phone from Diane. Reading it, she understood her solitude. The hunters had taken Nana and Josh to brunch while her empathic sisters were meeting her birthmother at the airport.

After heading to the ground floor, Layla wandered the hallways of the order's headquarters. She found the empty study where Liam investigated her history and that of her son, and she stuck her head into its confines. Papers and folders were strewn about over desks, and one of the hunter's laptops showed its blank screen. She entered the room and crossed it to its far door, but when she tried the handle to the library, the locked latch resisted.

She withdrew from the room and explored the building further, seeing a few friars gathered in a dining hall next to a kitchen. Moving deeper into the building, she reached a hallway with worn carpet lined with multiple doors that issued to offices.

As she kept walking, she reached a staircase that she assumed climbed towards berthing areas serving the half dozen friars who comported themselves with the confident familiarity of permanent residents. One such friar, one who seemed young compared to the others, descended the stairs and greeted her with a smile. She gave a hasty salutation and then reversed course towards the main entrance.

When she reached the lobby, she waved at the steward behind the counter who was one of the friars she recognized as a resident, and then she sank into a comfortable couch. Jet lag took hold, and she dozed off into a light slumber.

She snapped her head forward to the sound of the outer door cracking open. Turning her jaw, she saw her empathic sisters escorting an older woman into the lobby. Her heart raced as she realized her birthmother was walking into the room. She leapt from the couch and walked to her.

With a smile across her face, Diane announced her birthmother's name. "Layla, this is Farah."

Amid squeals of joy and the random anxious gibberish she uttered, Layla embraced the stranger. After releasing her, she realized she was less emotional than she'd anticipated, and she internalized the lesson that telepathic connections mimicked the real world in uniting their participants. Although it was her first physical embrace with Farah, their true reunion had occurred during the prior evening's link.

Farah's voice was deep with a thick Persian accent. "I can't believe it."

"Me neither. I don't know what to say." Layla had considered the woman a meaningless concept until her sisters had escorted her into the ethereal introduction. Now, she was an immediate and integral part of her life. It was too much, too fast, but somehow the rapid reunion resonated as logical and appropriate.

"There's so much we have to catch up on. I don't know where to begin. I was afraid I'd die without ever seeing you. I mean, without seeing you again. I remember the moment I had to give you up."

The words were an unexpected answer to a question Layla had wanted to ask. "You had to give me up?"

"I had no choice." Her birthmother's tone was firm.

Layla felt like saying that everyone always has a choice, but she gave the woman, who appeared at most sixty years old, a chance to explain. "What happened?"

Diane preempted the answer. "Let's all go sit down." The Chaldean psychic led the foursome to the couches.

Her back straight, Farah sat on the edge of a cushion. "I was only seventeen when I got married. I hardly remember the so-called courtship. Your father was twenty-six and making good money and was from a connected family. So, my parents made me marry him. That's what mattered to them, having a daughter married to someone who was successful. What was I supposed to do? I didn't know any better."

Layla found the oppression theme familiar. "That's sounds about right. Young woman gets screwed because someone has the power to screw her."

"It gets worse. Your father worked for the shah. I didn't know it when we got married, but he was crooked, like so many in the shah's government. He apparently knew someone who knew someone who was related to someone and so on and so forth. He was born into the right family at the right time. He had no skills or ability, and he was a mean man. He hit me, not much at first, but as the shah's rule crumbled, he took out his frustrations on me more and more. Getting pregnant with you didn't slow him down."

"Great. I'm the bastard of a mean bastard."

"We had to flee before the revolution, and he sent me ahead to the United States while I was pregnant with you, to stay with his cousin's family. But I looked at my trip to America as a chance to get away from him."

Layla scoffed. "I don't blame you."

"But his cousin was a bad man. He kept me prisoner in his house. It's like he feared I'd run away if I could, not that I had any money, or knew anyone, or could even speak the language. I was a hopeless mess. Then when he learned that your father was killed in the revolution, he had you taken from me at birth. He said he'd give you to another Iranian family."

"Well, at least that part was true. I was. My adopted father left my mother while I was a baby, though."

"I had hoped for better for you."

"Don't worry about me. Back to you."

"Your birthfather's cousin said he couldn't afford to pay for another mouth to feed and that I wasn't ready to be a single mother. Then when he decided that he no longer had an obligation to look after his dead cousin's widow, he sent me away on my own."

Layla was beginning to see the woman as a victim, instead of seeing her as a source of abandonment. In a moment of self-awareness, she recognized her recent personal growth since joining her sisters. The older version of herself would've condemned her birthmother for weakness, but her evolved self had empathy. "That's tough. How old were you?"

"I was nineteen when you were born."

"I can't believe that jackass kicked you out."

Farah shrugged. "I didn't know my husband or his cousin long, but I can't argue that they were corrupt, bad men. And it was the worst of times for them because their easy life of power was breaking down. It was a bad time to be related to the shah. It brought out the worst of the bad people."

"Is my birthfather still alive? Did he try to find you?"

"I don't know. I gave birth to you, then the cousin himself, who lied and told the doctor he was your father, took you and walked away with you. I never saw him again. He had his wife drive me to a hotel when I left the hospital. They paid for a week of my stay, left me a hundred dollars, and that was it."

While Layla absorbed her birthmother's history, Diane continued the inquiry. "That's terrible. You must have felt horribly alone."

"It was tough."

"What did you do?"

"I thought about trying to find my husband, but that was too desperate. Finding him would be harder than just starting over in America, and why the hell would I want to go back to him? I knew America was the supposed land of opportunity, and that gave me hope. I could see the affluence all around me. It seemed like anyone could succeed."

Diane frowned. "But you said you didn't speak English. You didn't know anyone."

"True, and I didn't know anybody. So, there I was in some affluent Chicago neighborhood, and I walked those clean, pretty streets until I found a church. They took me in, they helped me find some friendly people in an Iranian community, and a family took me in as a nanny. I took care of someone else's little girl, but I pretended she was you." Farah broke down into tears.

Reactively, Layla got up from her couch, moved to her birthmother's side, and draped her arm over her. "It's okay now."

"I'm sorry. I don't mean to be a sniveling old woman."

Layla thought her birthmother's smooth, swarthy skin retained much of its youthful allure. "Old? You hardly look fifty-five."

"You're too kind. I just turned sixty-one."

"I must have got your youthful good looks. People still accuse me of being in my thirties."

Farah gasped and then wiped away her tears. "I almost forgot. I've got more than good looks for you." She fished through her purse and pulled out a necklace. "This was my mother's. I think I'm supposed to give it to you." She extended the amulet.

Layla grabbed it and held it under her nose. "Diane, Emma? Can I see your amulets?"

The sister empaths hovered over the new jewelry and extended their pendants. All three were exact replicas of each other.

Before putting on her new charm, Layla looked at her birthmother. "You don't seem too sure that I should have this."

"I don't know because my mother never told me. I got the feeling growing up that we were supposed to be special with psychic powers. I can't believe I'm talking about this openly, but you three get it because you use your powers. Whatever skills I have or was supposed to have must be dead. My mother never taught me anything. All she wanted to do was climb a social ladder."

"I'll try it." Layla clasped the chain behind her neck and then slipped the pendant under shirt. An immediate calmness overcame her. "Whoa."

Her birthmother studied her. "It's got some effect on you?"

"Yeah. It feels... nice. It feels right."

"Now I wish I'd worn it once before giving it to you."

A cold sensation washed over Layla. "Hold on. I... something's wrong. I don't feel him anymore." She reached for the amulet to snap it away, but its soothing essence slowed her hand. "He's gone. I can't feel my son."

Diane intervened. "I'm sure he's still alive. I didn't sense anything changing, and I think I would have. Did you, Emma?"

The German psychic shook her head.

"I should always be connected to my son."

Diane shook her head. "If your amulet's protecting you from sensing him, it must be a good thing. But it might still hurt."

"It does, like an open wound, I think. I... I don't know. It's like I think I've just been cut deeply, but my brain hasn't registered the pain yet. I just know I miss him. I miss him terribly."

Farah extended her arms. "I'll take it from you."

Her birthmother's behavior reminded Layla of a drug addict fighting herself over the desire for a recreational dose. With a pang of anxiety, she stood and put distance between her neck and her birthmother's hands. "I don't mean to be demanding, but do you also have a book?"

Farah seemed mesmerized by the amulet, like it had wielded a secret power over her, despite never having worn it, and its absence left a scar.

Unsure how to address her birthmother, Layla called to her by her name. "Farah?"

"Oh. Yes. Sorry." She fumbled through her purse and pulled out a manila folder containing yellowing papers. "It's not really a book, but I remember my mother saying it was a copy of an ancient text." She extended the papers.

Layla grabbed them and thumbed through them. The characters were foreign. "What language is this?"

"I have no idea."

Diane canted her head. "Aramaic. Just like mine and Emma's."

The exterior door opened, and the rest of the team strolled into the lobby. After introductions and updates, Layla scanned the room and noticed her manuscript resting on the computer tablet in the hands of the Chaldean empath's brother.

Diane looked over Josh's shoulder. "Anything interesting?"

"No."

"You seem interested, Josh. Are you enjoying your reading?"

He grunted.

Diane looked up and addressed whoever was looking at her. "I don't think he's finding anything new here."

As Josh closed the papers, his eyes radiated a momentary but impossible green glow. "There's nothing new, but there's a common place mentioned in all the documents. It's called Media."

Layla sensed a hidden meaning in his declaration. Something in the young man's statement promised to help heal her many wounds, old and new. "Josh? Why does that matter?"

"It's where wraiths come from. It's where your son's going. It's where we need to go."

CHAPTER 25

Liam scratched his temple while mulling over Josh's statement. Failing to understand it, he blurted out the obvious question. "So, does anyone know where Media is?"

Blank stares and shaking heads.

"Well, then. Does anyone know when Media was? It probably doesn't exist anymore, at least not by that name."

His father tapped his fist against his head. "Oh, dear. I should know this."

With a confused scowl, Nana looked up from her chair. "What are we looking for?"

Diane raised her voice. "Media!"

"Oh? Is that where the old Medes people were?"

Connor snapped his fingers and pointed at the grandmother. "That's it! Media's a reference to the Medes peoples. I remember it from my studies. They were adherents of Mithraism or Zoroastrianism. I believe their area of influence spread from Western Afghanistan to Southeastern Turkey, roughly."

Liam scowled. "I don't remember any of that. Why would you have studied it, but not me?"

"Well, lad, do you think I twiddled my thumbs for fifty years waiting for you to arrive at my doorstep?"

Liam smirked. "Well, yeah. That and drinking beer and hunting."

Connor waved dismissive fingers at his son. "Bah. There's a lifetime of learning ahead of you–possibly... normally... I mean, well..."

"You mean if Diane and I don't get married?"

"Yes. That's what I mean. Which won't happen unless we find Amir, who apparently has taken flight to a land Josh has defined for us as a huge chunk of the Middle East."

Liam inhaled, lifted his phone, and aimed his face at Josh. "I'm going to research Media, but if anyone has an idea of the century when the empaths' original books were written, it'd help me know how big Media was at the time."

Having missed the hint, Josh kept thumbing through Layla's pages.

The young man's autism frustrated Liam. "Josh? Do you remember when the books were written?"

Nothing.

Liam raised his voice. "Josh, can you remind me when the books were written, why you think Media's important, and give me some sort of bloody clue as to how you helped scare a demon out of a wraith?"

Josh scowled, sought the nearest wall, and walked away.

Her eyes black, Diane appeared in Liam's face. "You screwed up, and I'm not fixing it for you this time. Tuck your tail between your legs and go coddle him like you mean it."

"I'm sorry."

"Now!"

Amid silent watchers, the young hunter slinked towards Josh, who'd retreated to a corner of the lobby. When he reached him, Liam lowered his head. "Uh, Josh?"

No answer.

"Josh?"

A grunt.

"Look, I didn't mean to be... so mean."

Another grunt.

"It's just that you're doing so many impressive things, and I guess I got too excited about it. If I promise to be nicer, will you talk to me?"

"Maybe."

"Well, I'm going back to your sister. Will you come talk to me when you're ready?"

"Okay."

"Thanks, Josh." Liam walked back to the group, which focused on his father.

Connor updated his son. "We're discussing the option of using our empaths' daggers to find Amir. I don't think the Media clue alone will get us anywhere useful, but it can guide us."

Without thinking, Liam bought into the concept. "What are

you thinking? Getting some bearing separation and triangulating?"

"Exactly. The good news about the Media clue is that we can get a good fix with prior planning. I propose to send one dagger team to Dubai for bearing separation. The problem is, I asked three empaths for a volunteer, and three hands went up. However, someone needs to stay here to get our lines of bearing to cross."

"Got it. Can I have a moment alone with Diane?"

Connor nodded as Diane moved to him, and Liam led his desired future fiancée to a private space near the wall. "How bad do you want to go to Dubai?"

She rolled her eyes. "How bad do you think anyone wants to go to Dubai with someone else paying for it? I want to go to the top of the Burj Khalifa. I want to eat in a five-star restaurant. I want to set foot on a man-made island. Can't a girl have a little fun?"

He weighed his words. "If we come out of this alive and get married, what if I promise to take you there on our honeymoon?"

"From a guy sworn to poverty?"

"If we get married, I don't think I'll be stuck with all my vows."

"You don't think, but you don't know."

"I'll find a way to get you to Dubai, I promise."

She groaned. "Ugh. Fine. Let the other two go."

As he realized the psychics had used their daggers to find fellow sisters but not Amir, Liam rethought the approach. "First let's test this in the sanctum before we waste our time. I think everyone, including me, was buying into groupthink. We don't know if this'll work."

The Chaldean empath frowned. "I don't think anyone in the world can hide from the three of us."

"That's a bit arrogant."

She shrugged. "Maybe."

"You're doing a great job leading the others in learning your powers, but I've got a nasty feeling about this. I think the demon that killed Ethan's going to embed himself in Amir, dig in, and put up a hellacious fight."

Her eyes sought the floor. "Okay, maybe you're right. I'll watch it. Getting cocky's not going to help anyone."

He softened his tone. "I know you know better. You just needed some reminding. Just because you've got Emma and now maybe Layla on your side–"

Lifting her gaze, she exposed dark eyes. "Maybe Layla?"

"You trust her because she's your partner in telepathic crime, but I can't afford to trust her."

"Fine. Whatever."

"No 'whatever'. That means I'll be keeping an eye on her. Father will, too." He leaned close and lowered his voice. "You know that I have to consider her expendable."

Her voice was venom. "Then I'm expendable, too."

"I'm not talking about you. You're not expendable to me."

"Not even for accomplishing your mission? Your job's stopping a wraith, not protecting me. Don't worry. We've been through this before. I'm used to it."

"What good would it do me if I accomplish my mission but couldn't be with you?"

"I know how you think. Don't pretend otherwise."

Under the influence of her allure, he'd lost track of how he thought. "Can we just get on with it? Do you want to run some experiments or not?"

Her tone relaxed. "Yeah. We should probably see what we can do without letting Amir know that Layla's still with us."

The tactical consideration impressed him. "Good thinking. If you and Emma can find him while keeping her hidden, that'll give us the option to separate from Layla later."

She struck with cynicism. "Okay. That might save her from you getting trigger-happy when you stop finding her useful."

"That's not what I meant by 'expendable'."

"Forget it.

"Thank you. Can we run the experiments now?"

"Yeah. Let's go."

He looked to the gang and raised his voice. "Dubai's going to have to wait."

In the sanctum, Liam watched the empaths. They stood in a triangular formation with their daggers at their feet.

The scowl on Diane's face told the story. "Nothing's happening. We're trying telepathy with ourselves. We're taking turns leading the trances. We're trying it alone and together. We can't make them point at anything."

"You didn't try contacting Amir directly, did you?"

"No. Not yet."

"Good. That's a last resort, since it gives up any element of surprise." Aiming his finger at the daggers, Liam voiced a theory. "Do you think they've become exclusively tools of telepathy?"

She shrugged. "I guess."

"I mean, they don't work as pointers for you anymore."

"Maybe. The last time Emma and I used them as pointers, we found Layla. Layla never used hers as a pointer."

The Persian psychic clarified. "That's right. I never had a pointer. I always used detectives to find Amir the normal way."

Liam shook his head. "We don't have time to find him the normal way before the next full moon, and we're pretty sure that's the deadline before his next murder, whether he goes after Layla or someone else."

"Why wouldn't he come for me? I thought that was something you were all sure of?"

"We are sure, but wraiths can change targets. We've seen it before." Liam pushed further into his theory. "But I have an idea. If everyone but Father will leave the room, I want to try something."

Diane called his bluff. "If you're going to see if you can turn them into pointers by looking at them, we could just look away."

Liam chuckled. "You got me there, but I think your very presence with the daggers is overpowering."

"What are you talking about? We tried just closing our eyes in the cabin in Arizona."

The young hunter disagreed. "We did, sort of. But in Arizona, it was two empaths, two hunters, and one dagger. Now it's three empaths, three daggers, and we're on the holy ground."

Diane shrugged and replied in falsetto. "So?"

"So, just humor me. My hunch is that you three are too powerful for us here in the sanctum. But if your daggers can't see you, so to speak, they'll default to pointers in the eyes of us hunters."

"Fine. Come on, girls. Let's go." Diane led the empaths out of the room.

When the last empath closed the plywood behind her, Connor raised an eyebrow. "If this works, I'll owe you a pint."

As the young hunter burned his eyes on the daggers, two of them remained inert. But Layla's glowed with its natural bronze hue and began its slow rotation. "You were saying?"

"I think I'll be buying you some beer, lad. In the world of daggers, I see that empaths trump hunters. If you remove the empaths, the daggers default from tools of telepathy to pointers."

The moving dagger settled, and Liam eyeballed its direction relative to the floor's compass. He then tapped the bearing into a mapping program on an open laptop on the council's bench. The line ran through small rural areas but touched two major population centers. "We'll need to get a couple more bearings while we travel, but I think I know where we're going."

"Do tell."

"Somewhere in Northeastern Iraq. The origin of this demon's power is either Mosul or Erbil."

CHAPTER 26

Diane sat in the waiting room with her new extended family–her biological relatives and her empathic sisters. "Knowing Liam's luck, he'll be exactly right."

Seated on the opposite couch, Emma nodded. "He's got good intuition for a... what do you call him?"

"A caveman."

"Yes. Your caveman will make at least one dagger move. I think it was a good theory."

"He's not my caveman until we get through this."

The plywood creaked open, and Liam's head jutted from the sanctum. "Hey, everyone. It worked. Diane and Emma's daggers didn't move, but Layla's is pointing towards Mosul and Erbil. They're on the same bearing. Other than that, it's pointing at small cities and mountains. We'll get a tighter fix while we travel."

Nana's face lit up. "My sister, she lived in Mosul until ISIS forced her away."

Diane recognized the news as an opportunity and an obligation. "That means we'll be staying with her, right? She's in Erbil now?"

The grandmother frowned. "No, not stay. They have only a small apartment, but we need to visit her after we're done."

Liam stepped into the waiting room. "Our travel's going to be complex. It's hard to get flights. The best I could find was a flight from Amman, Jordan to Erbil, but there's nothing direct to Mosul. We have to start in Erbil."

The grandmother shrugged. "Okay. So, we meet my sister before we do what we need to do."

Diane drew a breath to explain to Liam the family's expectations of hospitality, but her brother stood.

With an unnatural green glimmer, his eyes commanded attention, and his voice carried startling authority. "We need to start in Mosul. From there, we go to Erbil. That's where he is."

Diane gasped. "He's in Erbil? You're sure?"

"The line of Nineveh begins in Mosul. A demon's stand would be distant from the origins of his enemy's power."

Liam nodded. "Good point, but we can't get a flight to Mosul."

Josh, or the entity that Diane considered a confident replica of her autistic brother, stood his ground. "Then we cross into Iraq from Turkey, on the ground."

Two days later, Diane watched through the delivery truck's windshield as a border guard wearing combat fatigues and carrying an assault rifle over his shoulder approached the driver seated beside her. As the Kurdistan soldier pressed his palm against the truck, the driver, one of Diane's many distant relatives from Mosul, rolled down his window and spoke in the Iraqi dialect of Arabic. "Good morning, sir."

"Good morning. Identification, please. From all of you."

From Diane's right, her grandmother extended her passport. The psychic took it and added hers, which the driver stacked on his own.

With three passports in hand, the guard thumbed through pictures and eyed each of the vehicle's occupants. "Two Americans?"

The driver, a man in his early sixties with hard lines on his face, shared a truth that Diane expected to carry weight. "My cousin and her granddaughter."

In flawless Iraqi Arabic, Nana added her unsolicited emphasis. "I was born in Mosul. I want to show my granddaughter her heritage."

The guard held the passports. "Yes, of course. But why are you passing here from Turkey? There are quicker and easier ways to get to Mosul."

Nana's performance was perfect, and Diane would've considered it brilliant acting had it not been authentic behavior. "Do I look like I'm made of money? My sister and brother-in-law's entire business was shut down when ISIS took over Mosul and destroyed their factory. Getting a ride with my cousin on his business route was the only way I could afford coming back home with my granddaughter."

The guard nodded at Diane. "She speaks Arabic?"

"I do. Not as well as my grandmother, but I speak."

While tucking the passports into his breast pocket, the soldier faced the driver and pointed towards the vehicle's rear. "I will check your cargo. Come with me and open the back door."

As the driver stepped from the cabin, Diane reached for the dagger in her purse. With haste, she found her way into the guard's mind and saw through his eyes.

He stood from the vehicle while the driver opened the door, revealing a cargo bed filled with raw materials intended for cutting into blouses and dresses. "Turn on the lights."

The driver stepped up and flicked a switch, and the tight packing of rolled, folded, and stacked fabrics became visible. "It's just material for clothing."

"I need to see more." The guard pulled a flashlight from his belt and lifted it.

But before the solider could aim between the rolls, Diane spoke into his mind and willed him back. "Stop. You've seen enough."

The man froze and then grunted. "Very well. I've seen enough." He slid his flashlight back into his hip.

Carrying a mirror he'd used to examine the truck's underside, a colleague of the guard approached from the vehicle's far side and shook his head. "Nothing."

The guard nodded and then handed the passports back to the driver. "You're clear."

Two miles later, the border crossing disappeared behind bends in the road, and the low, sand-colored buildings of the Kurdistan city of Zakho appeared on the horizon.

Stark panic filled Diane's mind, and she sensed a presence. "Who's there?"

"We need to stop!" Josh was terrified. "Get out of the truck!"

She knew the answer, but his demand's bizarreness forced the question. "We're only a couple miles from stopping. Can't it wait?"

"No! Now!"

She snapped her jaw towards the driver. "Stop the truck! We need to get out."

"Why?"

She screamed. "Just do it!"

He pulled to the side of the road, and the tires kicked up dust.

Nana stepped from the door, and Diane followed her. As an SUV passed from the opposite direction, the Chaldean empath trotted to the truck's rear, where she met the driver. "Open it."

He fumbled for keys, unlocked the bolt, and lifted the door.

Crawling below the cabin's roof, two empaths appeared atop the nearest fabric rolls. Emma landed on the hard dirt first, followed by Layla, who appeared terrified. "Josh is going nuts. He says we need to get out."

"I know. He contacted me telepathically."

The hunters appeared atop the fabric rolls, followed by Diane's brother. Liam seemed distraught. "I'm not sure what's gotten into him, but he says we need to get clear of the truck." He ushered the group away from the vehicle.

But the driver doubted the guidance. "What's this? I'm not leaving my truck open for someone to steal. Family or not, I barely know you people."

Diane scowled. "You have to."

Josh trembled as he marched along the highway's shoulder. "Follow me! The truck's not safe."

Twenty meters away from the vehicle, Diane caught up to her brother and whispered in his ear. "What's going on?"

He stopped, and his eyes flashed with a supernatural green sparkle. "An ambush."

"What?" She scanned their surroundings. "We're in the middle of nowhere."

A streak of reddish light pounded the truck and knocked it over. Cutting through the chassis, the bolt of energy tore open the gas tank and invoked an explosion that engulfed the cabin.

As the blast pushed Diane back, Liam appeared by her to

shield her from flying debris, which fell short of the group. Connor moved to protect Layla.

Black smoke billowed and flames crackled from the toppled truck while Diane scanned her group. With the driver in the cabin, she called out to the hunters. "We need to get him out."

Josh stepped in front of her. "He's gone. Stay here. This is a battle."

"What battle? We're not even close to Erbil yet."

Her brother's voice assumed an impossible authority. "Get your dagger out. All three, hold hands and unite."

Though clueless, Diane trusted him. "Come here, girls. Get your daggers ready." She formed a triangle with Emma and Layla, blades held upward. "What are we looking for?"

Josh turned his back and faced the burning wreckage, over which a glimmering red light hovered. "You'll know."

Sensing Emma and Layla, Diane brought the trio into a transcendent link in which emotions riveted meaning upon minds with understanding beyond words. The highway, their team, and the burning truck entered a lethargic near-timelessness and then slipped into a vapid void.

As a symbiotic, triune super-empath, they floated in the center of a blackness backlit by stars of empathic sisters.

With an unspoken effort, the Diane-Emma-Layla creature harkened to the brightest star, a light with an angelic azure aura. But instead of the world retaking form in an empath's body, a spiritual being joined the ladies' consciousness.

It was an angel, and as it merged with them, wordless knowledge flowed between all minds.

The psychics wanted to know how an angel could appear in the void when they'd never contacted anyone other than fellow empaths.

A simple answer flowed back. Josh was a beacon who allowed the angelic connection.

Was Josh here, in the void, with them?

Yes, and the angels respond to his presence. This one, fused with them, understood their predicament but lacked the power to help.

Can any angel help?

There are only seven among us with the strength to face the demon who attacks.

A demon's attacking us?

The very one they'd seen in the face of wraiths. The angel with whom they communed agreed to summon one of proper power.

As Diane felt the angel leave, she lost the link with her sisters and reemerged in reality.

The departed angel's promise proved true as a streak of pulsating green raced across the sky and stopped atop the burning truck. It engaged the cloud of red energy with sparks of bright white flying from their exchange. As quickly as the battle between the two supernatural entities had begun, it ended in what Diane assumed was a stalemate with both beings of light careening over the horizon.

Liam stared at the sky with his eyes wide. "What the bloody hell was that?"

While Diane framed her thoughts to render her best answer, Josh flashed sparkling green eyes over his shoulder. "An ambush and a display of the demon's power. He tried to defeat us here, but we were warned."

Diane stepped forward. "Who warned us, Josh?"

The green hue fell from his eyes, and the docile tones of his natural voice returned. "I don't know."

Liam was upset. "Well, that's just great. We're facing a demon in the desert, we have no vehicle, and our equipment is burning."

Connor calmed him. "The weapons are far enough behind the fire. They'll be fine. Let the fire burn itself out."

"And then what? We walk to Mosul?"

Josh tucked his hands into his pockets. "I don't know about getting to Mosul. But I know that we'll need to walk to Erbil."

Liam scowled. "Seriously? Do you know how heavy those weapons are?"

Josh shrugged. "I'm not sure you'll need them. This is a spiritual battle. What I do know is that we need to walk, in order to build the spiritual strength to win."

CHAPTER 27

Liam observed the commotion surrounding him. A police car was parked behind the spot where the demon had pummeled the truck, and two officers questioned the ladies who spoke their native language. After ten minutes of questioning, the policemen released their witnesses and turned their attention to the arriving firetruck.

Her grandmother beside her, a smirking Diane walked to the young hunter. "That went well, thanks to some fancy answers and a little psychic assistance." Referring to her dagger, she tapped her purse.

After seeing a demon topple a truck and fight a summoned angel, Liam was ready to believe anything. "If you say so."

Nana clarified. "That dead cousin of mine, I called my sister. She said he was no-good. He's been separated from his wife for years after he cheated on her. He gets easily angered, lots of outbursts."

Liam shrugged. "Maybe he wasn't a saint, but that's no reason to brush over his death."

Diane touched his arm. "We won't. We aren't. Nana's just saying nobody from her family's going to blame us."

"Blame us? For a demonic attack?"

"For putting him at risk of being attacked by one."

"Well, bloody hell, we didn't know it was going to start today."

Standing next to the young hunter, his father raised his palm. "Enough, lad. The demon may have made his home in Media at the dawn of time itself, but we're responsible for waging this war here and now."

A police officer shouted in Arabic, and Liam thought he understood the meaning. But he verified with Diane. "Did he just say we could go into the truck?"

"Yeah. Let's grab our equipment and start walking."

"Walking? It's eighty kilometers to Mosul."

"Relax. I'm kidding. Nana's sister's coming with her son and two cars. We'll be checked into our hotel in time for dinner."

The restaurant's ambiance fell short of Liam's experiences of dining with his Chaldean colleagues. Outside the building, a berm of dirt and busted concrete outlined an open ditch to a watermain an Iraqi Army mortar round had carved while expelling ISIS from the city. Despite the unsavory view through the window, the young hunter found the food fresh. He swallowed a mouthful of shredded beef and grilled pepper. "What's this called again?"

Nana turned to her sister, a younger, thinner version of herself with reddish hair, and she repeated the question in Arabic.

Her sister looked up and smiled. "You like it?"

"I love it."

The Chaldean psychic undermined his compliment. "He eats like a caveman. He likes everything."

"Come on, Diane. I don't like everything. This is really good. It's fresh. I like the spices, too."

She rolled her eyes. "Not that you taste any of it, the way you wolf it down."

Nana's sister's English was impressive. "Please, Diane. Is that any way to treat your fiancé?"

Liam had suggested the semi-charade of their engagement to placate the curiosity of Nana's local family about the Irishmen's presence. "It's okay. She's right. I eat too fast."

Nana's sister answered the original question. "It's called *Tashreeb*. It's what they serve here."

"You mean it's their specialty?"

The woman shook her head. "No. It's all they serve now. They've been rebuilding their business one dish at a time since ISIS left and since a suicide bomber killed the prior owner and his brother took over the restaurant."

"Bloody hell. That's infuriating but impressive."

"We're a strong people. You're marrying into a good family."

He chuckled and glanced at a blushing Diane. "I sure am."

Nana's sister dug for more information. "So, tell me. Since our old house and factory are destroyed, what brings you to Mosul?"

Heads slowly turned towards Josh, who remained oblivious while reading his tablet and chewing his beef.

Diane probed for a response. "Josh? Can you say why we're here in Mosul, Josh?"

He grunted.

"Will you tell us why we're in Mosul, Josh?"

"Um, okay."

"Josh? Where are we going next?"

The autistic man's eyes briefly sparkled green. "To the Church of Shamoun Al-Safa."

Liam caught the meaning of "Shamoun" as "Saint", but the rest escaped him. "Saint who?"

Josh's voice carried its newfound periodic unnatural authority. "In English, Saint Peter."

The young hunter pressed for clarification. "That's in the ruins of old Nineveh?"

Josh nodded.

"Okay. Why?"

"Our journey begins there."

Liam scanned the faces of his fellow diners for defiance, but after Josh had warned them of the demon's attack on the truck, everyone seemed to accept his advice. "I guess it's settled, then. After lunch, we're crossing the Tigris into the old city." He looked to Connor for comment.

"Right, lad. As long as Josh is infused with some sort of divine gift, it's best that we heed his advice. In fact, before we head out there, I'm going to excuse myself and enjoy a stroll through the streets."

Liam thought he noticed fatigue in the elder hunter's face. "Are you alright, Father?"

"Oh, just a bit of jetlag, I assume. Nothing a walk and perhaps a respite on a park bench can't fix."

Surprising the young hunter, Josh stood. "I'll go with you."

After paying for dinner, Liam led the group from the restaurant into the clear, hot evening. Native dwellers of Iraq's second-largest city passed by in western-looking clothes, and the scent of fruity hooka smoke wafted over the young hunter's nose from behind a street vendor's cellular products display case. As Liam examined the wares behind the glass, as a disturbing vision caught his attention from the corner of his eye.

Holding Josh's hand, Connor appeared from a side street with his free hand covering his eyes.

Liam darted ahead of the group and checked on his father. "What's wrong?"

Connor's tone was grave. "I was reclining on a park bench when bird feces landed in my eyes."

"That doesn't sound so bad, but you look and sound horrible. Should we get you to a doctor?"

"Yes, lad. I'm afraid that I'm blind."

"From bird droppings?"

"This is most unnatural. I suspect demonic intervention."

Josh clarified. "There were at least five of them. They attacked him."

The rest of the group reached Connor and learned of his problem. Nana's sister offered her advice. "I know a doctor who can help. He stayed in Mosul through the ISIS occupation. He's not far."

Connor agreed. "Thank you."

With another episode of divine inspiration, Josh declared the team's direction. "The empaths and Liam must come with me to the church."

Nana nodded. "It's okay. We take Connor to the doctor. You do what you have to do."

Josh stooped, picked up a plastic bag, and stuck it in his pocket.

Curious, Liam withheld his question about the bag as he followed the autistic man down the street. "Do you know where we're going, Josh?"

"Follow me."

After walking over the Tigris on the Old Bridge, Liam saw children giggling on a merry-go-round. Wondering if Josh wanted to play in the amusement park, he was confused as the autistic man led him and the three empaths down a side street towards the riverbank.

Liam's curiosity became unbearable. "Where are we going?"

"To wash our feet."

"In the river?"

"Yes. For spiritual cleansing before we walk upon holy ground."

"That's weird."

Diane sat in the grass and pulled off her shoes. "Just go with it. I'm sure your dad's going to be fine. Chill for a bit here."

Liam joined the seated ladies by the flowing water. "Sure." He yanked off his shoes, pulled up his pants, and stuck his heels into the water, which felt cool. After immersing his legs to the middle of his shin, he leaned into Diane and lowered his voice. "You remember when the truck blew up this morning?"

She oozed sarcasm. "No, I forgot already."

"I mean when I moved to shield you from flying debris. Per the mission's goals, I should've protected Layla. But I instinctively protected you."

"That's romantic."

"Great. I'm romantic by accident, but when I try, I fail."

"Don't ruin it. Just accept that I was flattered."

"Well, Father wasn't. He reminded me about it being a mistake. Layla's the key to this mission."

Diane scowled. "No offense, but Connor can just... well, I'm not going to say it, especially when I'm concerned about him. He's a sweet old man, but he's wrong."

"Don't tell him he's wrong, or he'll..." Liam felt a tug at his foot. "What the hell?"

A large fish brushed by his big toe.

Diane leaned over and eyed the animal. "What's that?"

"It's just some freshwater fish."

After swimming away, the animal returned and rammed its mouth over Liam's foot. The attack tickled.

"What the hell?" He tried to kick, but his thigh muscles strained against the weight. "Bloody thing weighs a ton."

Diane laughed. "Is a fish outsmarting the mighty hunter?"

"I don't suppose you know if any fish around here are carnivores?"

She giggled. "Just that one."

"I'm going to beat it to a bloody pulp." He tensed his torso and pulled his body back with his arms. As the wiggling assailant slid onto dry land, Liam grabbed his combat knife from his belt and lifted it.

"Careful! Don't stab yourself!"

Despite being obvious, Diane's warning resonated. Liam reconsidered knifing the animal's brain when he realized his leg was under it. "Yeah, you're right." As he twisted his knee to give himself an unhindered thrusting arc, his encumbered leg moved like molasses.

Surprising him, Diane moved with swiftness and accurate ferocity. A blur of bronze arced downward from the end of her arm, and her dagger skewered the fish's head.

"Bloody hell, woman. That was half an inch from my leg."

"I could've gotten closer."

"Still, you didn't need to do that!"

"I got tired of watching you getting ready to stab yourself."

"My God, you can be emasculating."

She drove her knife downward to pin the dead fish into the dirt. "Pull your leg out and quit whining. If you want your manhood back, scale this thing and get it cooking on a fire."

"Sure. It looks like some species of carp. I'm sure it's tasty."

Josh addressed his sister and the hunter with his authoritative voice. "No."

Liam looked over his shoulder and saw a brief glimmer of green in the young man's eyes. "I guess you're right. With a demon attacking us, I should know better than to eat a possessed fish."

"Remove its heart, liver, and gall bladder. Use this to carry the organs." Josh extended the plastic bag he'd found near the restaurant.

Liam glared at the empath's brother. "Of all your recent weird behaviors, this one takes the cake."

The autistic man remained stone.

The young hunter wiggled his leg free. "Right, then. One gutted fish and three organs, coming up."

Diane squirmed. "Ew, gross."

Liam raised his voice and spoke in a serious tone. "What's going on with all these animal attacks? Is this the demon?"

Josh retained his unnatural calm authority. "The fish was not under demonic infestation. It is a gift from an angel."

The young hunter narrowed his eyes. "Which angel?"

Josh ignored his question. "You must use it as I instruct you, exactly, and only when the time is right."

CHAPTER 28

Liam followed Josh through the streets and into a hardware store. "Why are we stopping here?"

"Flashlights, bolt cutters, shovels, and a hammer."

The young hunter moved close to Josh. "If you're planning on looting from the church, you're wasting your time. They've all been gutted over and over again."

"Not all treasures."

"I wish you'd mentioned this in the hotel. I have most of what you need in my bags."

"I didn't know our destination back then."

Liam shrugged and walked towards an aisle with hammers. He reached for the largest claw head he could find.

Josh shook his head. "Bigger."

"A sledgehammer?" Liam scanned the aisle and pointed at a solitary example of the tool he suggested. "Like that?"

"Yes."

"At least you're not half-assing whatever we're doing."

After Liam paid for the equipment, Josh led the team on a tedious walk slowed by tools carried on shoulders until they reached the border of the church's excavation site.

As the sun set, it cast long shadows through the chain link fence that served more as a suggestion than as a barrier to looters. Liam lowered the bolt cutters from his shoulder. "I doubt it matters, but everyone look around and make sure nobody's watching." He scanned his surroundings, saw unpopulated hills, and then put the teeth of his tool around a lock. After the metal snapped, he dropped the cutters and jingled open the gate.

Josh stepped through the opening and continued down concrete steps that restoration teams had installed leading to the ancient church, buried five meters below ground.

Diane's phone rang. "Hold on." She answered it and exchanged rapid words with her grandmother. Then she hung up. "Both of Connor's retinas detached. The good news, great news, really, is that he can make a full recovery and see again. The doctor can do the surgery tomorrow. The bad news is, he'll be in bed for three weeks."

Liam did the obvious math. "He won't be able to hunt with us."

"I know. But you've got three empaths and whatever divine angel that's helping Josh. If you need her, you've got Machinegun Nana, too. Have faith."

Josh shook his head. "We're not equipped to succeed yet. Follow me." He continued into the sloping entryway.

As the fading sun disappeared behind him, Liam found the passageway confining. He illuminated his flashlight, and each member of the team did the same. Overhead lights mocked him in their unpowered state, which he attributed to the lack of a generator. To lighten the mood, he admitted his anxiety. "This is spooky."

Shovels over their shoulders, the empaths responded with nervous giggles.

Striding with a purpose, Josh kept walking through the archeological tunnel.

Liam caught up to the autistic man as he entered a subterranean courtyard. He stopped to gather the team around him and flash artificial beams into the distant darkness. Excavated walls in the rising sediment set the space's boundary. "It must be some ancient courtyard."

"It was." Josh stepped onward.

Liam followed, bringing the empaths with him. Thudding footsteps on ancient stones echoed off the distant walls and low ceiling, and then the courtyard issued to another expansive space. Again, Liam stopped behind Josh and, with the psychics, aimed lights into the underground distance. Smooth walls, made long ago, surrounded him. "This is getting spookier."

"It's a cemetery. The walls are originals, to protect the sanctity of the dead." Josh stepped off the central path and onto hard dirt.

From behind Liam, Diane squawked. "Josh?"

At his sister's beckoning, the young man stopped.

Seemingly trapped between doubt and faith, the Chaldean empath shook her head as she overcame her apparent concerns. "Never mind. Keep going."

Passing several dozen tombstones on a zigzagging path, Josh meandered through the graveyard. Abruptly, he stopped. "Dig here."

Liam studied the barren earth at Josh's feet, which he assumed had remained untouched for centuries. "You're sure? There's no headstone."

Josh's voice became stronger but remained calm. "Dig here."

"You heard him, ladies." Liam reached for Diane's shovel. "I'll take that."

"Why mine?"

"Well, um. You said it before yourself. You're scrawny."

While Diane glared at him, Layla shooed him back with her fingers. "Nice going, Casanova. That wasn't as bad as calling her fat, but you need to work on your game. Step aside and let us do some real women's work."

Liam backed away with Josh while the empaths dug. He whispered. "What game? I spent my entire life avoiding the temptation of women. I never was supposed to have a game."

Josh shrugged. "I don't know much about any game, but I know that you need to be more romantic. You're really stupid at it."

Liam snorted. "Well, at least I know that the real Josh is still in there."

Lowering his head, Josh failed to hide his grin.

"Don't think that being autistic and hopefully my brother-in-law gives you a free pass to mock me."

Josh chuckled. "But you make it so easy."

Liam had no choice but to laugh at himself. "Bastard!" He turned his attention from his shame to the working team and raised his voice. "I don't mean to be patronizing, but if any of you lovely ladies get tired, I'll relieve you."

Diane scowled at him. "Not on your life, buddy."

Ten minutes later, Liam admired the two-foot trench.

Diane straightened her back, wiped sweat from her brow, and dropped the shovel. "Alright. Female pride is gone. Back's getting sore. Get your caveman tail over here."

Liam suppressed his smirk while taking his place in the digging crew. "It would be my honor."

Another ten minutes later, Josh relieved Emma, and Layla abandoned the manual labor. The two men continued until Liam's shovel hit stone. "Is this what we're looking for?"

Josh wiped his forehead against his sleeve. "Yes. Let's clear the dirt around it. We need to break it."

After more personnel rotations and team laboring, the stone's identity became clear as the top of a tomb. As he dug, Liam stood upon it and realized he had ample clearance to swing a hammer. "I can break in now."

Josh stepped up from the trench they'd created. He pointed to Liam's feet. "Hit it where you're standing."

"Okay." Liam reached for the hammer and then cracked the stone. After several whacks, rubble fell inward, and a stale stench arose. "Now what?"

"Keep going. A little more."

Liam opened a hole large enough to see into the tomb. He set aside the hammer, knelt, and aimed his flashlight downward, expecting to find bones. Instead, he saw an urn. "It's some sort of jug or vase."

Josh's voice was authoritative and reverent. "This is the tomb of our family's ancient ancestor. She is the matriarch of all empaths in our line, and the original scrolls of our family's book are buried with her."

The young hunter flicked droplets from his forehead. "Well, hell, Josh. That's fascinating, but this looks like something and someone we shouldn't be disturbing."

"The scrolls are at risk of looting. They must be under holy protection before we can defeat the demon."

Liam looked at the three empaths. "Is anyone getting a bad vibe about this?"

Three heads shook.

The young hunter wasn't appeased. "Why now? What's so special about this team and this time that we need to take something from the matriarch that's been buried for a thousand years?"

"This is the final battle."

"How can that be? "There are two more wraiths and daggers out there other than Amir. "

Josh spoke in his most authoritative tone yet, and the green glimmer shone through his eyes like stars. "If you succeed against the demon, all seven lines of wraiths will break–forever."

CHAPTER 29

In Connor's hotel room, Diane knelt at the elder hunter's bed-side. "Does it hurt?"

"Not at all. It's just frustrating and admittedly a bit frightening. I don't want to become a burden to anyone."

"You'll never be a burden."

Dark temporary sunglasses hid his ailing eyes, and his voice carried sadness. "You're too kind. I wish I could come with you and be useful."

From over her shoulder, she heard her brother speak with his newfound unnatural confidence. "You must come."

"Oh, Josh. I appreciate your desire to include me, but I'm an old man trained for using my eyes. I'm afraid I'd be worse than a burden. I'd be a risk to your safety."

"You must come."

"I can't imagine a scenario in which I could help."

Flustered, Diane sought within her mind a way to make sense of her brother's demand, but nothing materialized.

Standing on the bed's far side, Liam tried to engender some enthusiasm. "You've said it yourself, Father. While Josh is gifted with whatever divine guidance he has, we need to listen. If he says you're coming, you're coming."

"I can't see your faces. Is this what everyone wants?"

Diane scanned the room. Her sister psychics nodded, as did her grandmother. She spoke for the team. "Yes. Everyone's with you."

"But the doctor said I had to remain immobile after the surgery or that it wouldn't heal."

Josh retained his authoritative air. "There will be no surgery."

Connor rotated his nose towards Josh. "Are you saying that I need to remain blind forever?"

"No. Your son will heal you."

Liam raised his eyebrows. "Huh?"

Josh turned towards the door. "Follow me."

Heeding the new prophet's advice, the young hunter trailed

the autistic man into the hallway.

Alone with Connor and her extended family's female members, Diane canvassed her companions' faces for insight. "Did anyone understand what just happened?"

Heads shook.

The elder hunter aimed his dark glasses at Diane. "I was told by a doctor that I should make a full recovery, but that it would take weeks. I'm most curious as to what Josh has in store as a different plan."

Seated in an armchair, Nana lifted her nose. "That boy, he's special. Now he's even more special."

The elder hunter reclined against the headboard. "Indeed, he is. I'd say that we're seeing nothing short of a miracle."

Diane sensed the hunter's withheld wisdom. "Connor, I don't mean to pry, but you seem like you know something about miracles, maybe like the one we're seeing in my brother."

He smirked. "I can't hide anything from an empath, can I? Yes, young lady, I do. The study of divine intervention, or miracles, has been part of my formation. Of course, they're rare, but when they happen, they usually occur in isolated and powerful moments. But in the rarest of rarities, they can endure. You can think of it as the opposite of a demonic possession."

"An angelic possession?"

Connor shrugged. "Well, you've got the angelic part right, but angels don't possess people. Possession imparts the will of the demon upon the person, whereas angels who didn't fall from grace would never do such a thing."

"Then what is it?"

"I think it's a matter of Josh's will. He must desire something so profound and so important that he's earned divine support."

With the fledgling wraith's mother in the room, Diane avoided speaking of his possible death. "You mean, like getting Amir's dagger?"

Layla voiced her concern. "Without hurting him."

Connor nodded. "That's the desirable outcome, and I can't see Josh willing anything different. I don't know if a noble desire alone is enough to garner an angel's help. Nevertheless, I believe he's done it."

Diane sensed the end of the elder hunter's knowledge and decided to accept the unknowns as unknowns.

The room's door clicked open, and Liam entered. He held his palm outward and steady as he walked towards his father. "I've got a remedy Josh told me to make."

Diane thought it smelled fishy. "Is that the guts?"

Liam nodded. "It's a powdery concoction I made from the gall bladder." He reached the bed and braced his father's shoulder with his free hand. "Take off your glasses so I can apply it."

"If you say so." Connor complied.

"Open your eyes." The young hunter blew the powder, and with the eyes' moisture, he spread a thin salve across the wounds.

Connor reached for the bridge of his nose. "Dang it, that stings."

"Josh said it would. Take courage, Father."

"If you say so."

"Leave it there a while. When it stops burning, you can take it off."

Diane saw the pain in Connor's face. "I don't like this. Where's Josh?"

Liam kept his eyes on his father. "He was in my room. Why?"

"If he's making you do something so bizarre, he should be here."

As if hearing his sister's command, Josh opened the door and stepped into the room. Without a word, he strode to the bedside, examined the elder hunter, and folded his arms.

Diane frowned. "There's no medical rationale for this, is there?"

Liam shook his head. "No. I'm trusting Josh."

Connor clarified. "We're all trusting Josh, and I suspect it's paying off. The burning's subsiding." He reached for his face.

Liam extended a hand towards his father and tapped his wrist. "Not yet."

Over the next few minutes, a whitish film formed over the elder hunter's eyes. "It feels like whatever's going to happen has happened. Can I peel this off yet?"

Josh offered a subtle nod.

"Go ahead, Father."

With both hands, the elder hunter peeled away a filmy coating from the corners of his eyes.

Liam darted to the bathroom and returned with a towel, which he placed in his father's lap. "Use this."

Connor groped for the cloth and then wiped his face and hands. Blinking slowly, he rendered his judgment. "It's amazing. I can see. My vision's good as new." He looked around the room. "It's wonderful to see you all again."

Diane shot a glance at her stoic brother. "How'd you know?"

Josh transformed into his true human self. "Know what?"

She inhaled and calmed herself as she realized she dealt with her mundane sibling. "Josh, can you remember why you told Liam to crush the fish's gall bladder into a powder to use on Connor's eyes?"

Josh shrugged.

Connor reached for his son for support in rising from the bed. "Never mind that. What's done is done. Let's celebrate with a nice dinner."

At dinner, Diane watched the elder hunter ingest a cube of beef with the voracity reminiscent of his son. "Slow down before you give yourself heartburn. You're behaving like a worse caveman than Liam."

He gulped his food. "I suppose you're right, young lady. I'm still too excited about having regained my eyesight."

Liam took a break from his devouring of meat. "Why'd you have to turn that into an insult against me?"

"Because it's too easy."

The young hunter sipped tea, washing down whatever food remained in his mouth, while giving the empath a stern look.

Connor wiped his mouth. "Let's turn our attention towards

our mission. We've had a few good scares, and I expect the demon to continue challenging us, either directly or with the infestation of animals, like the birds who attacked me. We must stay on our guard for such things."

Diane had considered the supernatural attacks and was eager to share her plan. "We should have at least one of us empaths holding a dagger at all times. I think that could give us some warning."

Connor angled his head in deference. "An excellent idea, young lady. Also, if we scout ahead, locate Amir's exact location in Erbil, and can work out an assault at a place and time of our choosing, we can set up our situation favorably."

Liam added his thoughts. "We'll take two cars to separate Layla from her dagger, at least while you and I use it to locate him."

The green glint returned to Josh's eyes. "No." In silence, everyone looked at him, and he continued. "The demon will not meet us until the full moon."

Liam scowled. "That's still a week away. We can't just wait for him. We're hunters."

"You won't find him until the full moon."

As the young hunter's face turned red, his father preempted his protest. "Let him speak, lad."

Josh laid out the team's upcoming week. "We must finish our spiritual cleansing. Three days of fasting followed by a walk through the wild to Erbil. Then, we will meet him."

Liam looked at his father. "May I?" After Connor nodded, the young hunter continued. "Josh, that's ninety kilometers. I could do that in two days if I humped it without equipment. But with our equipment, that's a hard three days for me. And you're asking everyone to do it."

Nana spoke up. "I slow you down. You go without me."

Diane hated the idea. "Nana! You have to come. I don't want to go without you."

Josh corrected his sister. "This enemy is beyond Nana. Only the hunters and the empaths may join me."

Diane had enough of the divine entity's secretiveness. "Who the heck are you? You're not talking like my brother."

Josh went quiet, receding to his human self.

Diane pouted. "Well, I guess I'm not getting an answer."

Connor waived his hand. "It's fine. Let Nana return to the order. She can escort the urn with your family's original scrolls. Who better to do so than your greatest living matriarch?"

"I guess that makes sense." Diane accepted her grandmother's absence and then reflected upon her brother's words. "Wait, what was that about a fast?"

Connor chuckled. "Eat heartily now, young lady. Fill your stomach. By the end of the three days, I promise you you'll relish the memory of feeling full."

CHAPTER 30

Three days later, the spiritual cleansing grated Diane's nerves. "I'm starving!"

Walking beside her, Liam corrected her. "Maybe, maybe not. Ketosis usually kicks in on the third day."

Keeping calories out of her mouth for nearly seventy hours had taken all her self-control, and with dinner looming, she was losing her patience. She was willing to handle another of the hunter's geeky anecdotes as a distraction from her discomfort. "Okay, Einstein. What's ketosis?"

"It's when the body burns fat to make ketones to burn as energy, instead of burning glucose from food. When you reach the third day of a fast, you lose your appetite. That's why people who do therapeutic fasts can go for weeks and even months."

"So, Josh has us fasting until the end of our hunger."

"I guess. I hadn't really thought about it that way."

"No. I'm sure you of all people were thinking about food. How the heck have you made it three days without eating?"

He turned towards the swings of the amusement park. "Father made me fast a few times for training. I don't like it any more than you'd expect, but I'm used to it."

She found an empty swing and removed the backpack Liam had forced her to wear for training. Lifting the hiking boots she was breaking in, she sat. "Push me."

He complied. "Watch your feet."

Tightening her abdomen, she kept her legs above the dirt. After several cycles back and forth, she felt dizzy. "Okay, stop."

Like a gentle vice grip, he grabbed her ribs. "That's enough fun."

She came to a sudden halt and stood. The sun was low and casting long shadows. "How long until we eat?"

"Soon enough. Let's get back to the hotel and join the others."

At the restaurant where she'd eaten her last meal prior to fasting, she wolfed down a full cube of meat. It was the most satisfying morsel of her life.

Their roles reversed, Liam nibbled half a cube. "Easy, Diane. Your stomach shrunk. Your appetite's bigger than your capacity."

She tried to slow her chewing, but it was pointless. She devoured the meat and jabbed her fork into another cube.

Connor addressed the group. "I know it's hard, but everyone remember to eat slowly. Your bodies need to get used to food again. Now, let's talk about our travels. Josh, do you have any insights other than walking towards Erbil?"

Josh shrugged.

"Alright, then. Good enough. Tomorrow, we leave at dawn. Liam and I will check everyone's backpacks tonight to make sure we're properly provisioned."

The next morning's alarm ripped Diane from her slumber. She was tired, but her stomach was full. She worked through her morning routine, dressed in her hiking clothes, and lifted her backpack over her shoulders. The equipment rested on her armored vest, which she wore for ease of carrying. With a final look at the last bed she'd sleep in for days, she headed towards the lobby. When she reached the team, she let the young hunter inspect her.

Tugging her straps, Liam checked her backpack for fit and balance and then opened her pack's zippers. "I'm moving the pistol to your belt." He lowered the weapon into her hip holster.

"I'm not ever going to use it. I've got my dagger." She agreed to carry the pistol as part of sharing the team's weight, but she'd use her bronze blade for defense if attacked.

"It's too heavy for your back, especially with the riot shield." He grabbed the bulletproof barrier and raised it behind her. After clipping it to her sixty-liter pack, he appeared in front of her. "How's that?"

As she wiggled under her straps, she appreciated the better fit, and the pull felt about the same despite the addition of the ten-pound shield. "It's fine. Thanks."

Liam responded while moving behind Layla's pack. "No problem."

After checking Josh and Emma, Connor faced the group. "Shall we begin our spiritual walk?"

The morning was warming under the risen sun as Connor led the hiking group along the highway through the low desert. Following the road to formally enter the self-governing Kurdish region of Iraq, the elder hunter led a single file with Josh behind him, then Layla, Emma, Diane, and Liam guarding the rear. "Keep a steady pace, everyone."

Breaking in the boots and becoming accustomed to the backpack during the three-day fast paid off. Diane found the load bearable, and her feet felt comfortable with each step.

Connor slowed the group and addressed the psychics. "Ladies, there's no need to use your powers. The order has given me papers that should simplify our entry, and I'm told a guard will meet us who speaks English."

While waiting in a short line of pedestrians inside a small building, Diane tapped her dagger, but she kept it at her hip as a uniformed guard behind a counter greeted Connor.

The elder hunter unfolded and extended a document. The guard disappeared for a few minutes and then reappeared with small papers Diane assumed were visas. Even with weapons in their possession, the group was granted entry.

With the checkpoint behind her, Diane caught up to Connor. "How'd you do that?"

"Not all our assistance is divine. Sometimes, it's good enough to have diplomatic connections. You can thank Friar Lucio when you get back." Minutes later, he led the group off the highway's shoulder and into the desert, following a compass bearing towards Erbil.

For the first four hours, Diane held her dagger in her hand as a sort of early warning against supernatural attacks, but the precaution earned her only a sweaty palm under the rising heat. "Who's up next for carrying a dagger?"

Her blonde ponytail whipped across her back as Emma turned her head. "Me."

Diane slid her blade into its sheathe and wiped her hand against her shorts.

As the sounds from the highway connecting Mosul and Erbil became a distant drone, Connor stopped in the shade of a grove of date palm trees. "Let's break for lunch and biological necessities."

Her stomach wrestling with the recommencement of her digestive process, Diane forced down two energy bars with swigs of water from her canteen.

Squatting with his back against a tree trunk, Connor raised his voice. "Easy, everyone. Only drink to quench thirst. Don't overdo it, or you'll end up urinating away your water supply."

Seated cross-legged next to Emma, Diane kept her voice soft. "Or we could head to the highway rest area over there and get some bottled water."

Emma lowered her head and chuckled. "Don't let Connor hear you say that."

"I'm more concerned about Josh. He's taken over as our spiritual leader."

"Sort of, but he's hardly talked for days."

"That's the normal Josh. It's the extra-weird abnormal Josh who's in charge. I'm afraid he's become schizophrenic."

The German empath shrugged. "It's not bad. He's either your sweet young brother, or he's a divine angel. Both versions are nice."

Connor strode to them. "Can I bother you ladies for some practice of your defenses?"

Diane stood. "Sure."

Emma also stood.

"See how fast you can lift your shields and deploy them in front of you."

Diane reached over her back and groped for air. "Oops. I'm a spaz. This is harder than it looks."

"That's why I asked you to practice. Watch. I'll show you." He reached with one hand, lifted the shield, and ducked under his arm.

"Oh, I see." Diane tried it, and the shield's weight bumped her forearm onto her head.

"That wasn't bad. A little more power into your upward lift, and you'll be fine. Now, hold it steady."

She ran her forearm through upper straps and then grabbed a handle lower down.

"Lower your hips. Brace yourself." Holding his shield in one hand, he pushed with his free palm.

Losing her balance, she rocked back. "You're strong."

"Try it again. Against a charging adversary, you'll want to brace yourself. But you also want to shrink your profile, make yourself tight and small. Against bullets, or, if it comes to it, a dagger, you'll want to present a tiny target."

"I think I got it."

"A little practice, and you will. Please get Layla and Josh involved, and then all of you can show off your new skills to me before we proceed with our march."

As the low sun slid below the horizon, Connor stopped under another grove of palms. "This is as good a place as any for the night. Let's get our tents up and eat some dinner. No fires and no phones. No light sources, so that we avoid drawing attention to ourselves. But feel free to take off your body armor."

Diane reclined against a boulder, removed the ballcap that protected her eyes from the sun, and bit into an energy bar.

Lowering his pack to the dirt, Liam sat next to her. "I thought you'd hate those, since you're so picky about your food."

The bar tasted delicious. "After fasting, these taste awesome. Maybe Josh foresaw that."

"How are you holding up?"

"This walk? It's not bad. I thought the heat would suck, but it's a dry heat. I hardly sweat. As long as I keep hydrating, I'm fine. I can see why this is cleansing for the soul."

"Right. We'll refill our canteens sometime around midday tomorrow in the Great Zeb River. I've got pills to purify it, but the water comes straight from the mountains."

Connor strolled to them. "I'm keeping you two apart on our watch sections. I want one empath awake with her dagger in hand all the time, but I don't want the two of you together. You share too many distracting topics of conversation."

Liam sighed. "Fine, Father. What's the rotation?"

"Diane and Josh first, while our danger's the least. Josh's role will be primarily to help Diane stay awake. I trust you, young lady, to know how to respond to any danger."

"I'm sure I can."

"Then me and Emma. Then you and Layla."

Liam stood and lifted his pack. "Well, shit. In that case, I should hurry off and get some sleep."

An hour later, moonlight bathed the desert, and Diane walked a perimeter around the quiet campsite with her dagger in her hand and with Josh by her side. Sleeping far from the others in the open air, Liam snored. The others rested in two-man tents.

Other than occasional headlights illuminating the distant horizon, the desert was peaceful.

Four hours after the boring patrol began, it ended, with Connor waking and bringing Emma to relieve the siblings.

As Diane slid into her tent and drifted to sleep, she hoped the rest of the trek would prove as cleansing and calming as her first day.

CHAPTER 31

Seated on a boulder, Liam watched the sun rise for a moment and then averted his eyes from the rays. He stood. "Come on. One more lap around the camp, and then we'll wake everyone up."

Her dagger in hand, Layla followed.

Liam patrolled the outer perimeter taking one last look at the barren distance. As he finished the lap, he prepared to wake his team. "You get the ladies going and I'll–" he sensed a presence behind him, turned, and whipped his rifle from his shoulder.

Josh stood facing him.

Liam lowered his weapon. "Shit, buddy. Don't scare me like that."

The autistic man's voice was authoritative. "We must delay our departure."

"How long?"

"Until noon."

"Why didn't you mention this last night?"

Confused, Josh scowled, and his voice became soft. "I don't know."

Liam slid his rifle over his shoulder. "You're cutting this close. We're barely going to make Erbil by the full moon. I hope you know what you're doing."

Layla stopped him. "Liam. He's gone. The angel or whatever's giving him insight is gone. It's just Josh."

The young hunter sighed. "Yeah. Sorry, buddy. We'll be fine. We'll stay here until noon."

After another meal of energy bars, which the team called 'lunch' due to the time of day, Liam lifted his pack's straps over his shoulders.

As Josh stood behind Connor and adjusted his equipment's weight, the team started forward under the intense overhead sun.

Six hours of walking put the sun behind the team and brought them within sight of an orb of light rising behind a small mountain from a small village on the Great Zab River. Following his compass, Connor led them north of the city towards a low mountain that rose between them and the closest bend in the water's flow.

Liam realized a problem with following the compass off the roads-no bridges. He called out from the back of the line. "Father!"

The elder hunter angled his jaw over his shoulder. "Yes, lad?"

"How do you intend to cross the river?"

"I honestly have no idea. I admit to expecting Josh to reveal that at the appropriate time."

Oblivious to the discussion, the autistic man kept pace behind Connor.

The elder hunter slowed and faced his followers. "I suppose now's the right time to ask if everyone can swim, in case it comes down to it."

Everyone nodded and responded in the positive, including Diane's confirmation that Josh knew how.

As moonlight cast a soft glow over their path, Liam ran through ideas to get the team across the water barrier. But first, they needed to cross over a low mountain. He called out. "Straight up, Father?"

"Straight up. Josh said to walk towards Erbil, and that's what we're doing." Connor led the group up a slope of hard earth. "Watch where you put your hands, since snakes will hide in small crevices. The Kurdistan viper is of particular concern. Liam and I have anti-venom for the local species, but let's try not to risk it."

"Should we make noise, Father? Scare away the animals?"

"Good idea. Singing, perhaps. But I surely can't carry a tune."

"Me neither. Singing's one father-son activity we'll never do."

Emma looked over her shoulder. "I can sing."

Diane chimed in. "Me too. What should we sing?" She squealed as she stumbled and then broke her fall with her palms.

Liam expressed his concern. "Are you okay?"

"Fine. I fall enough to know how to catch myself."

"What did you trip–"

"I tripped over myself, okay? I do that a lot. Get used to it."

Emma refocused the team on singing. "I like Country Roads by John Denver. It's always big at Oktoberfest." She started, and Diane joined.

Then Layla added her voice.

Liam found their voices pleasing, especially that of his desired future bride. He also hoped that every poisonous animal on the mountain would recognize the notes as a warning to scurry away. As the first song ended, he heard the ladies laboring for breath during the climb. "Keep singing. It's a small mountain. You can carry tunes the whole way."

Emma volunteered Sweet Caroline as another of her Bavarian favorites. The song kept hidden intruders away until the German empath fell silent and stood still during the final chorus.

Liam called out. "What's wrong?" He saw her dagger reflecting moonlight in her hand and realized she was the evening's supernatural sentry. "Father! Stop!"

Standing a meter below the summit, Connor halted the crew and looked downward. "Emma?"

She was groggy. "Danger... Demon."

Liam detached night vision goggles from his vest and scanned the rocks beside his comrades. Movement to the right caught his eye, and he identified a snake slithering towards the German empath. He lowered the optics into his vest, snatched his silenced rifle from his shoulder, and aimed the barrel at the silhouette. Six rounds immobilized the serpent, and the young hunter moved between Emma and the reptile. He checked the viper again with night vision and noticed it bleeding out. "It won't bother us. Let's keep moving."

Connor stopped at the summit. "I can see the river."

The young hunter shouted up to his father. "Can you see a place to cross?"

"Nothing easy. We'll have to swim it. I see a good enough location where the water looks calm, although it's a good thirty meters across."

Liam summited and then descended the mountain behind his team, who'd gone quiet after the failure of song to keep away the snake. He knew the serpent had been demon-driven, since the species avoided humans.

At the bottom of the slope, Connor stopped and awaited his followers.

A sedan drove by, marking a riverside road with its headlights.

After the team crossed the street and gathered to discuss crossing the river, Emma staggered from their ranks.

Diane reached for her but missed.

The young hunter lunged, crouched, and cradled the German empath's torso as her hip hit the hard dirt. "What's wrong?"

She strained for words. "I... danger. Danger... Demon."

"Another snake?"

Diane crouched with Emma and waved to the Persian psychic to form an empathic triangle. "No. It's something else. Let's see what we can find out. Come on, Layla."

Liam released Emma and stepped towards his father. "Let's scan our surroundings. I'll look behind us. You take forward." The young hunter placed his goggles to his face and looked across the river. The far bank was a quiet wilderness. In the southern distance, crossing headlights marked the eastbound and westbound sides of the highway connecting Mosul and Erbil. Closer to the group, the access road along the shoreline was empty. "Anything yet, Father?"

"Nothing. Keep looking. Remember to check the sky."

Liam made note to check for flying threats but kept his focus on the downward slope of the mountain. Descending the hill, a mass caught his attention. He froze his gaze upon it, recognized its form, and pointed. "Father! A wolf."

"How many?"

A second beast appeared in the young hunter's optics. "Two

so far. But if this is the threat that Emma noticed, I'd expect more."

Connor's voice was serious. "I count three to the right already. There's a lot of movement."

Liam lowered his optics, examined the slope with his naked eye, and lost count of the ominous silhouettes. "Shit. More than twenty. And they're big. Forty to fifty kilos each. Gray wolves. This is some unnatural bullshit."

From the ground, Diane called out. "We saw it in our vision. There's a big pack of wolves coming for us."

"Yeah, we already figured that out."

"What do we do?"

Liam ran the odds in his mind and announced his intention. "There's too many to stand our ground. Let's swim across and pick them off while they swim after us. Father?"

"Their numbers are still overwhelming. They're fast and hard to shoot in the dark."

Liam thought further. "We can use our riot shields to set up a v-shaped barrier and use the shoreline as the final side of a triangle. Then we'll have a clear field of fire on the river."

"So be it. Make for the river and swim for it. Let's go." He trotted towards the water. "Follow me. Run and swim for your lives!"

CHAPTER 32

The mountain-fed water felt frigid as it crept to Liam's groin. "Bloody hell."

Ahead of him with his backpack and head above water, Connor led the team, and his strong voice sounded tinny as it echoed off the babbling bank and the water's gentle surface. "The breast stroke is best. Use your legs for power. Steady strokes. Your packs have some buoyancy."

Liam verified everyone else was making good headway in the water before committing to his swim. A final glance over his shoulder showed the first wolf reaching the road and accelerating to a gallop. "Where the hell'd they come from?" Nobody responded, and he groaned as he thrust himself into the cold fluid.

Connor reached the far bank first and helped Josh to his feet. The men then helped the ladies up.

Liam arrived last and evaluated the barrier his father had set up.

Holding two shields at the far vertex of a triangle, an unarmed Josh buttressed the far flank. Crouched beside him, Emma and Diane held a shield each, and then by the waterline Connor and Layla held the last two buffers against wolves. The elder hunter had left space between the barriers to give the tight team room to brace themselves and to slash daggers into their assailants.

Seeing no room for him to stand on land, Liam waded in the shallow water. "Any special insights against these animals, Josh?"

The autistic man's soft voice revealed a lack of angelic intervention but carried a pound of common sense. "Kill the wolves."

"Fair enough." Liam withdrew his rifle and scanned the water. The first swimming wolf had traversed half the river's breadth. The young hunter squeezed off a round that splashed short of the canine's head. "Shit. Come on, Liam. Aim like a hunter." He calmed his breath, adjusted, and fired again. The animal's head sank, and its body rose sideways. "Bingo! I got one!"

From over his shoulder, his father opened fire. "I'm shooting until they get here."

Over his other shoulder, he heard a pistol pop and looked to see moonlit smoke rising from a weapon in Layla's hands. "You didn't expect me to waste a good gun either, did you?"

"Impressive."

"I'm a single mother. I learned how to shoot."

Liam turned back to the water and killed a wolf with every other shot until the pack got close enough for him to see their eyes. Their irises glowed red, chilling him but marking easier targets. "They're bloody demonic!"

"Keep shooting, lad. I've taken out three."

Hindered by the poor accuracy of a pistol over distance, Layla had worse luck. "I finally got one. I need to reload."

"I've hit four. But there's still more than a dozen." From the corner of his eye, Liam saw a lupine silhouette scramble from the water. "Careful. One's coming up from the right."

The first landed canine tested the barrier but bounced off Connor's shield as moist earth notched each buttress into the dirt.

Trusting his colleagues to defend their perimeter, Liam shifted his rifle to one hand and lifted a pistol from his holster. At short range, he leaned and leveled the smaller weapon at the ribs of the animal that clawed at his father's shield. The wolf whimpered and staggered away.

"Thank you, lad."

More dark silhouettes reached the shore, and loud bangs came from behind the young hunter as the assailants tested the shields. Diane squealed, but a deep thud suggested she'd held her ground.

Between squeezing rounds from both his weapons at the splashes in front of him, Liam heard growls and barks behind him. "Nothing's getting through me! How's everyone back there?"

An eerie silence lasted for a moment, and Liam risked a glance over his shoulder.

An airborne canine sailed over Layla's defenses and landed on Connor. Holding his shield with one hand, the elder hunter fended off the animal with his combat knife.

Also keeping one hand on her shield, Layla extended her enchanted dagger behind her back, and with supernatural guidance, the blade found the wolf's heart.

With its born fangs inches from Connor's face, the beast collapsed and fell into the water behind Liam's heels.

As the young hunter saw the final attacker climb to the shore, he unloaded his pistol at it.

The beast slowed and limped but kept coming.

Liam stuffed the emptied pistol into its holster and pulled his rifle's trigger. Nothing happened. He dropped the magazine, reloaded, and waded to his left.

Two wolves ganged up on Diane, who fell backwards under her shield.

The young hunter sent his boot's toe into the ribs of the animal that challenged Layla while he sent six rounds into the canines snapping at Diane's vest.

With impressive courage, Layla called out while slashing with her knife. "I've got this one! Help the others!"

Liam marched around the triangular perimeter shooting dark forms. He tallied five dead wolves as he rounded the two-shield vertex that Josh held steady. With four pairs of reddish eyes turning to him, he leveled his rifle and aimed. Again, he was empty. "Shit."

The four beasts charged.

A burst from his father's rifle dropped one.

As Liam grabbed his combat knife to face his deadly foes, he saw three streaks of bronze flash through the night, and a dagger landed in each remaining wolf. The growls and barks were gone, and only the panting of his teammates broke the silence. "Is everyone okay?" He retrieved the knives from the corpses.

A chorus of positive responses encouraged him.

Connor lifted his goggles to his face. "Check them for injuries, Liam. I'll verify that we're truly alone."

A flashlight in hand, the young hunter inspected his teammates. Having held the back boundary, Josh was untouched. Each psychic had claw and bite cuts on the arms of their dagger hands. When he reached Diane, he pulled her shield off her and helped her up.

He was impressed to find a dead and bleeding wolf underneath her. "Did you do that?"

"Yeah. Well, my dagger practically did it by itself."

"Let me see your arm."

She extended her bleeding wrist. "Do I need to worry about rabies?"

He snorted. "I know damned well the demon drove each one of them to attack us, but I wouldn't put rabies out of the question."

"Dang it. So, now what?"

"I carry the vaccine and immunoglobulin. We'll get you all cleaned up and start the first round of shots."

"Ugh."

"It's not a spinal tap, if that's what you're worried about. That went away long ago. It's just normal shots nowadays."

Exposing his bleeding wrist, Connor joined the conversation. "Count me in your list of patients."

"That could've been much worse. We're lucky Emma gave us enough warning."

"And we did some quick thinking and brave fighting, if I dare praise ourselves."

"Yeah. I guess."

"Oh, I forgot to mention. One of the wolves is still alive." Connor pointed towards the living animal.

Liam frowned. "You didn't put it out of its misery?"

"No. I figured I'd let an empath have a moment with it, to see what can be learned."

Her vest's outer cloth torn from fangs, Diane walked towards the fallen canine.

Liam followed her to the panting wolf. "I think that's the one I hit with my pistol."

Her dagger in hand, Diane crouched beside the immobilized body and laid her free hand on the wolf's ribs. "It's a girl. She's a mother. She's terrified."

"She knows she's dying."

"It's not just that. She doesn't know why she attacked. The alpha male led the attack, but there was no danger to the pack and no intent of hunting us for food. There were two packs, too."

"You mean rival packs united to hunt us?"

"I guess. The communication with an animal isn't that specific. She followed, but she doesn't remember what happened." Diane stood. "I think they were all possessed."

"Infested, technically, but I know what you mean. There was nothing natural about this."

She stood. "I'm scared, Liam. No wraith has had this much power before."

He steeled his nerves to feign confidence for her benefit. "Don't worry. He hasn't thrown anything at us that we can't handle."

"I guess not."

"Come on. We don't want to be found near two dozen wolf corpses. Let's fill up our canteens and get out of here."

CHAPTER 33

Naked in a tent she shared with Emma, Diane hid her body under a blanket.

Liam extended a stick through the canvass flap. "Anything you want dry, fold it over this. Father's allowing a fire for an hour."

From under her blanket, Emma extended a bare arm and draped her wet clothes over the stick.

Diane lifted her wet items from her grounded backpack and then folded them over the branch.

"Is that everything, ladies?"

The Chaldean psychic raised her voice. "Yeah, get your voyeuristic Irish arse out of here."

Emma giggled. "Is that any way to treat your future husband?"

"He needs to get used to taking orders from me, if it's ever going to happen."

"What do you mean if it happens? Think positive."

"A snake tried to bite you, two dozen wolves attacked us, birds blinded Connor, and a demon blew up our truck. I'm not seeing a positive trend yet."

"But we're okay. We have each other. And we have whatever goodness is helping Josh."

That part unsettled her. "We're basing everything on the assumption that Josh is being guided by an angel. What if he's not? What if it's a demon or worse screwing with us?"

"What could be worse than a demon?"

Diane squealed. "I don't know? Just go with it. I'm trying to make a point."

"Then we're screwed. But I think we'd know better. We're powerful empaths, after all."

"I guess you're right. But I can't stop thinking about that wolf attack. We would've been six hours ahead of them if Josh hadn't intentionally delayed us."

Emma glared at her. "Don't be like that. The wolves would've come for us no matter what. Josh's delay saved us by holding us back near the river so that we could defend ourselves."

The realization soothed the Chaldean empath's nerves. "You have a point. I hadn't thought of it that way. Maybe I should chill."

Diane awoke the next morning and saw the rising sun's early rays bring light into her tent. She flipped back her sheet and crawled into the cool air.

Layla trailing him, Liam patrolled the makeshift perimeter. "Good morning. How'd you sleep?"

"Good enough for a bed of dirt." She stood and stretched. "And good enough for being attacked by wolves before dinner."

"You've got about twenty minutes before we wake the others. You should do your morning private activities behind the palm tree while you're alone."

Taking the hint, she relieved herself and used moist wipes to clean her selected body parts, and then she buried the evidence in the dirt. With water from her canteen, she brushed her teeth and rinsed her mouth as the rest of the camp awoke.

She returned to her tent and worked on breaking it down until Connor called the group together for breakfast. Seated with her legs crossed and facing her teammates, she chewed on an energy bar.

The elder hunter addressed the group. "God willing, tonight we'll accomplish our goal. The full moon rises at six twenty-eight. The sun sets at five fifty-six. That gives us about half an hour of maneuvering in the darkness before moonrise, if we need it. The moon sets at six fifty-one tomorrow morning. That gives us more than twelve hours of moonlight to accomplish our mission."

Liam vented his frustrations. "But we don't know where we're going. Where are we going to face him? We may be walking into an ambush, which is the exact opposite of what we should be doing."

Josh offered a rare comment that mingled his own thoughts

with full awareness of his angelic support. "I'll know what to tell you when we get there."

Diane processed the information but knew too little about combat to judge her brother's statement as useful or accurate.

Liam, however, protested. "Is that you or an angel talking?"

Josh fell silent.

"Josh, please let me know if that's you or an angel."

Diane's protective instincts kicked in. "That's enough, Liam. It's Josh. Leave him alone."

The young hunter softened his tone but continued. "Josh, buddy, I appreciate the effort, but you don't know enough about combat tactics to know what you're saying."

Connor raised a quieting finger. "No. He doesn't. Neither did he know anything about demonic attacks on trucks, but he warned us of that. Neither did he know anything about stopping a pack of wolves, but he placed us at the river. We've come too far to doubt him now."

Liam sighed. "Against my better judgment, I have to agree. It's ugly and unconventional, but we'll have to go with it."

During the day's hike, the elevation within Iraqi Kurdistan rose, but the temperature maintained its late September desert highs near one hundred degrees Fahrenheit. In the dry heat, Diane wiped a bead of sweat from her brow and stuffed her dagger into its sheath. "Who's next up for dagger duty?"

"Me." Emma lifted her blade for Diane to see it, and then she lowered it to carry for the next four hours.

The walk was uneventful, even boring, compared to the prior day's animal attacks, except for the subtle change in scenery. The earth became darker and the vegetation denser as the travelers approached a fertile plain.

With the sun low at the team's back, Diane walked towards her long shadow. As the clustered buildings of Erbil became visible on the horizon, she felt comfortable asking her brother for clarity. "Josh, where are we going?"

Her brother halted his march. "We need to change direction."

Connor stopped and turned. "Where to?"

"We pass north of the city and continue to the mountains. Our destination is there." Josh pointed to the distant foothills.

The elder hunter raised his eyebrows. "That's an extra ten kilometers. We won't get there by moonrise."

"We will arrive on time."

"So be it. Everyone brace for extra walking this evening. We'll break for dinner north of the airport." Connor turned, and a Lufthansa airplane with a flying crane logo on its tailfin glided into its landing, marking the travelers' path.

Two hours later, Diane lay back on a blanket and watched the pulsating lights of an airplane fly above her. As it passed, she saw a red logo with the words "Emirates" identifying the carrier. "This doesn't feel like spiritual cleansing anymore."

Lying beside her, Emma spoke between chews of her energy bar. "I think that part's already done. From here on out, we're in a battle, even if we don't know it yet."

"With no idea where it's going to happen, other than in the mountains ahead of us."

"Now you sound like Liam."

"Well, he's got a point about walking into a battle with no idea what's going to happen. Aren't you at least concerned?"

"A little. I'm more worried about Layla than her son."

Diane curled her torso up and propped herself on her arms. She glanced at the Persian psychic, who sat alone. "You may have a point. She's been getting quiet the last day or so."

Emma sat up. "Wouldn't you get quiet if you were marching with a team of assassins to kill your son?"

"We're not going to kill him." Diane knew her claim was dubious as she said it.

The German empath shook her head. "I don't know about that, but I do know that Liam and Connor won't hesitate to do it. They have one-track minds about accomplishing their mission."

Diane sighed. She trusted the hunters to do the right thing, but she also knew they were pragmatic. Emma was right, and Layla, with her empathic abilities, must have sensed it. Despite the entire team's best intentions, Amir's life was at risk.

Connor appeared in front of Diane. "Look over yonder, young ladies. The moon's rising over the mountains. Can you see the divine elegance of Josh's direction? We're walking right towards it. He's set it up as a beacon for us."

The Chaldean psychic saw the moon peeking over the peaks. "Is it time to go?"

The elder hunter's voice carried gravity and enthusiasm, as if the promise of battle energized him. "Soon. First, it's time to put on communications units." He extended battery-operated short-range wireless units.

Diane clipped her unit to her vest and slid its speaker over her ear.

Connor then pushed her boom microphone against her neck and pressed a piece of tape over her skin. "There. That'll hold." He moved to the German empath and assisted her. Then he stepped back and turned away. "Can you ladies hear me?"

Diane heard him in her speaker. "I can."

Emma's voice landed in Diane's ear. "I can, too."

"Excellent. Let's get moving."

Two hours later, the lights of Erbil cast an upward yellowish orb over Diane's shoulder as she climbed a gentle slope in the foothills. Her legs ached with the journey's second uphill trek. Periodically, she scanned her surroundings for snakes, wolves, and low-flying birds, but the demon ignored the wildlife around her.

An hour later, she reached level ground and brushed between the green needles of fir branches. The team grouped together tightly and examined a circular field of grass onto which the moon cast the shadows of high branches through a gap in the trees. She felt a cold anger rising from the wilderness.

Connor grabbed his rifle and lowered it in front of him. "Everyone stay put, stay low, and stay quiet. Get your shields out in front of you."

Liam assumed the same posture, crouching and creeping around the perimeter of the unexpected circle of grass. "Listen to him. This looks like a site for an ambush."

To make herself a small target against unknown threats, Diane lowered her haunches behind her shield and glanced to either side at her psychic sisters, who also hid behind their barriers. Emma and Layla both looked scared and confused. Expecting Josh to also have obeyed the hunters, she was surprised to see him marching into the grassy circle, which appeared too perfect in shape to be natural.

Josh traversed a third of the diameter, turned, and raised his voice. "Set your defenses here."

The hunters rose from their crouches and walked to him. Liam addressed him first. "What defenses?"

"Draw a line here with your combat knives. Fill it with wood, which you will cover with incense and the crushed powder of the fish's liver and heart. Once that's done, you will set a fire."

"I've got the fish organs, but you didn't tell me to bring any incense."

Josh pulled a bag from his vest pocket. "I did."

"You're not making any sense, buddy, but if you say so."

Diane and the empaths helped the hunters gather branches and lay them in the line her brother had prescribed.

Liam knelt and lowered a lighter. "Now?"

Josh stepped behind the line, turned, and nodded. "Yes."

The young hunter set the small fire.

As incense wafted over Diane's nose, she sensed a wind rising. The moving air's strength grew stronger, and she knew it was something more powerful than a natural gust. Expecting the rush to extinguish the fire, she gasped as the flames grew stronger and rose as a wall.

Flickering flames illuminated a handsome young man with a face of haunting arrogance who appeared out of nowhere in the grassy circle's center. "Hello, Mother. I see that you brought some friends. Which one should I kill first?"

CHAPTER 34

Without hesitating, Liam carried out the action he'd promised himself he'd perform first in battle. He aimed his rifle at Amir's knees and squeezed off a burst.

Whittling a flurry of bronze arcs in the air, the fledgling wraith knocked aside each bullet. Surrounded by red, demonic irises, his pupils grew huge in a blackened rage. A haunting blend of screeches and deep baritones, multiple voices issued from his throat. "Keep your bullets, hunter. But you may borrow my dagger."

Liam sank deeper behind his shield as the wraith elevated his arm. With lightning speed, the bronze projectile raced towards him, but the flames rose in the knife's path, stopping the glinting blade in mid-flight.

Frustration visible on his face, Amir extended his fingers to recall the dagger. After hanging in a second of timeless motionlessness, the knife returned to its master's hand. "Impressive, hunter. But I'm not convinced." The wraith whipped the weapon the other way towards the elder hunter.

Again, flames rose and met the knife in mid-air. Again, the wraith summoned the weapon back to his hand. "I see that you've prepared a defense."

Liam pressed his boom microphone against his neck and kept his voice low. "The empaths need to get inside his head."

The elder hunter's voice was electrified through the speaker. "Agreed. Ladies, invade his mind and bring him down."

From their positions between the hunters, the three empaths formed a triangle of held hands.

The mountain shook, tree trunks swayed, and cracking branches fell to the earth. Liam widened his stance for balance.

When the trembling ended, Diane looked to him and shook her head. Her electrified voice sounded disheartened. "We tried to get into his mind, but we didn't get far."

Liam pressed his microphone to his throat. "How far'd you get?"

"We learned that the fire's a barrier against evil spirits. Daggers will return to owners when thrown, whether they hit or not. And this is cursed ground. It's an ancient burial site. That's why we're here. He wanted to face us here."

The young hunter scoffed. "That last part's hardly a surprise."

"I guess. I don't know what to do about it."

Liam thought of a new attack. "I won't ask Layla, but Emma and Diane need to throw their daggers at his legs. Father?"

"Agreed. Target his knees. Hobble him."

From their position between the hunters, the two psychics stood, lifted their arms, and hurled their weapons. Divine power accelerated the points towards the wraith, but he flicked the weapons away with his cursed knife. The diverted blades then twirled in opposite directions before returning to their owners' hands.

Amir regained his smugness. "A stalemate? How boring. Is that what you desire, hunters?"

Liam and Connor remained quiet.

"No answer? Very well. I can live with a stalemate... forever. Good luck finding me, or should I say, good luck to your great-grandchildren's great-grandchildren." He started to turn but froze when challenged.

Liam taunted him. "What's wrong, Amir? Didn't Mommy love you?"

The wraith hesitated and then scoffed. "If you're going to hide behind your enchanted fire, I have no time for you. As long as we're being childish, why don't you and your daddy show some courage and come for me?"

The young hunter glared at Layla. "Say something!"

"What?"

"Anything. Stall him while we think of something."

Layla yelled. "Maybe I didn't give you love, but I gave you a gift."

His mother's voice kept Amir in place.

Liam was encouraged. "Keep going."

"I made you a champion. I made you immortal, even knowing

you'd hate me for it. If that's not a sacrifice, I don't know what is. So, maybe I didn't give you love, but I did love you."

With demonic fury, the wraith howled. "Shut up!" He launched his dagger towards Layla, but the rising flames protected her, and the weapon flew back to its master.

Liam's frustrations overwhelmed him. "Screw it!" He plucked a concussion grenade from his vest, pulled its pin, and lobbed it towards the wraith.

Amir hurled his knife at the steel weapon and sliced it in half. Its inert components fell to the ground.

To prevent the wraith's escape, Liam sought a desperate tactic. "Bloody hell, nothing's working. I recommend hand-to-hand, Father. Four against one. The ladies have their daggers. We'll use batons."

Layla protested. "Five against one."

Connor took control of the radio net's conversation. "I forbid it, Layla. We can't have you second-guessing yourself. You'll become vulnerable to him."

"Damn it! He's my son."

As the net went silent, Amir postponed his retreat to taunt his assailants. "You know I can hear you fools. If you really want to challenge me up close and personal, I encourage it."

Josh spoke with angelic authority. "Stay behind the fire."

Liam challenged the order. "Josh, what's keeping him from just walking around the fire?"

Nobody answered.

The young hunter continued. "He could face us in hand-to-hand if he wanted to. So, why isn't he?"

Again, nobody responded.

Liam answered his own question. "Because he knows we can stand up to him. We have two, maybe three empaths with enchanted knives, and we have two skilled hunters. We can do this."

Hidden behind the ladies, Josh shrank under his shield.

Liam knew he'd challenged the mortal man, and not the angel, who had receded after issuing his latest command.

"Sorry, Josh."

Diane protected her brother. "I think he's trying to tell us that the center of this burial ground is the center of the demon's power. We can't fight him there."

Liam agreed. "Fine. Let's assume that. But we still need to do something. Does anyone have any ideas?"

While Amir strode away, the hunting team remained void of hope to stop him until Layla stood and shouted. "Get your ass back here."

Amir chuckled. "Sorry, Mom. I'm afraid you misunderstand our so-called family's hierarchy."

Liam was encouraged while the maternal challenge again halted the retreat. "Keep talking, Layla."

She complied. "Do you really want to spend your entire life killing innocent people?"

"Don't give me a morality speech. There is no 'innocent'. All of humanity is evil."

"That's a demon talking. That's not my son."

His voice was a gruesome mix of pain and demonic fury. "Stop calling me 'your son'!"

Liam jumped on the exposed wound. "His bond to you is a weakness. Use his name. Keep calling him 'your son'."

"Shut up, hunter!" The wraith hurled his dagger towards Liam, but the fire again forbade the damage.

Layla continued her plea. "Amir!"

"You have no right to use my name!"

"I do. I am your mother."

"I am not your son!"

Liam cheered Layla on. "Keep going. You're doing great." He leveled his rifle at the wraith's knee and awaited a moment where he hoped to notice a vulnerability. Then he realized he needed an empath's help, but he wanted to avoid speaking and warning his target of his plan. He glanced to Emma and then to Diane, but each empath watched the verbal exchange.

Layla continued her inspired performance. "If you've done things you regret, it's not too late to turn back."

"Really? Should I apologize for what I am? For what you made me?"

Liam glared at the quiet empaths and cleared his throat. After the subtle approach failed, he got blunt. "Diane, Emma, look at me!"

The duo obeyed.

From the corner of his eyes, Liam verified the wraith's focus on his mother. He raised his rifle and mouthed the word 'when'.

The empaths frowned.

Liam slumped his shoulders. "Come on, you're flipping empaths. What am I asking you to do? Think about it." He pantomimed shooting his weapon and mouthed the word 'when'.

The empaths leaned into each other and called a telepathic link. Time stopped, and Liam felt himself frozen in a private mental conversation. "Do you know what I want?"

Within his mind, Diane answered. "You want us to tell you when to shoot him, right?"

"Yes!"

"You're going to try again?"

"If Layla can keep him off balance, it might work."

"We'll watch for it."

"Scream 'shoot' when it's time."

"Okay."

The link broke, and time recommenced. But as he scanned the situation, he saw Layla undermining his plan. She was abandoning the protection of her shield and walking towards the fire.

CHAPTER 35

As she walked towards her son, Layla questioned the sanity of each step.

The young hunter yelled. "Layla! What are you doing?"

Connor protested with less disbelief. "If you cross that fire line, you'll be beyond our reach to protect you."

From behind, Diane snapped. "We can't do this without you."

One step from the fire, Layla stopped and looked over her shoulder. "And I can't do this with you. I need to do this alone."

"What are you doing?"

Layla shared the advice of the ghost. "The Maiden of Toronto said my sickness arises from a lack of love. She said I was seeking my son from a desire to control and that I need to yield my need for dominion. Love is the power of the empath."

"I know that." Diane looked to Emma. "We know that. But this is still too new to you."

"Maybe. But in the short time I've been with you, I've seen more love than in my entire life. Friends... family... romance. I spent my life escaping pain and victimhood by wanting power and control, but I can see how lonely that is, how ugly and pointless. Only love matters."

"So, you're going to commit suicide?"

The Persian empath raised her blade. "I don't know. My dagger's not telling me anything. Do you think I'm committing suicide?"

A tear streamed from Diane's eye. "Yes."

A sinking feeling pervaded Layla's stomach. "Then maybe I have found love." She dropped her dagger to the grass, faced her son, and stepped forward. She kicked aside burning branches that smelled of sweet incense and fish organs while passing through the gap she created in the fire. As the line of protection slid behind her, nausea consumed her stomach, despite any protection she'd expected from her amulet, but she forced herself to stand straight.

Amir glared at his mother. "What are you doing?"

Layla locked eyes with him. "You are my son. I'm doing what a mother does to protect her child."

Moisture covered Amir's eyes, but then they rolled back, revealing the supernatural whiteness beyond that of a seizure. The irises and pupils disappeared, indicating a demon's possession.

"Amir? Son?"

When the wraith's eyes refocused, they radiated red hatred. With a sadistic grin, the man standing before her lifted his blade and then whipped his arm forward.

The flash of moonlit metallic glimmering shot across the grassy plain, stopped underneath Layla's jaw, and then reversed over its return path.

Dizziness overcame her, and her knees dropped into the soft grass. She reached for her neck and stuck her fingers into a sticky fluid. Extending her hands, she saw blackish blood under the moon's illumination. Drawing upon a surprising strength, she kept her torso straight with her weight on her haunches and pressed her palms against the knife's wound.

The monster standing in the center of the grass grinned. "I told you to stop calling me your son."

Layla knew she was dying. A distant hope billowed within her that her team would rise to victory, subdue her son without hurting him, and recover the cursed dagger. A secondary concern was her receiving first aid and surviving. She realized she'd discovered love, the power of the empath.

Instead of the team rallying, soft footsteps moved behind her, and an authoritative voice issued from Josh. "Everyone stay back! I will face him." After Josh passed Layla, he stopped in front of her.

Amir's red irises glowed bright with fear. "You!"

"The fire blinded you from me."

"You hid, you coward."

"Silence!" Josh's voice thundered and echoed off the trees. While Amir remained hushed, the autistic angel lowered Layla's retrieved dagger and aimed it at the Persian empath's wound.

The blade glowed with a life-giving green hue, matching the luminescence of Josh's eyes.

Layla credited the angel's presence for the alleviation of her nausea, and she released her neck to grant her companion access. Numbing her nerve endings with supernatural painkilling, the blade's tip worked within her flesh and generated a healing heat, cauterizing her injury. As Josh withdrew the knife, she palpated her restored skin.

Her companion pressed her knife into her hands and then faced Amir, who regained his speech.

"Your power is limited here, angel. This is damned ground. You're in my territory."

Josh stood his ground but said nothing.

"What? No retort, angel? Or have you accepted that you cannot defeat me here?"

"Vile beast, I am one of the seven who can defeat you. You claim to know me. Yet you taunt me."

The wraith broke into wild laughter. "You can stop me from hurting them, but you can't touch me without an exorcist. You know the rules, holy angel."

Josh inhaled and then turned his head towards Connor. Gentle green cones of light shot from the autistic angel's eyes and illuminated the hunter.

Connor's features became stone, painting the sternest look on the old man's face Layla had seen. He ripped off his body armor, dropped his weapons, and kicked his way through the fire.

Amir glared at the hunter and seemed to recognize him as a mortal enemy. "You brought a damned exorcist." He turned to flee.

But the Josh-angel bathed the wraith with the green glow of his eyes. "Stay!"

His feet frozen to the grass and his eyes opened wide, the demon glared at Josh. "What allows you to immobilize me?"

A gentle hand fell to Layla's shoulder. "A mother's sacrifice. A mother's love."

Connor walked in front of Josh and dropped his backpack. He

fished within a pocket and pulled out a stole, which he wrapped around his neck.

Layla's words strained her throat. "Can I help?"

For the first time since the Persian empath had met him, Connor sounded afraid. "I may be an exorcist, but it's been a long time, and this is the worst of demons. You can help by praying for me."

She snorted. "I'm sorry, but I'm not much help in that area."

"Then think positive thoughts on my behalf. You're already in the correct position." He raised his voice. "Ladies, please join Layla and use whatever power's within you to bolster my efforts against this beast. But whatever you do, do not challenge him. Support me, send me your love and positive energy, but ignore the beast completely."

As her sisters knelt with her in the empathic triangle, Layla watched the young hunter move to his father's side. "So, you're an exorcist? I guess I should stop being surprised about what you've hidden from me."

"Trust me, lad, I'm running out of secrets. If have many more, I've probably forgotten them."

"What can I do to help?"

"From the looks of it, Josh and his angel need all their energy to keep the demon in place. I'll need you by my side to brace me if I fall."

"That's right where I belong, Father. Do you have a copy of the Rite of Exorcism you'd like me to hold?"

Along with a small wooden cross, Connor withdrew a pocket-sized book from his bag. "I'd rather hold the words when I can, but I'll give it to you when I need my hands free."

Liam frowned. "You said that was your diary! You told me not to look at it!"

"I'm not sure which is more incredible–that I lied to you about it or that you obeyed me and didn't look."

The young hunter shook his head. "Now's not the time to argue it. What about your holy water?"

"You've probably figured out that I'm qualified to bless my

own. I've been drinking it during the entire journey. Let's get started. Something tells me this will be a difficult exorcism."

With her dagger-toting empathic sisters joining her in a real-time trance, one in which their awareness kept pace with reality, Layla willed Connor forward as their champion. Bolstered by the riveting aura of the angel who'd infused himself within Josh, the power of the triune sisterhood was intense. The Persian empath felt her team harnessing every ounce of its available divine and psychic power.

Standing where Josh immobilized it, the beast within Amir glared at the exorcist. "This is cursed ground, and you're a terrible exorcist. You couldn't exorcise a kitten from a tree."

Ignoring the demon's taunt, Connor showed restraint. He opened his copy of the rite and read from it.

Beside him, Liam joined his father in reciting the Lord's Prayer and the Hail Mary, and the Athanasian Creed.

Connor handed the book to Liam and then touched the subject's neck with the hem of his stole while pressing his palm on Amir's head. He followed with a series of requests to saints for intercession and then issued his first command. "In the name of Jesus Christ, tell me your name." He dabbed water from the canteen draped over his shoulder onto his palm and flicked it over the beast.

The wraith grimaced but said nothing.

"In the name of Jesus Christ, tell me if you are held in him by necromancy, by evil signs or amulets."

The energumen chuckled. "Can we skip ahead to the part where I run away and torment your incompetent hunting ilk for centuries?"

"In the name of Jesus Christ, tell me the sign of your departure, so that I'll know when you have left God's servant."

Amir snorted. "Shut up."

"In the name of Jesus Christ, tell me your number."

Nothing.

"In the name of Jesus Christ, tell me why you entered God's

servant."

The beast wrenched the energumen's body backwards.

"In the name of Jesus Christ, tell me when you entered God's servant?"

More wrenching, with hissing and cackling.

"In the name of Jesus Christ, tell me how you gained access to God's servant."

"I'm bored, Connor the Shitty Exorcist."

"In the name of Jesus Christ, tell me your name." Connor flicked more holy water, making the demon writhe.

"We've already been through this."

"In the name of Jesus Christ, tell me if you are held in him by necromancy, by evil signs or amulets."

"I will kill women for countless centuries."

"In the name of Jesus Christ, tell me the sign of your departure, so that I'll know when you have left God's servant."

"Bring me my mother. Let me stab her."

Layla flickered from her trance, but her sisters retrieved her and assured her the demon spoke in Amir's stead.

"In the name of Jesus Christ, tell me your number."

"Bring me my damned mother!"

"In the name of Jesus Christ, tell me why you entered God's servant."

Behind Layla, tree branches split and fell.

"In the name of Jesus Christ, tell me when you entered God's servant?"

Silent, Amir writhed in a reptilian rhythm.

"In the name of Jesus Christ, tell me how you gained access to God's servant."

Tree trunks cracked like thunder around the circle, and roots started pushing through the ground as the trees defied gravity. Layla gasped within her trance.

His cones of green light holding Amir, Josh raised a palm. "No."

As the trees sank back to the natural positions, the demon wailed in pained defeat. "Damn you, angel!"

With a flick of holy water, Connor began the third litany of commands. "In the name of Jesus Christ, tell me your name."

The defeated beast answered in an ancient language, yielding his name to the exorcist.

"In the name of Jesus Christ, tell me if you are held in him by necromancy, by evil signs or amulets."

"The dagger holds me."

"In the name of Jesus Christ, tell me the sign of your departure, so that I'll know when you have left God's servant."

"I will appear as pulsating red light, and I will flee into the night."

"In the name of Jesus Christ, tell me your number."

The helpless demon answered. "We are eight."

"In the name of Jesus Christ, tell me why you entered God's servant."

"I took him as my slave to administer my rage."

"In the name of Jesus Christ, tell me when you entered God's servant?"

"I entered him when he stole the dagger from his mother."

"In the name of Jesus Christ, tell me how you gained access to God's servant."

"The dagger in his hand."

"I know your name, servant of darkness. In the name of Jesus Christ, I command you to depart from God's servant."

"You have not defeated me. This was a battle. There is a war."

Amir slumped to the ground as an amorphous field of red pulsating rose from him and raced towards the sky.

From Josh, a similar field of green shot forth and chased the first. As the green light reached the red, Layla heard the demon's screams. The luminous spirits wrestled, but the green enveloped its victim, changed its direction, and carried it westward into the sky behind the team.

As it disappeared into the heavens, the demon's howl of anguish issued an eerie echo.

CHAPTER 36

Liam pressed his knee into Amir's back and handcuffed his wrists. "Toss me yours, Father."

Connor lobbed his restraints. "Make haste. He's trained in martial arts."

Below the young hunter, the captive squirmed. "Why are you being so rough? I'm not resisting."

Turning one hundred and eighty degrees, Liam shifted his weight to his prisoner's hamstrings and cuffed his ankles. He rolled off him, grabbed his wrist restraints, and lifted. "Get up."

With the young hunter's assistance and stabilization, Amir staggered to his feet. "That wasn't me! That's wasn't me!"

Liam pushed and then pulled him, shaking him into silence. "We're not idiots. Shut up."

"It was the demon! It wasn't me!"

The young hunter leaned into Amir's ear. "You're no saint, either, but you're not on trial here. We're taking you out of here."

"Where are you taking me?"

Layla appeared in front of her son. She held his face, looked into his eyes, and said nothing.

Wresting his jaw from her fingers, Amir looked away.

"I'm sorry."

Amir frowned at his mother. "For what?"

"For pushing you away." When she finished her apology, she looked to the young hunter and stepped out of his way.

Liam nudged the prisoner. "Let's go."

Holding a satellite phone, Connor stopped him. "Not so fast, lad. I'm arranging for helicopter support. Friar Lucio's simplifying our trip home."

Liam glared at his father. "You'd risk a landing here, on cursed ground?"

"After what I just witnessed, I believe this ground is safe, at least for the remainder of this night."

After travel in a helicopter, a private jet, and a limousine,

Liam followed his father through the outer door of the order's headquarters. He pushed his prisoner into the lobby and handed him to two friars who flanked Friar Lucio.

Despite the morning's early hour, the council's chairman glowed with enthusiasm. "An amazing job. Wonderful."

Having released his prisoner, Liam felt his fatigue. He glanced at his father, hoping for a command to sleep.

After Connor embraced the friar, he turned to his team and gave the last order of their mission. "Let's find our cots and sleep until we're hungry."

As Liam walked towards the elevator, Friar Lucio placed his hand on his shoulder and whispered into his ear. "I'll make the formal declaration soon, but you're free now to do as you wish with your life."

Liam stole a glance at Diane, who appeared stunning to him despite her obvious exhaustion. "Seriously?"

"Yes. Keep it quiet until I have a chance to talk to your father. But if you want to take her as your wife, I suggest you hurry. A beautiful young lady like that may not be willing to wait much longer."

Alone, Liam awoke in the waiting room outside the sanctum. A spread of bagels, orange juice, and coffee awaited him on a foldout dining table. He stepped to the food and washed a bagel down with coffee before having his day's first coherent thought.

When the thought came, it terrified him.

He needed to buy a wedding ring, prepare his proposal speech, and steel his nerves to request Diane's hand in marriage.

While he examined rings on his laptop, his teammates rose from their slumbers at random intervals. Josh passed through the waiting room in silence, used the restroom, and then returned to the sanctum. To Liam's relief, Emma emerged from the sanctum next, before Diane. Jumping from his seat, he intercepted her on her way to the ladies' room. "Um, I don't mean to rude, but I need your help, big time."

Her blonde hair tussled from sleep, she glared at him with a puffy face. "Huh?"

"I want your help with something personal."

"I really need to pee."

"Sorry. I..." He blurted it out. "I want your help proposing to Diane. I'm seriously clueless."

She chuckled. "Don't worry. All men are clueless. Leave everything to me."

By the midafternoon, Friar Lucio had declared a meeting of the council for the next day, and Emma had convinced the friar to schedule debrief interviews with Diane and Josh together for two hours.

Freed from the Chaldean empath to shop with his German savior, Liam followed Emma into a jewelry store. "I... uh, haven't set a budget."

Hovering over transparent display cases, she scanned the wares. "You want something nice but not gaudy."

A salesclerk greeted them in Italian. "How can I help you?"

Anxious, Liam called out. "Emma?"

The German empath looked up and answered in English. "We're looking for a wedding ring."

The clerk switched to English. "Congratulations!"

"It's not for us. It's for him and my friend."

"Well, then, you're looking in the right casing."

Like a focused professional, Emma selected three tasteful candidate settings and asked to see them.

Liam liked them all, forced himself to pick one, and double-checked his choice of a full carat gem and a band of smaller diamonds against the German empath's judgment. After moving to a different display case and watching Emma select three candidate wedding bands for the groom, he decided on white gold surrounded by titanium. With his purchase in hand, he escorted Emma onto the sidewalk.

"How are you going to ask her?"

His stomach rose to his throat. "I'm not sure."

"You haven't thought about it?"

"It's all I've thought about. I've got too many ideas buzzing through my bloody brain."

"What are the top three reasons you want to marry her?"

Butterflies assaulted his stomach. "Geez. I love her."

She rolled her eyes. "Boring! She knows that. Give her something interesting."

"Well, shit. Because she's awesome. She's magical."

"That's not bad, but it's not very personal. Why does that matter to you?"

"She makes me feel special."

"She already knows you're special. You're a wraith hunter. Get more specific."

"You're brutal."

"You'll thank me when you do it for real."

He struggled in silence for several steps. "Dang it. I'm addicted to her. The more I'm with her, the more I want to be with her."

"That's better. I like the part where you say you want to be with her, but don't say you're addicted. That's weird. What else?"

"Um… she's the first person I've met whose problems I want to make my problems and whose joys I want to make my joys."

"Good, but mention only the joys and leave it at that." Emma slowed her gait.

"Are you okay?"

"Hold on. I'm getting something… a premonition."

He stopped, motivating her to do the same.

"Okay. It passed. Wow."

"What was it?"

"I've got your third reason for getting married. I felt it, but I don't think you should use it in your proposal."

"Tell me anyway."

"Your children have an important destiny."

Liam was a nervous mess wondering if he should propose to Diane over dinner, alone or with the team, or in some impromptu way. He flopped onto a couch in the waiting room and distracted himself by catching up on sporting events on his computer.

The plywood door to the courtroom opened, and Emma walked out. To Liam's horror, she held Diane's hand, dragging the Chaldean psychic behind her. The sisters stopped in front of him.

"Can I help you ladies?"

"Diane, Liam has something to ask you."

Emotions flooded the young hunter. "Huh?"

"Get on a knee and do it." Emma stepped out of their way.

Reaching into his pocket for her ring, he complied with the manipulative psychic's plan. Lacking time to get scared and overthink it, he appreciated the German empath's ambush. "Diane, you're the only person in my life whose joys are my joys, and the more time I spend with you, the more time I want to spend with you. I would be honored if you would agree to be my wife." He extended the ring.

She gasped and covered her mouth. "Yes."

He kissed her and hugged her.

Her mission accomplished, Emma offered a smile of smug satisfaction. "My work here is done. Let's share the good news with the others."

CHAPTER 37

In the sanctum, Diane sat at the familiar witness desk beside her fiancé. Emma and Layla sat on her other side.

Friar Lucio called the group to order, verified the identities of the hunters in front of a glowing dagger, and then addressed the attendees. "Where to begin? I admit to being a bit overwhelmed by what this group has accomplished."

Diane exchanged a high-five with Emma, and then she turned and risked the gesture with her future husband. Slapping his hand felt right, despite their recent and still semi-secret engagement.

"I'll begin by answering the questions that are probably at the forefront of your minds. I've already met with the councilmembers and have some decisions to share."

Under the table, Diane extended her hand to Liam's lap, and he interlaced her fingers with hers.

"Retiring four daggers has freed Connor and Liam Brady from further hunting obligations. From this moment forth, Connor and Liam Brady may, at their choosing, be absolved from their vows of service to the order."

Hearing the declaration filled Diane with glee, and she squeezed her fiancé's hand.

"Connor and Liam, you may each address this newfound freedom with me in private. It's a huge decision that I want neither of you to rush."

Seated on the young hunter's opposite side, Connor responded. "We'll give it the consideration it deserves."

"I'm sure you will. Also, I'm pleased to announce that the enchanted daggers of the other two hunting lines glowed green and rotated last night."

Releasing Liam's hand, Diane gasped.

Friar Lucio continued his report. "One of the teams has already used their dagger to find its cursed twin abandoned by its former wraith owner, and I'm confident the other team will soon succeed. Apparently, when you defeated the demon on the mountain, the angel who assisted you gifted us an end to the horrors we've been combatting for a millennium."

Seated next to Nana in the audience, Josh called out. "The scrolls we found in the church said this would happen."

"Yes, Joshua Yousif. We transcribed multiple copies of the scrolls, one of which you've obviously digested, and our researchers arrived at the same conclusion. It was indeed prophesized long ago that defeating the demon who serves as the Master of the wraiths would break their line. Now that it's happened, the two remaining hunting families will be called upon to guard the seven cursed daggers within this room. The demon is defeated, but he is not dead, and our guard will remain vigil."

Liam faced his future wife. "Bloody hell. We did it."

Friar Lucio continued. "On to more somber matters. Amir Jazani will remain imprisoned in these headquarters while awaiting trial before this council. Although we have no civil authority, we must pass judgment for ourselves on his past behavior. Depending what we find, we may hand him to the proper civil authorities."

Seated at the end of the witness table, Layla covered her face while shedding a tear.

"I'm sorry for having to remind you of your son's situation, Miss Jazani, especially after your great sacrifice. You've been through a lot. I assure you that we'll consider all extenuating circumstances, such as the possibility of demonic oppression prior to his possession."

Layla managed a response. "I know. Thank you. I'd hate to think what his future would've been without you, all of you." She looked around the room.

Emma gave her a hug.

Diane stepped from her seat and joined in the embrace.

Friar Lucio glanced at the other six councilmembers for additions to the agenda but saw shaking heads. He tapped his gavel. "This concludes these proceedings."

In the waiting room, Diane fumbled in her pocket for her engagement ring and then showed it to Liam. "Can I put this on?"

"I should probably see Friar Lucio first. I don't want him to see my decision on your finger before I've talked to him."

She returned it to her pocket. "Yeah, you're right."

Friar Lucio joined the betrothed. "Pardon me, but you appear to be discussing something important. Could it be Liam's future with respect to the order?"

The young hunter shrugged. "Yeah."

"I've spoken with your father, and he accepts any decision you make. And so do I."

"I appreciate it."

Diane glared at her fiancé and cleared her throat.

Her dense caveman understood her message. "In fact, I've made up my mind. I want to marry Diane."

The friar's face lit up. "Excellent. I'm thrilled that you've arrived at a decision. In fact, I'd be honored if you'd let me preside at the ceremony."

Diane loved the idea. "Of course!" She hugged the old man and then released him.

"Well then. Let me know when you've chosen a date, and I'll be sure to make myself free." Friar Lucio departed.

"Can I put on my ring now?"

"Yeah. No more secrets. I'm free to... wow. I'm just free. Period."

She wiggled her ring finger. "Not for long, buddy. This means your mine!"

"I look forward to it." As he fell silent, a shadow covered his face.

"What?"

"You just jumped at the chance to have Friar Lucio marry us, but that's the first of a ton of decisions we need to make."

The prospect of designing her marriage celebration energized the Chaldean empath. "I know. It's going to be awesome."

"For you, maybe. This is going to be the Diane Show, starring Diane, featuring Diane, and also with a cameo appearance by Diane. I'll show up in a tuxedo and do what you tell me."

"I knew I was marrying a smart man."

"But I get a husbandly veto on the post-ceremony stuff, like where we live, who lives with us, and what we do for a living. If you really want to go to Dubai for our honeymoon, that's fine by me, but I'd like this to be a partnership after our big night."

She agreed in the legitimacy of his concerns, but for their enormity, she postponed addressing them. "Ugh. Can't I just have my moment?"

"Yeah, sure." He lifted his eyes as people passed through the plywood doors. "But not yet. This isn't a happy day for everyone. You and Emma should spend some girl time with Layla."

"Yeah. We'll take her to lunch."

"I've got a feeling I need to take care of Father, too. This is a great victory for him, but while the rest of us are planning new lives, he's getting put on a shelf."

Diane hadn't considered Connor's de facto retirement. "You've got a point. Maybe you can be sensitive when you try."

"Look, I'll take care of him. You have Nana take Josh to lunch and also see what you can do to console Layla."

"Deal." She kissed him on the cheek and then turned to find her sisters.

On the sidewalk outside the order, Diane studied Layla's face. "How are you coping?"

The Persian psychic's shoulders slumped. "Okay. It could've been worse. At least I know where my son is, and he's safe."

"Do you want to bring your birthmother into this? I mean, you're not close to your mother, but maybe you could use the help of another empath from our bloodline."

Layla shrugged. "I'm not ready for that. I need to keep Farah at a distance for a while. I'd rather think about your wedding and help with the planning than worry about my messed up blood relatives today." She forced a smile.

Diane had an idea. "You know what we should do? We should have a telepathic link with some of our sisters to get some ideas. We can go anywhere in the world we want for my wedding, and

I want you both as bridesmaids. So, you get to help me choose where to go and what to do."

Emma shrugged and smiled. "I'd be honored."

"Me, too." Layla pulled her dagger from her purse and extended her hands. "Is Dubai still in play?"

"Yeah. Sure. Let's see if we can get some other ideas." Diane reached out, clasped the wrists of her sisters, and entered the starry void.

A bright speckle of light grew into a powerful orb and invited the entity of triune empaths into union.

Stripped of her milky ghost form, the Maiden of Toronto welcomed her sisters into a wordless conversation in a shapeless stoppage of time. She congratulated Diane on her engagement, expressed compassion and hope for Layla's son, and shared her relief in having been redeemed.

The three psychics expressed their gratitude for the ghost's helping Layla through her tough times and wished her a peaceful eternity in her freed redemption.

Before relinquishing the empaths to seeking their other sisters for wedding planning, the maiden imbued them with a final piece of advice–they needed to stick together.

Although they'd defeated the demon of the murdering wraiths, evil would endure. Other heinous masters stoked the fires of wickedness across the globe, and the world needed good psychics–noble empaths–who would risk their lives to champion the cause of justice.

But such challenges and adventures could wait until after the wedding celebration, since they were stories for another time.

THE END

About the Author

After graduating from the Naval Academy in 1991, John Monteith served on a nuclear ballistic missile submarine and as a top-rated instructor of combat tactics at the U.S. Naval Submarine School. He now works as an engineer when not writing.

Join the Wraith Hunters to get news, freebies, discounts, and your FREE Prophecy of Eden (Book #5) early bonus chapter!

Wraith Hunter Chronicles:

PROPHECY OF ASHES (2018)
PROPHECY OF BLOOD (2018)
PROPHECY OF CHAOS (2018)
PROPHECY OF DUST (2018)

Rogue Submarine Series:

ROGUE AVENGER (2005)
ROGUE BETRAYER (2007)
ROGUE CRUSADER (2010)
ROGUE DEFENDER (2013)
ROGUE ENFORCER (2014)
ROGUE FORTRESS (2015)
ROGUE GOLIATH (2015)
ROGUE HUNTER (2016)
ROGUE INVADER (2017)
ROGUE JUSTICE (2017)
ROGUE KINGDOM (2018)

John R Monteith

PROPHECY OF DUST

www.ingramcontent.com/pod-product-compliance
Lightning Source LLC
Chambersburg PA
CBHW030305200626
46816CB00002BA/769